ALSO BY KAREN CLEVELAND
Available from Random House Large Print

You Can Run

Keep You Close

THE NEW NEIGHBOR

THE NEW NEIGHBOR

A Novel

Karen Cleveland

RANDOM HOUSE
LARGE PRINT

All rights reserved. Published in the United States of America by Random House Large Print in association with Ballantine Books, an imprint of Random House, a division of Penguin Random House LLC, New York.

Cover design: Carlos Beltrán
Cover photograph: Silvia Otte / Getty Images

The Library of Congress has established a Cataloging-in-Publication record for this title.

ISBN: 978-0-593-60820-3

www.penguinrandomhouse.com/large-print-format-books

FIRST LARGE PRINT EDITION

Printed in the United States of America

1st Printing

This Large Print edition published in accord with the standards of the N.A.V.H.

For my family

Every man is surrounded by a neighborhood of voluntary spies.

—JANE AUSTEN

THE NEW NEIGHBOR

PROLOGUE

THERE IT IS, THE SOUND I'VE BEEN WAITING for, the crunch of dried leaves underfoot. It's faint, drowned by the rushing river, but it's there. It's not my imagination. **None** of this is my imagination.

I crouch low in the brush, one hand flat on the cold packed dirt, the other gripping the gun at my side. Eyes on the clearing, just barely visible in the moonlight. The jagged boulder, marked with an X, fresh white chalk. And I listen. The steps are slow and methodical, each louder than the one before.

There are bears out here. Coyotes, too, and snakes. It's why we never let the kids play here alone. Hundreds of acres behind our home, unspoiled, untouched. In my mind, **this** was where predators lurked. The cul-de-sac itself was safe, a refuge, a haven.

How very wrong I was.

But these—these aren't the steps of an animal.

My breathing is shallow. The footsteps are growing louder, closer. I shouldn't be here. But this is **my** cul-de-sac. My friends. My neighbors.

Except one, who isn't. Who brought this danger into our lives.

Wind whistles through the trees, rustles the branches. The footsteps stop.

A beam of light filters through the brush. A flashlight, pointed toward the clearing, toward me, hidden just on the other side.

I wait, breath held. The footsteps begin again. Closer, and closer.

I lift the gun. My finger curls around the trigger.

And I watch through the sights as a figure appears.

ONE

Three Weeks Earlier

"PERFECT," I SAY, EYEING TYLER THROUGH THE viewfinder of my Nikon, pressing down gently on the shutter release. I lower the camera, check the image captured on the screen. Tyler's smiling broadly, bathed in early morning sunlight, leaning on the handle of his rolling suitcase, the freshly painted front door behind him, the stone planters on either side bursting with late summer color. It's true, it's the perfect shot, Instagram-worthy, if I were into that sort of thing. The last picture I'll snap of one of my kids in front of the home where we raised them.

But it shouldn't be the last, should it? Perfect as it is, it's all wrong.

Tyler's already walking past me, heading toward the driveway, suitcase in tow.

"One more," I say.

He turns. "Really, Mom?"

"Right there, with the cul-de-sac behind you."

He smiles again for the camera, this time with a touch of exasperation, and I get the shot. I lower the camera and check the screen. Better. There's the FOR SALE sign in the yard, UNDER CONTRACT tacked to the top. But I can Photoshop that out.

"It's just an empty street," Tyler says, looking out at the loop.

I follow his gaze. The Kanes' and the Johnsons' and the O'Malleys'. Softly lit houses, lush lawns, mature landscaping. Everything quiet, everything perfect. And he's right—the street is empty.

"Well, **now** it is," I say.

He continues on down the path to the driveway, suitcase wheels clacking over the breaks in the concrete. In the driveway, Mike's starting the car, the engine sputtering softly. Everyone's ready but me.

I'm still staring at the loop of pavement, and in my mind's eye it becomes full again. Figures appear, almost ghostly at first, but gradually coming into focus. Children on bikes, some still with training wheels; others drawing with sidewalk chalk; the younger ones toddling around, unsteady on their feet. Their mothers, sitting in lawn chairs arrayed in a half circle, chatting and laughing—

"Mom!" comes Tyler's voice from the drive-way, and the figures vanish. The cul-de-sac is empty once again.

"Coming." I start walking toward the driveway, and can't help but steal one last glance at the street. That scene was so clear in my mind I would have sworn it was real.

IT'S A TWO-AND-A-HALF-HOUR DRIVE TO the University of Virginia, another half hour to wait for a parking space to open up. When it finally does, the three of us make our way to Tyler's dorm, an old brick building near the center of campus, past a courtyard with big shade trees.

The room itself is small, a typical dorm room, with two of everything: extra-long twin beds, desks, dressers, all the furniture solid and well worn. We're the first to arrive.

I start unpacking while Mike and Tyler head down to the car for more boxes. Place stacks of clothes into the dresser drawers. Books and school supplies on the desk. I'm placing a couple of pairs of shoes into one of the small closets when they walk back in, maneuvering the TV box through the door.

"I don't need you to unpack," Tyler says to me as they set down the box on the carpeted floor, leaning it against the dresser.

"I want to."

The door opens before he can object, drawing our attention.

A skinny teenage boy with a smattering of acne stands in the doorway. Must be the new roommate. He and Tyler have chatted online, followed each other's social media accounts, but they haven't met in person yet. "Hey," the boy says, lifting a hand awkwardly.

"Sweetheart, can you walk all the way through the door, please?" comes a terse voice behind him. He steps forward into the room, and a woman follows, giant-sized Target shopping bags in each hand. Two blond grade-school-age girls trail behind her, sullen looks on their faces, bickering. She shakes her head at me. "Kids." She rolls her eyes, then adds, "Hi. I'm Beth."

"Well, that'll be easy to remember," I say. "I'm Beth, too."

"No way."

She must be the mother, but she's **young**. Mid to late thirties, maybe. Tight-fitting workout clothes, hair that looks freshly styled, flawless makeup, not that she needs it. I'm instantly conscious of my own appearance. Loose-fitting clothes, air-dried hair, ChapStick. And my **age**. I have a decade on her, at least.

We might have the name in common, but the similarities end there.

"Where are y'all from?" she asks.

"Near DC. McLean." I watch for any spark of recognition. In the DC area, McLean is synonymous with Langley, which inevitably leads to questions about the CIA. Fortunately, though, her expression remains blank, and I don't need to be evasive about my career. "What about you?"

"Richmond."

One of the girls elbows the other, who instantly shouts, "Mom!"

"Girls, cut it out," she says curtly. Then, to me, "I should have brought their iPads."

The room, already small, now feels almost claustrophobic. The two boys are helping Mike pull the TV out of the box; there's barely room for the three of them between the two beds.

"It's a madhouse out there," she says to me, moving the shopping bags to the unclaimed side of the room.

"Sure is."

"Would have left earlier if I'd known." She shakes her head. "Rookie mistake."

I smile. She reaches into one of the shopping bags, pulls out an unopened set of sheets, then a new pack of smart plugs, the same kind the kids talked us into getting at home. Everything's controlled with a voice now, or an app.

"Is this your first time, too?" she asks. "Sending someone off to college?"

"Actually, third. Our girls are already **out of college**."

"Yeah?" she says, pulling out a plastic-wrapped pillow, then reaching back into the bag. It looks like she raided the back-to-school section of the store. "What are they doing now?"

"My oldest is a teacher. She just got married in June."

"No way." She pauses and looks at me, a boxed Bluetooth speaker in her hands. "Gosh, you might have **grandchildren** soon."

The words are cringeworthy. I'm not old enough for that. And Aubrey's too young to be married, let alone have kids. I mean, she's the age I was when I had her, but still. "Well, they want to get a house first. Settle down. But they're looking for one, so it might not be long. . . ." I realize I'm rambling. "And my younger daughter just graduated from Georgetown in May. Took a job as a travel reporter. She moved to London last month."

"How exciting. What a summer for your family."

What a summer, indeed. "And your girls? How old are they?"

"Ten and eight. We're still in the gymnastics and soccer stage of life."

The girls are sitting on the bare mattress of one of the twin-sized beds, still looking petulant. The older one says something quietly to the younger one, who immediately says, "No I didn't!"

"Girls," she scolds, turning toward them. "I said **enough.**"

She turns back to me. "So you're going home to a quiet house." She gives a wry laugh. "Lucky you."

I force a smile.

It's really hot in here. Mike and the two boys have the TV out of the box now, packing material strewn about. She's opening up the second shopping bag.

I check my watch. Ten minutes until eleven. "Well, I think Tyler's things are mostly unpacked, so I'll get out of here, give you all some space to move around."

"Tight quarters in here, huh?"

"No kidding. It was really nice to meet you."

"Likewise," she says with a smile.

I turn toward Mike. "I'm going to wait outside. Come get me when you and Tyler are ready for lunch, okay?"

"Sure."

Tyler's focused on unwrapping cables and cords, doesn't even look up. I watch him for a moment, then turn and let myself out of the room.

I SIT ON AN EMPTY bench under a large shade tree, just outside the entrance to the dorm. The air is fresh and pleasantly cool, and the leaves are rustling softly. I pull my phone from my purse, open up the HomeWatch app. A live feed appears. It's from the default camera, the one mounted above our front door, looking down at the porch, and the street beyond. Street's empty, porch is empty. Everything's quiet.

I set down the phone on the bench beside me and watch the passersby. Anxious teenagers, parents loaded down with boxes and suitcases and shopping bags. New beginnings for some, chapters closing for others. Bittersweet.

I check my watch again. Two minutes until eleven. I reach for the phone again, unlock it, tap the HomeWatch app. The live feed appears. There are two cars parked on the street now, in front of our house. A sedan and an SUV. Three people walking to the front door. An older man leading the way, a young couple following behind.

That's them. The Sterlings. Madeline and Josh.

I can't get a good look at her; she's blocked by the Realtor from this angle. But I can see Josh. He's tall, dressed in jeans and a casual button-down, sleeves rolled up to his elbows.

The Realtor reaches for the lockbox on the front door, and then I see her. Madeline. She looks tall, too. She's dressed in slim-fitting white ankle-length pants, a silky cream-colored top. She's tan, like she's just spent a week at the beach. She's **young**. They both are.

She looks over at Josh and smiles. She looks relaxed, content.

The Realtor pushes open the door—

I tap the screen, swipe left to reach the next camera view. This one's inside our front foyer, from a camera mounted in the top corner of the room.

"Shouldn't we take it down?" Mike had said last week, looking up at the camera.

"Shouldn't we figure out what they think?" I'd replied. Because really. If they're going to back out, isn't it best we know as soon as possible? And it's not like we're hiding the cameras. Our Realtor disclosed them.

The foyer's empty, just cardboard boxes stacked neatly against one wall, as unobtrusive as possible.

Madeline's the first to walk through the door, followed by Josh, then the Realtor. My eyes are locked on her as she looks around—

"Oh, Josh," she breathes. "It's even better in person."

"Beth?" Mike's voice startles me. I close the app and lower the phone in one quick motion, look up. He's standing right in front of me. I was so absorbed in the video I didn't hear him approach.

"Finished with the TV?" I ask.

"Yeah."

I stand up, slide the phone back into my purse, sling the bag over my shoulder. "Where's Tyler?"

"He's staying."

"What about lunch?"

"He's grabbing lunch with the new roommate at the cafeteria."

The words feel like a blow. "Oh. Okay. Well, let me go say goodbye."

"They've already left."

"What?"

"He said he'd call later."

"Okay," I say, because what else **can** I say? He wants to start settling in here. As he should.

I just thought we'd get to enjoy lunch first. And that I'd get to say goodbye.

"Just the two of us, then?" I say brightly. Too brightly. It doesn't cover my disappointment.

"Actually, if we head home now, I can make it into the office. I called Britt, and she's going to put a few things back on my calendar. You don't mind, do you?"

"No," I answer. Perhaps a little too quickly. But really. We'll have plenty of meals with just the two of us. Plenty of **time** with just the two of us. More than enough.

Because that's what it is now. It's just the two of us.

THREE HOURS LATER, I WALK through a double set of sliding doors into the lobby of CIA headquarters, stepping across the giant seal on the floor to the bank of turnstiles, past the watchful eyes of numerous armed guards. I hold my badge to one of the scanners, press my index finger to the reader, wait for the green light. Access granted.

I had requested the whole week off, but it's more than I need. The house is mostly packed. Tyler's settled at school. And I was off last week, too, on vacation. Ocean City with the family—the majority of it, anyway, now that Caitlyn's overseas. I'm itching to get back in the swing of things. This will be a welcome distraction.

I work counterintelligence for the Agency. In the division dedicated to Iranian intelligence services, one of our hardest targets. My focus is Quds Force, their external operations wing. And in particular, a high-ranking Quds Force commander named Reza Karimi.

Karimi's mission is gaining undetected access to JWICS. The Joint Worldwide Intelligence Communications System. The intranet system the intelligence community uses to send top secret information.

If Iranian intelligence agents hack into JWICS without detection, they have the keys to the kingdom. Access to any top secret, compartmented information they want. There's nothing more dangerous, from a national security perspective.

And if anyone can do it, it's Reza Karimi.

He's brilliant. Persistent. Patient. And Quds Force is technologically advanced, extremely capable, especially in the cyber realm. None of us would be surprised in the least if they've managed to plant malware **outside** the intelligence community, in places like power plants, if it's lying dormant, waiting for activation. But inside the intelligence community is another story. Our **intranet** is another story. They're not getting in, not if I have anything to say about it.

I'm the one who discovered Reza Karimi—I pieced together his identity through call chain analysis and covertly obtained Iranian tax records—and I've been working him for nearly two decades. In that time I've disrupted numerous attempts to gain information about JWICS, to gain **access** to JWICS. I've helped stop more than a dozen of his recruits before they could hurt our country. The Jackal. The Goalkeeper. The Anchor. So many more.

But there's one that's evaded me. One I can't figure out. The thorn in my side, for almost fifteen years now.

The one Reza Karimi calls "The Neighbor."

The Neighbor is an access agent—and by extension, a notoriously difficult target. Put simply, access agents are recruits who take over the role of recruiting. Individuals who agree to work for a foreign intelligence service, sell out their own country—by recruiting **more** traitors. And they're nearly impossible to find, because they **blend in**. They're locals. They might work in sensitive positions, but they might not; it's enough to just be in the same orbit as people who do.

We don't know who The Neighbor is. We get crumbs from intercepted conversations, bits and pieces about what The Neighbor has done, but no actionable leads. We don't know who The Neighbor has recruited, either, but intercepts suggest the recruits are from within the U.S. intelligence community: employees with security clearances who are now feeding sensitive information to our adversary, and have been for years.

Most worrisome of all, we've intercepted internal progress reports that make it clear Reza Karimi is getting close to mission success—all thanks to the work of The Neighbor.

That can't happen. Because if Karimi's mission succeeds, nothing else we do matters. The Iranians will have **everything**.

The FBI's focused on finding The Neighbor's recruits, learning what secrets they've exposed. And we're focused on finding The Neighbor, putting an end to all of this before it's too late.

I wind my way through the halls down to the Counterintelligence Center—CIC—the same place I've worked for what feels like forever. It's not uncommon to move around here, switch accounts every few years, work in different mission centers.

It's encouraged, in fact. But I've stayed put. I'm going to find The Neighbor eventually. I won't give up until I do.

If there's any silver lining to the empty nest, anything I've truly been looking forward to, it's the freedom to focus **fully** on The Neighbor, and to do so guilt-free. I'll be the first to admit I struggled to find balance when the kids were young; even when they hit the teen years, when Aubrey left, and then Caitlyn, when it was just Tyler at home, I always felt the need to get home before six, to make sure he was doing homework, that we were eating dinner together as a family. Now there are no kids at home who need me. The Neighbor is what will keep me busy.

I hold my badge to the reader beside the door to Iran Division, wait for the lock to disengage, but nothing happens. "Come on," I murmur, holding the badge up again—

The door opens, someone pulling it open from the inside. "Oh! Beth. You're back." It's Annemarie, who sits in the cubicle across the aisle from me. She's one of the long-timers in CIC, though not nearly as long a tenure as mine. She's wispy and quiet—and smart as a whip.

"Couldn't stay away," I say with a smile, and walk past her into the office. It's windowless in here, and expansive, with long rows of cubicles. Feels as familiar as a second home. I turn down the third row and start heading toward my own desk—

There's a stack of white cardboard file boxes outside my cubicle, against the exterior wall. Four high. All labeled on the side with black permanent marker. **Kent School**. Apparently in the week I've been out, someone decided to use my cubicle as storage space.

Who's headed to the Kent School? I rack my brain but come up empty. It's the Agency's school for intelligence analysis, and it's out in Reston, deep in the suburbs. Away from the action. Tends to be a good place to park washed-up analysts, the ones who'd be too hard to fire. Or part-timers, or occasionally a decent analyst looking for the crucial "broadening experience" needed for promotion— though if that's the only option, I don't think a promotion is worth it, to be honest.

I step into my cubicle. There are two more cardboard boxes sitting on my desk. Also labeled **Kent School**. These are set at an angle, though, and I can see there's writing on the other side of the boxes. I turn one slightly—

Beth Bradford.

"Beth?"

I turn. It's Dale. My boss. Wiry and bespectacled, and dressed in a suit, as always. "You're back," he says carefully.

"What **is** this?" I gesture to the boxes.

Dale follows my gaze. He seems to be considering what to say, or how to say it. "I was going to call you, Beth. Tomorrow. This is certainly not how I wanted you to find out."

"Find out **what**?"

"You've been selected for a position at the Kent School."

I give my head a firm shake. "I don't want it."

"You don't have a choice."

I stare at him, try to read his expression, but it's blank. "Dale, I'm not leaving this account. I work Reza Karimi. I work **The Neighbor**."

"Well, that's just it. Your work on The Neighbor . . . it hasn't exactly been successful."

The words sting, especially coming from **him**, from someone who knows how committed I am to this case. From someone I trust—and who I **thought** trusted and believed in me. "It's a hard target."

"No one's denying that."

Annemarie slides quietly into her chair across the aisle, doesn't look at us.

"We're getting closer," I say. "I can feel it. And I'm doubling down, especially now that Tyler's gone. I'm here on my day off, aren't I?"

He smiles sadly. Uncomfortably.

The vault has gone silent. I know everyone around us is listening.

The gravity of this, the reality of this, is starting to sink in.

"Dale, you can't move me."

"I'm sorry, Beth." He looks like he **is** genuinely sorry, but he's my boss, and even if he wasn't the one who suggested the move, he obviously approved it.

I look at the boxes, the ones at my desk, with my name on them. Then around the office, this office that's been mine for as long as I can remember. My gaze lands on the electronic board beside the conference room, the one with the week's schedule. **Friday 9 A.M.: Interagency meeting on The Neighbor.**

"**Interagency?** What the hell, Dale? You're kicking me out and bringing in the **Bureau?**"

I stopped working with the Bureau on the case ages ago. Frankly, there's no point. I mean, come on. **I'm** the one who's uncovered every other one of Karimi's recruits. **I'm** the one who's kept our intranet secure. There's been just **one** target that's evaded me, one target that's gone on to recruit others, and they haven't been a lick of help. We're talking spies within our own government, and they've never uncovered a single one. They just keep interviewing the same people—the IT folks, ones who work on JWICS—over and over again. Poring over financial disclosures—the annual asset-and-liability form everyone with a clearance is required to fill out—and taking a hard look at any big deposits.

This case, for them, has always involved a

revolving door of ambitious agents, all of whom move on as soon as they realize the case is tough to crack. Plus they don't share their own information; there's really nothing in it for us.

There's historic distrust between the CIA and FBI, and in my opinion it's well founded. If anyone's going to catch The Neighbor and root out the spies, it's us. If anyone's going to tip off Iranian intelligence, it's them. We know how to keep secrets, and our tradecraft is immaculate. They leak like a sieve, and they're sloppy.

"Something came in," he says. "Something that . . . Well, it's a good transition point, Beth. And we feel—"

"Who's 'we'?"

"**Senior management** feels that it's time for a fresh set of eyes."

The words seem to hang there in the silence. Everyone heard them, didn't they?

"What came in?" I ask, my voice low.

"I can't get into that."

"It's **my** case. My target."

"Beth—"

"Was it another intercept?"

The intercepts are everything in this job. They're **key**, as few and far between as they are. Pulled from an encrypted channel between DC and Tehran, between the head of Quds Force in the U.S. and Reza Karimi himself.

Dale says nothing.

I look past him, across the aisle. "Annemarie, **was** it?"

She looks over, glances from me to Dale, shrugs helplessly. She knows, but she won't say, won't contradict her boss. They all know, everyone but me.

"You can't do this, Dale." **You can't betray me like this**.

"It's already done. We've removed your accesses."

The words stun me into silence. I can't even see what's happening in **my** case anymore?

That's why my badge didn't work at the vault door, isn't it? That's why **they're** packing up my desk, instead of me. I'm no longer allowed to touch most of what's here: the raw intelligence, the reports I wrote. It's all compartmented information, that intelligence that's even more secret than top secret, and now they've cut me out of it. Someone's going to remove all of those papers, shred them, burn them, send me on my way with whatever's left.

No. If there's something happening in my case, I need to know. I look around again, almost in a panic this time. The computer at my desk is off; I wouldn't have access to the content I want anymore, anyway. The whiteboard—

I turn around, look behind me, at the enormous whiteboard hung on the rear wall of the office. Our brainstorming spot, a place for analysts to write down key information that others should be aware of, to gather other analysts' input, especially for intel that isn't clear. A jumping-off point for discussion.

I remember clear as day the first time I wrote something there. The phrase we picked up in an intercept, the one that ignited my passion for this case, that's haunted me ever since. The reason I've never left the case, and never will, not until I track down The Neighbor.

Use the children.

Now there's a new phrase in the center of the whiteboard. Red dry-erase marker, someone else's handwriting. Could be about any case, really, but it's **not** just any case. It's **my** case. I can feel it. I know.

The cul-de-sac.

"What was the rest of it?" I ask, my eyes still on the words, even though I know he won't tell me.

Cul-de-sac. Code for something. Maybe the group of The Neighbor's recruits. Or the network of employees who work on JWICS. Or a multi-pronged way of penetrating the network, taking out one "house" after another.

Whatever it is, it could be key to us finding The Neighbor. And if it's up on the whiteboard, it's unclear.

To **them,** anyway. Maybe it wouldn't be to **me.**

"Beth, you need to leave."

"What else did it say? What else did we collect?"

"Beth." His tone has a note of warning now, almost like an unspoken threat. Security could be here in an instant if someone makes the call. I'm not going to find out any more, and I know it.

"This is a mistake, Dale. No one cares about this case like I do."

"I know," he says, gently this time. "But it's time for a new chapter. For the case, and for **you**."

"I don't **want** a new chapter." The words sound pained, pitiful.

"I'm sorry, Beth. You don't have a choice."

THE CUL-DE-SAC.

I can't get those words out of my mind. They're stuck there, eating away at me. I've always known **everything** there is to know about The Neighbor. The fact that there's something out there, something new, and I don't know what it is, it's unbearable.

They told me to leave, to head home, start fresh at the Kent School next week. But I can't go, not yet. Can't let **this** go, and won't.

I sit on one of the benches along the pathway from the entrance to the parking lots. There's a steady stream of people leaving for the day—the early birds, no doubt; the ones at their desk by seven every morning, who've already put in a full eight hours.

Annemarie should be joining them soon. She's out the door every day by four, off to pick up her daughter at daycare.

I keep an eye on my watch, and another on the foot traffic. Wait for four, wait for her.

Finally I see her, walking alone, part of the stream.

I watch her as she approaches. Stand as she gets close. The movement catches her eye. She sees me, and her expression changes. Falters, almost. She doesn't break her stride, but she ever so slightly alters her path, arcs away from me.

Doesn't matter. I walk toward her, fall into step beside her.

"What are you still doing here?" she asks as she walks. Doesn't look at me, doesn't slow her pace.

"What do you think?"

"I can't talk to you about this, Beth."

"Just tell me what it was. It was an intercept, right? What did it say?"

She gives her head a brief shake. Still doesn't turn to face me.

"Please, Annemarie. You have to tell me."

She has other targets she's responsible for, but she knows this case. **My** case. Just like I know hers. We're each other's backups at work. She covers for me when I'm out, and vice versa—though nine times out of ten I'm the one picking up the slack.

She owes me. And she knows how important this case is, and how much I care about it.

If anyone's going to talk to me, it's her.

She keeps walking, eyes forward, doesn't say a word. Veers off to the right, down a row of cars.

I follow her. "What if **this** could lead us to The Neighbor?"

She reaches her car—a black Prius—and finally stops. She looks uncertain now, like I'm getting through to her.

"What if this is the break we've been waiting for?" I ask. I sound like I'm pleading. I **feel** like I'm pleading.

She opens her mouth to speak, closes it again. Almost like she catches herself, reconsiders. Her eyes are boring into mine.

"Let it go, Beth," she finally says. There's a note of warning in her voice, in her look.

Before I can respond, she turns away, slides into the car. Starts the engine, pulls away. And I stand there in front of the empty parking space, watching her go, left with more questions than answers.

TWO

I DRIVE THE SHORT ROUTE HOME IN A DAZE. Past Langley High, where all three kids graduated. Past Langley Park, where Tyler played Little League for so many years. Into our subdivision, Langley Oaks. Everything around here shares its name with the most well-known Langley of all: CIA headquarters. And really, just about every family in the neighborhood has some sort of connection to the Agency.

The location was one of the big draws for us, when we first moved here. Less than a ten-minute commute for me, and just twenty into the city for Mike. We maxed out our budget to buy the place, but it was one of the best decisions we've ever made—and it paid off, too, when property values skyrocketed.

I wind my way slowly through the neighborhood. Past the pond; no sign of the ducks today. Past walkers and bikers, pickup basketball games in driveways.

When we first moved in, I didn't think we'd ever leave. But the house is too big for just the two of us; we realized that as it started emptying, as Aubrey left, and then Caitlyn. We don't need the top-ranked schools anymore, or the giant backyard, and all the upkeep that comes along with it. Our plan at first was to sell the year **after** Tyler graduated. But inventory's low and prices are high. Other homes in the neighborhood have been selling for ungodly sums, twice or even three times what the owners paid when the homes were first built. We didn't know if this was a bubble that was going to pop, and we didn't want to take that risk.

Still, though, I didn't want to sell the home—or even get it ready to sell—until Tyler was off to college, so our plan was to wait until fall. Our Realtor, Robert, talked us out of it. Said we'd get far more if we could list by midsummer. We hemmed and hawed—and then hurried. Got it on the market in July.

The day the house was listed, we had an offer, sight unseen. Full asking price.

Seemed strange at first, but Robert explained that the family was out of town, on an extended summer vacation. And they sent a note, written by Madeline. **When we saw pictures of the cul-de-sac,**

we knew: this is the perfect place to raise our three children. . . .

We signed the contract, then a lease for a six-month rental on a townhouse in McLean, not far away. We're going to sell the house, use the cash for a hefty down payment on a new one. Something close to here, because this is where our lives are, where all our friends are: our neighbors, our coworkers, parents of our kids' friends who we grew close to over the years. Maybe we'll find a good deal in the fall, or wait for something perfect next spring. But this way we don't need to rush.

Movers arrive tomorrow. Closing's the day after that. It all worked out for the best.

I'm all the way to the back of the neighborhood now, the last street, Riverview Drive. I take a left.

I drive slowly down the street and pull into our driveway, park there, since the garage is full of boxes.

Then I get out of the car, walk to the front door. Unlock it and hesitate, look back out at the street. Perfect houses in all directions. Quiet, serene.

It's always looked so welcoming here. Always put me at ease.

Now, though, something seems off. I feel unsettled.

Let it go, Beth.

I can still hear Annemarie's words, still see the

look in her eye. I don't know what she meant by that. Maybe nothing at all.

I open the door and walk inside, and an old adage runs through my head, unbidden, unexplained.

If it seems too good to be true, it probably is.

I CLOSE THE DOOR BEHIND me, slide the dead-bolt closed. The click of the lock seems to echo in the silence. **Every** sound seems to echo lately. Most of the area rugs are gone, donated; much of the furniture, too. We're downsizing, after all. Décor is packed, shelves are empty. It's one thing I hadn't anticipated, hadn't remembered from the time we moved in. When the house is this barren, this sterile, there's little to soak up the noise.

I walk into the kitchen. The countertops are bare, all the appliances packed up. Cabinets are cleared, dishes and glassware in boxes. The pantry's empty, except for some paper plates and disposable cups, some plastic utensils. We've been living off takeout for a week now.

On the built-in desk in the corner, there's a single bottle of wine—a pinot grigio, my favorite—and a fancy corkscrew, our gift to the new owners.

"How do you know they'll like this one?" Mike had asked, picking up the bottle. "Maybe we should leave a red."

"They'll like it," I said.

"But how do you know?"

I shrugged. "Because they're like us. Because **she's** like **me**."

"You don't know her."

"I just have a feeling. Besides, it's **wine**. Wouldn't we have appreciated wine—**any** wine—when we moved in?"

I stare at the bottle. Then, abruptly, I walk over and reach for it, cut the foil off the top of the bottle, place the corkscrew on top, start twisting. I can pick up a new bottle for them tomorrow.

I pour a generous-sized portion into a clear plastic cup from the pantry, take a sip, then another longer one.

I'm sorry, Beth. I can't tell you what you want to know.

It's time for a new chapter, Beth.

I walk over to the sink and look out the kitchen window into the yard, the wide expanse of grass leading to the fence, the wooded area beyond that. Can't see it from here, but the river's about a half mile away. I'd trek down there occasionally when the kids were young. There's a clearing where it curves; the kids liked to play on the large rocks, throw stones into the rushing water. Sometimes we'd walk a half mile farther along the bank of the river until we came to Langley Park.

I take another sip of wine and focus on the part of the yard where the kids' playset used to stand. I can almost see the wooden beams; the three swings, side by side; the wavy green slide; the fort at the top. And there's Tyler as a boy, in his pirate dress-up vest. I smile at the sight of him. He's at the top of the ladder, peering through a telescope—

The scrape of a key in the front door lock draws my attention. I blink—the playset is gone—and reluctantly turn. Mike's stepping through the door, brown paper bag full of takeout in hand.

"Hi," he says, walking into the kitchen, and his gaze shifts down to the nearly empty cup of wine in my hand, the open bottle on the desk. He shoots me a quizzical look. "I thought that was for the new owners."

"I need it more than they do."

"Beth." He uses that chiding tone, the one that drives me crazy.

I finish off the last sip, just because.

He sets down the brown bag on the island, reaches in and pulls out a plastic container, then another. Pasta from Antonio's. "You're taking this harder than I thought."

"Taking **what** harder than you thought?"

"Tyler. Leaving." His brow furrows, and he shoots me a concerned look.

Of course Tyler.

"Everything okay at work?" he asks.

"I was **selected** for a new position." I sink down onto one of the bar stools.

"Oh?"

"Teaching new analysts."

"I didn't realize that was something you wanted to do."

"I don't."

An awkward silence falls over us.

"Then did you turn it down?" he finally asks.

"I can't."

He slowly sits down on the stool at the other end of the island. "Why? What's going on, Beth?"

"My case." I stare down at the empty plastic cup in my hands. "There just hasn't been a break."

That seems like a reasonable way to put it. And that's about as detailed as I can get. Mike doesn't know exactly what I do. He knows I work counterintelligence. That I work Iran. That I'm focused on one target in particular, and one **sub**-target. But that's it. That's as much as he needs to know, as much as I'm allowed to share.

"They think it's time for a fresh set of eyes," I add. I can hear the bitterness in my voice.

"Oh, Beth. I know how hard you've worked on that case. I'm sorry it never worked out."

I nod. I still haven't looked up at him. I'm focused on the drops of wine left behind in the bottom of the plastic cup.

"Teaching won't be so bad, will it?"

It will, actually. And it's not the **teaching**. The teaching I can handle. It's having what I **want** to do ripped away from me. It's being forced to let go of something that's been such an important part of my life, when I'm not ready.

"It's just a lot at once," I say. "Tyler. This. The move."

The kind of statement that'll hopefully put an end to the topic, because I don't want to talk about it anymore.

"Speaking of which," I say, in an attempt to change the subject. "The move. Guess we can talk about a new place now."

When we first decided to list the house during the summer, I had one condition: I didn't want to start house hunting—or even **talk** about house hunting—until Tyler had gone off to college. There wasn't a rush; we had the six-month rental. And I wanted us all to savor those last few months in our home without focusing on what was next. Mike agreed, and we've stuck to it.

He leans forward, forearms resting on the granite, hands clasped. "Are we really doing this, Beth?"

"Doing what?"

He holds my gaze, says nothing, then looks away. "We can talk about it another time."

Unease courses through me. I understand the

look, the words. Twenty-five years of marriage will do that, I guess. "No. We can talk about it now."

He shakes his head.

"Are we really doing **what**?"

"I'm not talking about it now."

The unease has settled into something else, something heavy, something **real**. "Because it's news I don't want to hear," I say. "Because you can't deliver it right after I tell you I've essentially been demoted."

"Let's just discuss this another time."

"You don't know if we're staying together."

I say the words, and in the silence that follows, I wish I hadn't. Or maybe I just wish they weren't real. That Mike would deny them.

But he doesn't. He holds my gaze, searches my face. "Our relationship is shit, Beth. Don't act like it's a surprise."

"And we're going to work on it."

"I don't think there's enough there to work with."

The words sting, in the way only the truth can. "The rental will be a fresh start for us."

"I'm not going to the rental."

"What are you talking about?"

"I signed a lease on an apartment."

It's like one blow after another. Like this is some sort of bad dream. "When were you going to tell me this? Why didn't you **tell me**?"

"Because I didn't want Tyler's last days at home

to be about **this**. I wanted things to be as normal as possible for him."

Same reason I didn't want to house hunt. Why we pushed the move, and the closing, until after Tyler left. Keep things as normal as possible until the last possible moment.

I don't know what to think. I know our relationship is terrible. We have nothing in common anymore, besides the kids. The passion's long gone. We're like roommates, not spouses. Co-parents, not a couple.

But we were going to work on it. We **said** we were going to work on it. When we hit that last rough patch years ago, the one when we first hurled around the word **divorce** in a particularly blistering fight.

We can't, Mike had said quietly, the next morning. He avoided eye contact when he said it. **We need to try harder.**

And we did. At least, I **thought** we did. The fights stopped. Indifference took the place of passion—in arguments, and in life. We tried to overlook the faults that used to drive each other crazy, or at least to stay quiet about them. We found ways to compromise when our priorities and preferences differed—mostly by doing our own thing.

We found peace by growing apart.

How did I not see this coming? Up until now, I would have sworn this didn't happen outside novels and movies. One partner being blindsided by a breakup. But here I was, blind to the truth right in front of me.

"So that's it, then?" I say. I never thought this would be the end result. I don't think I ever really believed we'd **fix** our relationship, that it would be like it used to be, but I thought we'd find a new normal. That we'd be content to just **be**.

"It's not like we're never going to see each other again. We'll always have the kids. We'll always be part of each other's lives. We just . . . I think we're better apart. And I think this is the right time for a fresh start."

"A new chapter," I say bitterly.

"Yeah," he says, then catches himself. "Beth—"

"When does your lease start?"

"It already did."

"So you're staying there tonight?"

"If you want me to."

"I do."

I slide off the stool, head toward the desk. Reach for the wine bottle and refill my cup slowly, my back to him.

"Beth?" he says.

I set down the bottle, but I don't turn. I don't want him to see the tears in my eyes.

"I'm sorry."

I don't say anything, keep my back to him, and finally I hear his footsteps leave the room.

Unnaturally loud, echoing in the emptiness. When I turn, he's gone. The foyer is bare.

"I'm sorry, too," I say quietly.

I STILL REMEMBER THE FIRST time the front door opened, the first time I stepped foot into our home.

"It's perfect," I said to Mike.

Truth is, I already **knew** it was perfect. It was the neighborhood we wanted, and just the kind of lot we'd hoped for: end of a cul-de-sac, backing to trees. I'd already made up my mind, but seeing it in person sealed the deal.

He walked in and stood beside me, taking it in. We were in the foyer, and our eyes were on the great room straight ahead: bigger than our entire first apartment, filled with natural light, with huge windows that looked out on the woods, a beautiful stone fireplace. Everything was open and fresh and new, a blank canvas begging to be decorated.

"It's something, isn't it?" Robert said, walking in behind us.

"It's beautiful," I said. I stepped forward into the center of the great room. The kitchen was just off to the left, open and connected, a huge island in the center, tons of cabinets, gleaming appliances.

"There's so much **space**," I said. We were moving from a townhouse, too small for the five of us, with too many flights of stairs. Here the kids would each have their own bedroom, and a playroom on top of that. And it was in the shadow of Langley, a ten-minute drive at the most. Mike's commute would be shorter, too; we'd both have more time with the kids.

We'd been fine in the townhouse when it was just the girls; cramped maybe, but it worked. The public schools were terrible, but we had Aubrey in a private one, and our mortgage was low. But with the thought of three in private schools, and a house that barely fit the four of us, let alone five, we knew we had to leave.

We always knew the townhouse wasn't our forever home; we'd been saving up for the next down payment for years. Langley Oaks was perfect: great location, great schools. But by the time we started looking, after Tyler was born, all the decent lots had been bought. There were just a handful left, too close to power lines, on too-busy roads.

Months passed, and we didn't find anything that was just right. Probably because I had my heart set on this neighborhood. And then Robert called. A buyer had backed out in Langley Oaks. Financing issues. The house was fully built, ready to go.

"Want to see the upstairs?" Mike asked.

"Sure."

Robert stepped into the dining room to make a phone call, so Mike and I walked up the curved staircase, just the two of us, our footsteps echoing. To the right first, to the two large rooms at the end of the hallway, ones that shared a bathroom. "Aubrey and Caitlyn," I murmured.

We walked into the room that would be Tyler's next. The one nearest the master bedroom, with its own en suite bathroom. The floor plan was just right for our little family. The girls had their own space, and Tyler would be close enough we might not even need the monitor. I couldn't stop the smile from spreading to my face.

Mike wrapped his arms around me, pressed his body against mine. "Are you happy?"

"So happy."

Then he kissed me, long and slow.

"The beginning of our next chapter," he said when he finally pulled away, his arms still around my waist. "The place where we'll grow old together."

"I don't want to think about getting old."

He smiled and nuzzled my neck, sending a shiver up my spine. "Then just think of it as the place we'll be in love, for the rest of our lives."

I smiled, feeling like life couldn't be any more perfect. "That's more like it."

FOOTSTEPS ECHO ON THE STAIRS, and then Mike comes around the corner, duffel bag in hand. He pauses in the foyer.

"I'll be back tomorrow," he says. "First thing. Before the movers arrive."

"Okay."

He looks like he's going to say something else, or thinks he **should** say something else. But there's nothing left to say, really. He gives me a sad smile, and a nod, and heads to the door. Reaches for the handle, pulls it open. Turns around one last time.

"Are you okay, Beth?"

"I'm fine."

Another nod, and then he steps outside, closes the door behind him.

I stare at the door. Then, slowly, I walk over to the bay window in the living room. Look out at the street. Watch as his car backs down our driveway, stops, then accelerates, forward this time. I watch as it leaves the cul-de-sac, past Jim's house, past the Patels'. It takes a left at the cross street, then disappears from view. Everything is quiet, once again.

I should be feeling sad. Distraught. Angry. **Something.**

I don't feel anything at all.

I STAY AT THE WINDOW, watching the empty street, devoid of emotion. My husband just left. My marriage is ending. **And I don't care.**

My mind isn't on him. Or **us**. It's on The Neighbor.

There's something out there, some piece of information that I don't know about.

And I need to figure out what it is. If it'll lead me to my target.

It's not too late. It's not like my marriage, that slow and steady decline that deep down I know we can't crawl back from. This **just** happened. I can fix it.

There's so much riding on it. **Everything** is riding on it. If Reza Karimi uses The Neighbor to hack into JWICS, it's over. All of our intelligence will be fed straight to Iran. It's the absolute worst-case scenario. And I might be able to prevent it.

I pull my phone from my back pocket, find Annemarie's number in my list of contacts. Press send.

One ring, then another. And another.

Voicemail.

I end the call, stare at the screen. She saw that it was me, didn't she? That's why she didn't answer.

Fine. She doesn't want to talk. Not right now, anyway.

I slide the phone back into my pocket and focus again on the street outside.

I'll find the information I'm looking for, one way or another.

I can't make the kids young again. Can't convince Mike we have something we don't—and not sure I'd want to, anyway.

But this case—this case is different. It's something I can **change**.

I'm close to finding The Neighbor. I can feel it. I might not have proof, might not have concrete leads, but gut feelings count for something. I've been on Reza Karimi's tail for twenty years. I've listened to everything we've intercepted him say about The Neighbor, and I know this: something's changed. There's something different about his voice lately. He's scared.

The coming months will be crucial for the success of The Neighbor. Karimi's own words, spoken at the start of the summer. I believe with all my heart he knows we're onto him. He knows we're close to The Neighbor.

I'm close.

I **have** to be.

Because right now, I don't have anything else.

THREE

A KNOCK AT THE DOOR. IT STARTLES ME, PULLS me back to the present. I realize I'm staring out at the empty cul-de-sac, the darkening sky. How long have I been standing here?

Another knock. I walk over and open the door. There's Alice, a bottle of my favorite pinot grigio in one hand, a lawn chair in the other. She lifts the chair slightly, gives me a smile. "For old times' sake?"

THE SUN WAS INCHING LOWER in the sky by the time our moving van finally made its way down the street, away from our home. The girls were watching from the bay window, waiting.

"It's gone," Caitlyn yelled.

"Can we go outside now?" Aubrey asked.

I walked into the room, Tyler on my hip, peeked out the window, saw the taillights of the truck down the road. The street in front of the house was empty. "Sure."

The girls bounded out the front door, ran through the front lawn with glee, twirling in circles. Mike and I followed, and I set Tyler down, watched him toddle around, bend down to examine a blade of grass. Mike put his arm around me, pulled me close. "We're here. All moved in."

"Finally."

"Mommy, Daddy, can we ride our bikes?" Aubrey asked.

Mike and I made eye contact, that sort of wordless conversation we'd perfected since becoming parents, and I shrugged. "There's still a bit of daylight."

Luckily, the bikes were easily accessible in the garage, and before long, both girls were in their helmets and riding their bikes in a circle around the loop, bright streamers trailing from handlebars. Mike and I stood at the bottom of the driveway with Tyler, watching.

The night was warm, the sky streaked with pinks and oranges, everything quiet, none of that street noise we'd grown accustomed to in the townhouse. Just the happy chatter of the girls, the scrape of training wheels against pavement, and then the sweet ding of a bell, the one mounted to Aubrey's bike.

At once, as if summoned by the bell, the front door of the home next door swung open, and two kids raced out onto the front lawn, a girl and a boy, similar ages to Aubrey and Caitlyn, maybe a touch older. They ran straight to small bikes lying in the grass.

A woman walked out behind them and briskly across the lawn, her eyes on Mike and me, her hand raised in greeting. She was short, built like an athlete and dressed in workout clothes, with close-cropped hair and a friendly face. "You must be the new neighbors," she said as she approached. "I'm Alice. Alice Kane."

"I'm Beth," I said. "And this is Mike. We're the Bradfords."

She looked down at Tyler and smiled. "How old are the little ones?"

"Six, four, and one."

"Oh, that's wonderful. We have three, too. Piper and Paxton are seven and five." She motioned to the kids on the lawn, who were strapping on helmets. "And our youngest, Preston, is one."

The front door to their house opened again, and a man walked out, carrying a toddler on his hip. He was tall and broad-shouldered, and even from a distance I could tell he had a distinctive air of confidence about him. "The new neighbors," he said, approaching. "We've been looking forward to meeting you. I'm Charles."

Mike introduced us as I snuck a peek at the street. All four older kids were riding in a circle now. Our girls were smiling ear to ear. Charles set down Preston—a chubby little boy with blond curls—on the grass beside Tyler. The two looked at each other warily.

"What do you do for work?" Alice asked.

"Government," I said. My standard answer. I wasn't undercover, so I was allowed to tell people where I worked, but it was frowned upon. Around the DC area, "government" was generally understood to be code for **something sensitive I don't want to talk about.** Most people just accepted the answer and moved on.

She gave me a knowing smile. "Charles is 'government,' too." She used air quotes. "He's CIA."

"Alice," Charles chided. He was so tall, and she so short, that he actually had to look down to talk to her.

"We're **neighbors,**" she said to him. "We'll all know these things about each other eventually, won't we?"

"I'm Agency, too," I said.

"Oh?" Charles said. "What part?"

"CIC. You?"

"CTC."

I glanced over at Mike, who looked a bit befuddled by the acronym. "Counterterrorism Center."

"What do you do?" Alice asked him.

"I'm a lawyer."

"Oh yeah? Me, too. What kind?"

"Contract law. Sullivan and Mulhern. You?"

"Good firm! I'm with the DA. Where'd you go to law school?"

"Stanford. You?"

"Yale."

"Ivy Leagues. So you must be drowning in student loan debt, like my wife," Charles said, putting his arm around her.

Alice rolled her eyes. "He likes to remind me of it, constantly."

"Just every month when we make the payment." He winked at her.

"Actually, Mike's lucky," I said. "His parents paid his way."

"**Mostly**," he corrects, with a smile at me.

"Damn. **Lucky** is an understatement," Alice said.

The sound of a garage door opening, from the house on the other side of ours, drew my attention. Two little girls ran out into the driveway. A woman followed behind them, a lawn chair in one hand, a bottle of wine and a sleeve of clear plastic cups in the other. She had a big smile, big hair, and— I could tell immediately—a big personality.

"Our new neighbors!" she said as she approached, arms outstretched. She had on a bright fuchsia patterned dress with chunky boots and chunky jewelry, and she looked almost giddy. "I'm Desiree Johnson. Everyone calls me Des."

"Beth Bradford," I said. "It's so nice to meet you."

Alice took the sleeve of cups and bottle—something white and cold with a screw top—and Des kicked open her chair, set it down in the street. "No chairs tonight?" she said to Alice.

"I'll grab them," Charles said, and headed up his driveway toward the garage.

"We usually sit out here and watch the kids play," Alice said to me.

"More kiddos," Des said, looking at the street. "Love it."

"Jada and Jasmine are the same age as your girls," Alice said to me, pouring wine into one of the plastic cups, then handing it to me.

"You're kidding," Des said.

"How lucky is that?" I said with a smile.

"Where'd you move from?" Des asked. Alice handed her the second cup of wine, then began pouring a third.

"Not far. Alexandria."

"Let me guess—better schools?"

"Schools and **space**."

"Well, you've got that here. What do you do for work?"

"Government."

"Ah. Agency?"

I was a bit taken aback—again—by the direct-
ness of the question.

She must have seen my look, because she quickly
added, "Langley's practically just around the corner.
I think every house on this street has someone who
works there. In our house, it's me."

"Yeah, Agency," I said, somewhat comforted by
the fact that I was talking to another CIA careerist.
"I'm in CIC."

"Nice. I'm in Security. Polygraph Division."
She cast a glance at Mike. "And my husband—
Darryl—he works in IT. Private sector."

Charles returned with two lawn chairs, opened
them up, set them down beside Des's.

"Go ahead, sit," he said to me.

"You sure?"

"I've been sitting all day." He smiled.

Alice, Des, and I settled into the three chairs.
Something caught Des's attention as she was sitting
down. I followed her line of sight and saw another
woman approaching, from the house beside the
Kanes', two doors down. The fourth of the four
houses sharing the end of the cul-de-sac. She was
slight and fair, with long red hair, and she was carrying a chair of her own.

"Hi," she said when she got close, giving me a
shy smile. "I'm Erin O'Malley." She was dressed
in slim-fitting black pants, black flats, and a nondescript tan top. No makeup, or very little—I could

see a smattering of freckles across the bridge of her nose. A far cry from Des's bright pink lips and attention-grabbing outfit; Erin immediately struck me as the type that wanted to blend into the crowd.

"Beth Bradford. It's nice to meet you."

"I live there," she said, stating the obvious, pointing to the house from which she came. She opened her chair, set it down next to Alice.

"They're **both** Agency in that family," Des said, "Erin and Sean."

Erin looked at her in surprise. Alice handed her a cup of wine.

"It's fine," Des said. "She's Agency, too. And she's our **neighbor**."

"I work the Middle East," Erin said. "Regional issues. Sean's in the Directorate of Support. Facilities."

"I'm in CIC," I said. "Is it just the two of you? Any kids?"

"Not yet." She gave me another shy smile. "But hopefully soon."

The older kids had abandoned their bikes and all six were playing a game of tag. Tyler and Preston were toddling around the gutter, Tyler clapping gleefully, while Mike stood nearby, talking with Charles.

I chatted with the new neighbors, listened to the happy shrieks of kids at play. After a while, Darryl walked over to join us. He was built like a linebacker, sported a shaved head and a booming laugh, quick to crack a joke. And then Sean joined, too, on his way back from a run. He was lean and young and quiet, like Erin.

I watched as the streaks of pink and orange in the sky turned to dusty rose, dark violet. When cups went dry, Alice brought out a new bottle and refilled them. Before I knew it, both bottles were gone and the streetlights had flickered on.

I leaned back in the lawn chair and looked over at Mike, who was standing with Charles and Darryl and Sean, three of them with bottles of beer in hand, Sean with a bottle of water. Mike caught my eye, winked, smiled. He looked as content as I'd ever seen him.

"I think you guys are going to fit in really well here," Alice said, watching me.

I believed it. I felt like this was where we were meant to be, all along. "Good, 'cause we're not leaving. Never moving again."

She and Des laughed, and Erin smiled.

"Honestly, though, this is really nice," I said.

"Sure is," Des agreed.

Alice looked over and smiled. "It's perfection."

ALICE AND I SIT IN our old lawn chairs, rusted at the joints now, the fabric faded, in the street between our two houses. We hold plastic cups of wine and stare out at the empty street. Everything is quiet.

"Mike left," I say, without looking at her.

"I know. He told Charles."

I spin toward her. **"What?"**

"He just texted."

Typical Alice bluntness. She doesn't beat around the bush. Never has.

I take a sip of wine. It seems like a betrayal, that Mike shared the news before I could. Even if Charles **is** his closest friend, just like Alice is mine.

"God, I'm sorry, Beth." Her forehead creases, and I can see the sincerity in her eyes. She hasn't changed much in all these years. Same short, no-nonsense cropped hair, same athletic build.

I shrug. "It's not like it's **completely** out of left field."

She nods.

"I knew we were growing apart. It's just . . . I thought we were going to work on things."

"I know you did."

I take a sip of wine, and she does, too.

"I remember when you first moved in," she says. "How close you were . . ." She laughs and shakes her head. "Remember the first time we had you over? Trivia?"

"Trivia?"

I rack my brain. I do remember the first time

we went over to the Kanes'. They'd invited us to have dinner. I remember trying on a few different outfits in my bedroom, desperate to make a good impression, unsure whether it would be a backyard barbeque or a fancy dinner party, if all five of us were even invited, or if they assumed we'd get a sitter. If the bottle of wine we were bringing was nice enough. I was standing in front of the full-length mirror, smoothing out a sundress, when Mike came up behind me, wrapped his arms around my waist, nuzzled my neck. **Stop worrying,** he said. **They'll love you, just like I do.**

"You don't remember?" She sounds incredulous.

"No. Not the trivia, anyway." I remember she answered the door in her usual workout attire, and they ordered pizza. They were our kind of people after all.

"After the kids ate, we put them in front of some Disney movie, and the four of us played some stupid couples trivia board game in the other room. I say **stupid** because you two got every single question right." She laughs. "Charles and I got most of them wrong."

The memory comes flooding back. Mike and I on the couch, his arm around me, each of us practically reading the other's mind, scoring point after point. Watching Alice and Charles screech and laugh each time they got something wrong. Giggling, but being secretly pleased. **We sure do know each other well,** I had said quietly as we walked hand in hand back home at the end of the night.

"Guess there's more to a relationship than knowing each other well," I say.

"I didn't mean that," she says, looking chagrined. "I just meant . . ." She trails off, seems uncharacteristically at a loss for words.

"You didn't think it would end like this."

"No, I didn't."

A car turns down our street, takes the left onto Riverview, headlights washing over us. Jim's Buick; we know them all. Only six driveways in this direction; the four of us at the end of the cul-de-sac, and Jim and the Patels farther up the street.

The Patels are the only ones on Riverview who aren't original owners, though they've been here practically a decade now. They're retired, and they've always kept to themselves. Jim and Rose did, too, and she passed away a few years ago. Jim works at the Agency; I've seen him in the halls at headquarters, though I couldn't tell you what he does there. We never really got to know either family as well as we should have.

The car turns in to his driveway, pulls into the garage.

I wonder what he thought, if he saw us down here. We probably look crazy. Two middle-aged women sitting on old lawn chairs in an empty street, drinking wine.

This was the norm for so many years, when the kids were younger. We'd gather out here, with Des and Erin and our spouses, watch the kids ride bikes, or scooters, or draw with sidewalk chalk. Catch up on our days, drink wine as the sun set and the streetlights came on.

Over time, the kids outgrew the chalk, and the scooters, and the bikes. They had homework after school that kept them inside, and myriad after-school activities. And of course there was the inevitable lure of screens: tablets, video games, then their own cellphones. The wine nights moved inside, around kitchen islands, and became fewer and further between—in part because **we** were busier, too. Alice worked her way up to a federal judgeship; Charles is head of CTC. Des is a senior polygraph examiner; Darryl is president of his company. Erin manages a team in the Office of Middle East Affairs, Sean manages one in the Directorate of Support, and together they run their church youth group on the side. Mike is close to making partner, and I'm exactly where I want to be in my own career—or I **was**, until they took me off my own case.

Another garage door opens, this time from the house next door. Des walks out onto the driveway, a lawn chair and bottle of wine in hand. She walks over to us, kicks open the chair, brushes away some cobwebs, sets it down on the other side of me. "Haven't opened this thing up in years," she says, sitting down. The chair creaks under her. She's always been curvy, but those curves have become much softer over the years.

"Mike left," I say. It feels like the elephant in the room.

"I know."

She reaches for the bottle that's already open, refills my cup, then fills her own. The bracelets on her wrist—there must be a dozen—clang as she moves. She still has a sense of style that's all her own: outfits full of layers and textures, jewelry designed to make a statement. Nonconformist, just like her.

"Why do I feel like I was the last to know?" I ask.

"You weren't. Alice just texted me."

I steal a glance at Alice, who avoids eye contact, reaches for the bottle.

"News travels fast around here," I say.

"It always has," Alice replies.

Isn't that the truth.

"Have you learned any more about our new neighbors?" Alice asks.

I've already filled them in on what little I know. The names from the contract, the information that turned up when I googled them. He's a physician, sports medicine. Couldn't find anything on her, not even a social media page.

"Maybe a stay-at-home mom?" Erin had asked.

"In this neighborhood? With the home prices today?" Alice said.

"Well, if he's a physician . . ."

Alice had shrugged, unconvinced.

And I know they live in Bethesda right now. Their home is zoned for good schools, so they're not moving for that. But property records show their house is a four-bedroom. Maybe they want that fifth room. The extra space. We wanted that, too, once upon a time.

"They were here today," I say.

"I saw them," Des says.

"Yeah?" Alice says. "Spill."

"Silver Audi SUV, Maryland tags. Just the two of them, no kids. They looked young. Thirties. Cute. You know, how we all looked when we moved in."

"Any feedback?" Alice asks me. "They're not backing out, are they?"

"Haven't heard anything. I started to watch the security camera footage, but—"

"Whoa," Des interrupts. "You were taping them?"

"It wasn't like it was a secret," I say, defensive. "We disclosed it to the Realtor. Perfectly legal."

"So you were able to watch them **and** listen?"

"Yeah."

"That's awesome. And a bit creepy."

"Figured it was better to know if they're going to back out before closing." I shrug.

"So what'd they say? What'd they think?" Alice asks.

"Actually, I haven't watched it." I only started it, when I was sitting outside Tyler's dorm. God, that feels like a million years ago.

"But you still can?"

"Yeah, it's recorded."

"Who in the world doesn't see the house they're buying until two days before closing?" Des says, shaking her head.

Movement catches my eye. Erin, approaching from around the side of her house, lawn chair in hand. She's in tailored pants and flats, like always; her hair—shoulder length now, still a vibrant red—looks polished as usual. "Does she know about Mike, too?" I say.

"She knows," Alice replies, reaching for the second bottle of wine and the sleeve of plastic cups.

Erin pulls open her chair—it's bright and new and lightweight, unlike the ancient chairs the rest of us are using—and sits down beside Des.

"Nice chair," Des says.

"Soccer," Erin replies. The twins are fourteen now, and deep into soccer, both of them on competitive travel teams. Erin and Sean spend a good chunk of their time sitting on the sidelines of fields.

Alice hands her a cup of wine, and she takes it, then turns to me. "I'm sorry about Mike."

"Yeah, me, too."

We lapse into silence, the four of us just watching the darkening sky, nursing our cups of wine.

"I still can't believe you're leaving," Alice finally says. "The cul-de-sac won't be the same without you."

Des murmurs her agreement.

"We're right behind you, you know," Erin says.

"**What?**" Alice and Des say in unison.

"We're listing in the spring."

"You can't be serious," Des says.

"But the kids—" Alice begins.

"We'll be moving right before they start high school. Up to Maryland. Their travel teams are based there, and the high school teams are better. It'll be better for them, in the long run." It's an uncharacteristically detailed explanation for her. She's still the quiet one, always has been. Much prefers listening to us talk than sharing things herself. Usually we have to drag things out of her, ask questions to encourage her to share more.

"Oh, wow," Des says. Alice looks like she's in shock. I am, too; I figured they'd be the last to leave.

"It'll be just us, then," Alice says, turning toward Des.

"Actually"—Des shifts uncomfortably—"Darryl and I have been talking. . . ."

"Oh no, not you, too," Alice says.

"Come on, you know what Beth's house is going for. And how fast it went. What if this is a bubble and it pops?"

"Nothing's popping," Alice says.

"The kids are out of the house now." Des shrugs. "We're looking at new construction. We found some neighborhoods we like."

Alice just stares at her.

"Come on, Alice, you must have considered it."

She shakes her head adamantly. "We're here for the long haul."

Des says nothing. Erin takes another sip of wine.

Down the street, Jim's porch light flickers on.

"Man. All three of you?" Alice says. She shakes her head. "It's the end of an era."

Des reaches down for the bottle, realizes it's empty. Sets it back down again. No one speaks.

It's time to pack up the chairs and go, but I don't want this to end. I'm not ready.

"I should be getting back inside," Erin says. "Check on the kids."

"Yeah, it's getting late," Des says.

I can hear the reticence in their voices. No one makes a move to leave.

"Well, someone's gotta say it," Des says, breaking the silence. "I sure am going to miss this. And I'm going to miss **you**, Beth."

"Same," Alice says.

"Same," Erin echoes. There are tears in her eyes.

"I won't be far," I say quietly. I smile at each of my friends, and I know it looks as sad as it feels.

"Beth, you're going to be okay," Alice says. I like that she put it that way, a statement instead of a question.

"I know," I say. And I **do** know. Part of me is relieved at the thought of Mike being gone. Not having to make awkward conversation. Not being frustrated by the myriad little things he does that annoy me. Being able to watch whatever I want on TV, or eat whatever I want for dinner, all the time, no compromising.

I'm not sure how much I'll miss him, to be honest.

The truth is, I don't want **him**. I just want the life we used to have.

BACK INSIDE, INTO PAJAMAS FOR the night, I settle into the couch cushions, remote in hand. Turn on the television, pull up the HomeWatch app. Find the time I'm looking for—11 A.M.—and press play.

There she is. I watch her walk into the foyer again. **Oh, Josh. It's even better in person.**

He comes up behind her. "It is, isn't it?"

I lean forward, remote at the ready. As soon as she takes a step forward, I press the right arrow on the remote, switch to the next camera angle, the one in the great room, facing the kitchen.

There are three cameras downstairs and one up, strategically placed to provide maximum coverage of the house. I won't be able to see **everything**, but I'll follow them as best I can.

She's walking toward the kitchen, her back to the camera.

"Look at that island," she says. I'm completely focused on her; I can't take my eyes off her.

"Huge," Josh says.

"Granite," says the Realtor.

"Oh, this window." She stands in front of the sink, looks out. "I think a playset could go right there, don't you?" She turns to Josh.

"One step at a time, Maddy," he says with a smile. "Let's get through the move first, okay?"

Maddy.

Maddy and Josh. Josh and Maddy.

She turns around, circles the island slowly, eyeing the appliances, the cabinets, then steps into the dining room. I can't see her from here, but I can hear her.

"Our table should fit nicely in here," comes her voice.

Footsteps; I think they're heading to the living room.

There they are. She walks to the bay window, stands in front of it, looking out, while Josh peruses the room.

"Nice natural light," he says. "We might have to paint, though. This color might clash with the couch."

In my mind I'm seeing couches, trying to imagine what style might be theirs, what color. What would Mike and I have picked if we were a decade or two younger?

"Maddy?" Josh says.

She finally turns from the window. "Sorry. I'm just admiring the view. You can see everything from here."

You can, it's true. I could have sat there at the window and watched the kids play, but I never did. I was always outside with them. With Alice, and Des, and Erin—

"Upstairs now?" the Realtor says.

I switch back to the foyer view, watch them climb the stairs, Madeline in the lead. I switch to the upstairs view, watch her reach the top. She heads to the right, toward Aubrey's and Caitlyn's old rooms, then disappears into Aubrey's room. I can't see her from the camera angle. I turn the volume up as far as it will go.

"Oh, look at this, Josh," she says. "The layout's perfect. The two girls' rooms share the bathroom."

I watch as the Realtor disappears into Aubrey's room, too, behind Josh.

"We couldn't quite tell from the pictures," she says, probably to him.

A phone chimes, and then I hear the Realtor's voice. "If you'll excuse me, I'm going to take this. Please keep looking around." He appears again in the hall, heads toward the stairway, makes his way down.

I still don't see Madeline and Josh. I can hear the murmur of voices, but they're indistinct now. They probably walked through the bathroom into Caitlyn's room—

There they are. They're in the hallway again, exiting from Caitlyn's room. Walking down the hall, toward Tyler's room.

She stops at the door. "Look at this. Light blue. Perfect for Theo."

She walks inside, Josh following behind. I can see part of Tyler's room from this angle; the camera's mounted just outside.

"I think the crib should go right against that wall." She points to the same wall where we had Tyler's crib when we first moved in. I feel like my heart is being squeezed.

"So it works?" Josh says. I can't see him from this angle; he must be standing beside the closet.

"It's perfect. I love that it's so close to our room. We'll be able to hear him when he needs us."

Josh moves into view now, comes up closer to her, puts his arms around her, so they're chest to chest. "**Now** it's good. But what about when he's older?" He leans down, kisses her neck. "I mean, he'll be able to hear **us,** too."

She arches her head back, her long hair falling away from her body. He slides his hands down her back, holds her low at the waist. She's so thin. I was that thin once.

She laughs. "When he's older, we'll close his door. Lock ours."

"Mmm. I like the sound of that." He kisses her, and his hands slide lower down her body. She playfully swats them away.

"It isn't our house **yet,**" she says with a coy smile.

Footsteps, and Josh drops his arms, pulls away. Madeline runs a hand discreetly down the front of her top, smoothing out invisible wrinkles.

And then the Realtor appears, blocking my view of her. "What do you think?"

"We love it," she says.

"Excellent."

He turns and walks back into the hall, and Madeline and Josh follow, exchanging a smile as they walk out of the room, like there's a secret between them.

The three walk into our bedroom and disappear from view once again. I hear the murmur of their talk, indistinct words, something about internet service providers, then watch them head back down the hallway, down the stairs, to the front door.

They leave my house, step out onto my front porch, Josh's hand resting lightly on the small of her back. As they walk down the steps, she reaches for his hand, and they smile at each other again.

I hit pause, and they're frozen like that on my screen. Their backs to me, bodies angled toward each other, hands clasped, a loving look between them.

I feel sick to my stomach, but I can't take my eyes off them. In my mind it's not **them** anymore, it's **us,** Mike and me, back when **we** were in love.

I reach for my phone, check the screen. No missed calls, no texts.

Tyler was supposed to call. Mike said he was going to—

He probably **did.** He probably called Mike's cell.

They'll always call him first, won't they? I mean, Aubrey will, for sure. She's always been closest to Mike. Tyler too, probably. And Caitlyn—who knows about Caitlyn. She's the unpredictable one, the one who flouted our rules whenever she could, who didn't just move away, moved an **ocean** away. The independent one.

What will happen on holidays? Where will Tyler stay when he comes home from school, or Caitlyn when she's stateside, or even Aubrey and Austin, before they find a home of their own?

I unlock the phone and tap out a text to Tyler. How's everything going?

I wait for a response, for those little dots that indicate he's responding, typing his answer, but there's nothing.

I always feel vaguely concerned when the kids don't respond right away, same as I did when they were young and they were out of my sight.

Mike wouldn't have told him, would he? No. He'd wait for me, let us tell the kids together. He'd do the right thing.

The screen eventually goes black. I tap it again, bring it back to life. Still nothing, just the screensaver, a picture of all five of us from the last family vacation we took, years ago. I suppose it's time to change that, isn't it?

I open up the photo app, then tap one of the folders. **Old pictures**. Ones I uploaded from the laptop years ago, a trip down memory lane before Aubrey's wedding.

I scroll through, find just the one I'm looking for: the three kids in front of the house, the day we moved in. Aubrey and Caitlyn on either side of Tyler, sitting on the front steps, their arms around him, squeezing him, big grins on their faces, tickling him to get him to smile, too. I remember it like it was yesterday.

I set it as my new screensaver. In my mind I can picture them at that age. Tucking the girls into their beds at night, making sure their teddy bears are secure in the crooks of their arms. Laying Tyler down in his crib, tiptoeing out of the room.

Madeline's words echo in my head. **We'll be able to hear him when he needs us.**

When he needs us.

I look down at the phone. Still no response from Tyler, just the picture of the kids when they were little. When they still needed us.

When there was still an **us.**

I set the phone down and walk into the kitchen, refill the plastic cup. Then I take the cup and the rest of the dwindling bottle back to the couch, settle down into the cushions, and hit the rewind button on the remote. All the way back to the beginning. I press play and watch Madeline as she steps into my house for the first time, this woman with the perfect life, with **my** life, the one I used to have.

FOUR

I WAKE UP THE NEXT MORNING TO THE TINNY chimes of the alarm on my cellphone. I'm disoriented—I'm still on the couch, television still on, displaying the HomeWatch logo—and my head is throbbing. The wine bottle on the coffee table is empty. I fumble for my phone, silence the alarm, squint at the screen. New text message, from Tyler, from last night.

I'm fine. Everything's good here.

I get up off the couch, stiff and uncomfortable, slightly nauseous. Throw out the empty bottle, force myself upstairs to shower and dress. Movers are coming at eight. Mike will be back before that.

He arrives at quarter till. Knocks on the front door, which must be as strange for him as it is for me. I let him in. I'm dressed and ready and drinking a cup of coffee from the Starbucks down the road—the coffeemaker's already packed up, and this is **not** the morning to be without caffeine. The Advil hasn't done a thing, and the Gatorade I knocked back only made me feel sicker. It's been a long time since I was hungover.

"So how are we doing this?" I ask. Everything was supposed to go into storage until we pulled it out for our new place. Now there's no **our** place, just his place and my place.

"We'll just have them move it all into storage, like we planned. We can figure it out later."

I nod.

"You doing okay, Beth?"

"I'm fine." I wonder if he can smell the alcohol on my breath. I'm trying to stay far enough away that he can't.

"Good."

"Look, I'm going to go into work today," I say. I decided as I was getting ready. Not because I'm anxious to get to the Kent School, but because I don't want to be **here**, with him. And because that information on The Neighbor's still out there, and I'll be damned if I don't figure out what it is.

He looks relieved. "Yeah, no problem."

An awkward silence follows.

"Did Tyler call last night?" I ask.

"Oh yeah. I forgot to mention it. He did."

"You didn't . . . **tell him**, did you?"

"No, of course not. I said you were at work. I

figured . . . we'll tell them together, right? Each of them, when the time's right?"

"Yeah."

More silence.

"Aubrey called, too," he says.

"Oh?" I'm not surprised. She's the most communicative of the three kids, though Mike's phone is almost always the one she dials. Says it's because **Dad** comes before **Mom** alphabetically, and it's only fair. But I've always thought it's because he's the one she really wants to speak to. She's always preferred him, ever since she was a toddler. **Daddy's girl,** we always said. Not that she and I don't have a good relationship; we always have. The two of them are just closer.

"Yeah. Just to chat."

"How is she?" It hurts to ask, but this is the future, isn't it? I won't know everything that's going on in her life. I won't find out right away. She and Mike might grow even closer. And that's fine, but I'm terrified now that it will come at the expense of my relationship with her.

"Fine. Nothing new on her end. Or Austin's."

"Okay."

We stand there in silence. No need for a perfunctory kiss anymore, is there?

"I'll see you later, then," I finally say.

"See you later."

———

THE DRIVE TODAY IS IN the opposite direction, away from Langley. Watching the cars heading toward the city, a steady stream of traffic, when I'm traveling **away**, the lanes around me empty, makes it all the more brutally clear that I'm not part of the action anymore. I'm an outsider.

The Kent School is housed in a nondescript office complex. There's a guard post, but it's discreet, not like the heavily fortified ones at Langley. And quite frankly, it doesn't need to be: this place just doesn't matter nearly as much.

I park beside the building and take the elevator up to the third floor. There's a check-in desk just outside the elevator, staffed by a young guy in jeans. I hand over my badge, and he scans it, then hands me a new one. A Kent School badge. White, on a white lanyard. "You won't be needing that old one around here," he says.

"Thanks." I slide the lanyard over my head.

"Through there," he says, gesturing toward the door on my right.

I hold my badge to the reader and the door unlocks. I push it open, step into a hallway, office doors on either side, big windows into each one. A few are lit, but most are dark. The hall's empty. None of the bustle that Langley's sure to have at this hour. There's a different vibe here. A different pace. Different work being done.

I start walking down the hall, checking the name

placards beside each door. I pass one open door, one office with lights on, and my eyes linger as I pass. The computer's on, screen open to the classified search engine, no one sitting behind it, no one in the office. Leaving a computer unlocked like that at headquarters is grounds for censure, and just doesn't happen.

It's a different world out here.

The placard with my name is about halfway down the hall, on the left.

I step inside and turn on the light. Dull and drab, a desk with two computer screens—one for the classified system, one for the open internet—a bookcase, and a table near the door with a printer on top. A stack of six cardboard file boxes in the corner—all the belongings from my old office.

My own office for the first time, not a cubicle, but God, I'd prefer the cube.

I sit down in the rolling chair and turn on the computers, log in to the classified system. Then I bring over a box and start unpacking.

The first one's books—tomes on Iranian history, Iranian culture, and the Farsi language. Even one on Persian flowers; there was an obscure NSA intercept years ago that indicated Iranian intelligence agents were displaying red roses—the national flower of Iran—to signal the presence of a sympathizer, and I always wondered if they were using other flowers, as well. The second box is books, too—an assortment on spycraft, counterintelligence, and analytic techniques. I set them all on the bookcase.

The next box is awards—plaques and framed certificates, Exceptional Performance Awards, recognition for contributions to the mission. I've done a lot here, a lot of good work. The Neighbor's the only area where I came up short. And it's all they see, all they care about, and the most frustrating part of all is that I **would** find my target if they'd just give me a chance, let me stay on the case.

At the bottom of the box are the framed pictures I kept on my desk at the office. One of the whole family, all five of us, from Aubrey's high school graduation, and one of just the kids.

I pick up the picture of all of us, and look at it closely. Big smiles, like we're the perfect family. I place it facedown in my bottom desk drawer.

The next frame holds one of the three kids, one of my favorites from when they were younger. Tyler couldn't have been more than three. It's in the front yard, at the height of summer, and they'd been playing in the sprinklers. Their clothes are wet, their faces are flushed, and their smiles are huge and genuine. I remember standing on the front porch and snapping it.

I set that one on my desk.

Next box now. This one's full of old stuff, really old, the kind of stuff that sits untouched at the bottom of a desk drawer until you need the space.

Old financial disclosure forms, listing our bank account balances, the mortgage on our townhouse, our car payments. The form I filled out when Mike and I got engaged, granting the Agency permission to interview and investigate him, make sure there were no counterintelligence concerns. The kind of thing I would have gone through and purged if I had been the one to pack my belongings.

I lift out a stack of paper, jumbled and disorganized, much of it construction paper. The one on the top is a crayon drawing of our house, green scribbled grass at the bottom of the paper, blue at the very top for a sky, a giant yellow sun with long rays. Tyler signed the bottom, big shaky uneven letters, some lowercase, some uppercase, a backward "E." A note from Caitlyn, with words sounded out, spelled inventively. Another note, this one from Aubrey, this one clearer, but God, these are old.

Stuck in the middle of the pile is a file folder. I pull it out. Written on the front, in black marker: **The Neighbor**.

I don't open it, but I know from the weight of it, from the way the edges of the papers inside jut out at various angles, from the specks of highlighting visible at the edges, that it's full of the very reports they were supposed to purge during the pack-out. Classified analysis, raw intelligence pulled from the encrypted Quds Force line. Key reports, the ones I printed out and saved for easy access, for reference, the most important parts highlighted. I haven't touched it in years, since they came up with a decent online interface that was actually quicker and easier to use.

I almost have to laugh. This was the whole point of them packing up my desk, wasn't it? To make sure I didn't have access to anything like this. I roll my eyes and stick it in the bottom drawer. Nothing in here's new, and it's the new information that I want. I'll deal with this later.

I roll my chair forward and open up my email on the classified system. The inbox is nearly empty. Three emails, all from the head of the Kent School. I'm used to hundreds of unread messages every morning, on top of thousands of older messages.

They reset my email. Removed me from all the groups I used to be part of.

I open up Alpha next, the system for cable traffic. It's my usual routine, after checking email, a way to see what new reporting came in overnight, the human intelligence reports and signals intelligence related—if tangentially—to The Neighbor. I've added myriad search terms over the years, overly broad in some cases, but designed to catch more than I need so that nothing falls through the cracks.

It's a blank page, no new reports pulled.

It's been reset. My search terms have been erased.

I curse softly. Those search parameters would take me ages to re-create.

I lift my fingers to the keyboard and type in the code name for the encrypted Quds Force line, Frozen Piranha, a nonsensical two-word phrase with a single benefit: its searchability. Nothing extraneous would get pulled into a search like that. It would only be information on the encrypted line, the information I want.

No results. Other information may be available.

I stare at the words on the screen, code for **nothing you're allowed to see.** They're not a surprise; I know they removed my accesses. But it stings.

I feel, once again, like something's been ripped away, like a piece of my life is gone.

I look down at the desk, at the scattered papers, so old. Focus in on the crayon drawing of our house. Impulsively, I pin it to the corkboard behind the computer.

Then I reach into the bottom desk drawer, pull out the file folder on The Neighbor. I open it up, feeling a strange sense of satisfaction. My own small act of defiance, of thumbing my nose at the powers that be. **You missed this. I still have it.**

The report on top is the one that started it all. The first pull from Frozen Piranha. The copy paper is starting to yellow, and it's bent at the edges, it's been thumbed through so many times. I run my finger over the subject line.

New Target: The Neighbor.

FIFTEEN YEARS AGO, THE REPORT dropped on my desk right in front of me, landed on top of a page I was halfway through reading, an obscure piece of signals intelligence related to Iranian intelligence officers. A friend will make himself known by displaying red roses.

"Got something for you," Dale said, standing behind my right shoulder.

My eyes settled on the subject line. New Target: The Neighbor.

"Intercepted communication," Dale said. "An encrypted line from the Quds Force station in DC back to headquarters in Tehran. To Reza Karimi."

I skimmed the report. Skipped over the technical specifications of the encrypted line, the Farsi words that were collected. Focused on the translation.

The Neighbor is in play. Ready to recruit A Good Friend.

Someone's in play.

Someone got by us.

And that phrase. **A Good Friend.** We'd seen it before. Code for an asset with a sensitive government position, someone with access to classified information. Karimi had tried to recruit a few already, used U.S.-based Quds Force operatives to do his bidding. Traditional approaches, traditional vulnerabilities: debt, blackmail potential, that sort of thing.

Each time, I stopped it.

But now it was someone else doing the recruiting. The Neighbor. They wouldn't talk about one of their own that way; it wasn't what they did. The Neighbor was a recruit, and if **that person** was doing the recruiting, if there wasn't a direct line of contact between Karimi and a local Quds Force agent and someone with a security clearance, then we were flying blind.

If Karimi was using an access agent, he was going to be harder than ever to stop.

"From DC Station?" I said, turning around to face Dale.

He nodded.

That meant the recruited asset was more than likely someone local to our area.

I looked down at the report again. It was going to raise alarm bells, as it should.

"No indication who's being recruited?" I'd stopped skimming, hadn't gotten to the end of the report, but I assumed if we knew, it'd have been mentioned up front.

"Bureau's on it."

"Any more on The Neighbor?"

"Not a thing."

"It's probably an American citizen, right? Isn't this more the Bureau's purview?"

"We don't know that. Besides, do **you** trust the Bureau to figure out who it is?"

Of course I didn't. But that didn't mean I wanted to figure it out. I said nothing.

"Look, for all we know it's a foreign national, which makes it ours. Let's not let the Bureau screw it up."

"Okay," I agreed, reluctantly.

I looked down at the report again. At those words. **The Neighbor is in play.** Racked my brain, tried to figure out what in the world I could do next, where I could go with this, how I could learn more.

"Is this all we picked up on the line?" I asked. "Was there any response from Karimi?"

"There was. Turn the page."

I flipped to the next page of the report, scanned past the Farsi, to the translation:

Remind The Neighbor to use the children.

The words made my stomach turn. " 'Use the children'? Are you serious, Dale?"

"I had a feeling that would catch your eye."

Of course he did. He knew me better than anyone at work.

He gave me a steady look and a quick nod, and it was almost like an unspoken conversation took place. We'd worked together long enough, and closely enough, that he didn't have to ask if I was prepared to take this on, and I didn't have to answer.

I watched him walk back to his office, and

my eyes drifted to the picture of my kids in a frame on my desk. It was a recent one, taken outside on the front lawn after they'd been running through the sprinklers. Their faces were flushed and their smiles were huge. Aubrey had a missing front tooth, Caitlyn sported messy pigtails, Tyler wore a grin so wide his eyes were scrunched shut. All of them looked so happy, and so innocent.

Using children to accomplish goals—that was a bridge too far. That was a red line in my book, and Reza Karimi had just crossed it.

There was something else about that phrase, too. It was a **lead**. It was the only thing we had to go on, really.

My gaze shifted to the whiteboard. In all the years I'd been in CIC, I'd never written anything up there.

I walked over and grabbed the red marker, wrote the words.

Use the children.

I reread what I'd just written, and nodded. I had a new mission.

A LIGHT RAP AGAINST MY open office door pulls me back to the present. I quickly shut the file folder, place it facedown on the desk, and turn toward the door. A familiar face—deeply lined, topped with a shock of bright white hair—shoots me a grin.

"Beth Bradford!" he says, extending one arm theatrically. The other is gripping an oversized mug with steaming contents.

"Cyrus Rooney," I say, with as much enthusiasm as I can muster.

He steps into my office, sets his mug down on the table beside the printer, then takes an awkward hop up so that he's sitting on the edge. There's a chair in front of my desk, but somehow it's just like Cy to prefer perching on a table. "How the heck are you, Beth?"

"Doing well," I say. "It's been a long time, hasn't it?"

Cy's an old teammate, the former senior analyst in Iran CI. Knows a ton, but got to the point he didn't know how to use it anymore. Didn't want to retire, but didn't really want to work, either. Just wanted to **talk,** to share his knowledge with anyone who would listen, and in the process made it difficult for anyone else to be remotely productive. Senior management moved him over here years ago, and productivity at headquarters increased dramatically.

"**Way** too long." He reaches for his mug, takes a slow sip, like we've got all the time in the world. "You know, I saw the nameplate on the door. Had no idea you were coming on over. No note from Kent School admin, nothing from CIC . . ."

"I was supposed to be on leave this week. Maybe that's why."

"Ah, you couldn't stay away, huh? I remember that about you." He wags a finger at me. "Hard worker. Dedicated."

I give him a tight smile. I don't particularly want to be talking to him right now, but there's no good way to make him leave.

"What will you be teaching?"

"The new analyst class."

"Oh, wonderful. Guiding the next generation. Nothing more rewarding."

Cy always thought that was his role, back when he was in CIC. Guiding the more junior analysts, imparting his knowledge. Slowing us down in the process.

They finally moved him out here, put him in charge of a one-day class on advanced CI techniques. A perennial favorite, one that includes demonstrations of the state-of-the-art spy equipment the Agency uses overseas for technical operations. Most classes here end early—it's generally acknowledged that taking a Kent School class means a shorter workday—but Cy's is one of the few that regularly runs over a full day. He's in his element showing off the spy equipment, being able to talk at length to a captive audience.

"Shame about the timing, though, with that new lead," he says. "The intercept on The Neighbor."

He knows about the intercept? He still has access to information, and I don't? I get that senior management needs to keep down the number of people read into compartmented programs like Frozen Piranha, but if there's room to keep Cy read in, why in the world was **I** cut out?

"Yeah, a shame."

"What do you make of it, anyway?" he asks, crossing his feet at the ankles, taking a slow sip from his mug.

"Hard to say, exactly." I don't want to admit I haven't seen it. This is my case, my person, and it's infuriating not to know.

He nods. "New target base of some sort, I would think."

"Probably," I say noncommittally.

It's too much. I'm seeing red now. I'm supposed to be at headquarters right now, supposed to be working on **this,** whatever it is. That was the plan for after Tyler moved away. That was my purpose.

All my plans are falling apart.

Cy sets his mug down on the table beside him, stretches, like he's here to stay. Classic Cy, wanting to just sit and chat—

"Cul-de-sac," I say abruptly. "Really curious about your thoughts on that, Cy."

It's all I know about the intercept. And hopefully it's enough to convince him I've **seen** the intercept, if there's any doubt in his mind.

I'm taking a risk here, pretending I've already seen the intel, trying to trick him into giving me classified information I'm not authorized to have. If—and **when**—he finds out I wasn't permitted to have it, I'll have irreparably burned a bridge with him, not to mention opened myself up to disciplinary action. But this is **The Neighbor** we're talking about.

"I'm glad you asked, Beth," he says, a pleased expression on his face. I'm pretty sure I just made his day.

Keep him talking, Beth.

He tips his head to the side, looks thoughtful. "Naturally, I'd have liked to see more than a line. But it's a line that's full of meaning."

"And that's where your expertise comes in," I say.

He nods soberly.

" '**The Neighbor has found a new cul-de-sac,**' " he says, enunciating each word.

The words echo in my brain, even as he continues to talk.

"**New cul-de-sac.** My guess? Different agency. If it's NSA they've penetrated, they're moving on to CIA. Or vice versa."

"Maybe," I murmur. "No way of knowing, really."

"Not until we catch him. And we will. Well, **they** will. Not you and me anymore, right?" He chuckles.

I just stare at him. I can't force a smile to my lips.

"You know, back in '05, when we were watching

Ahmadinejad, we didn't have much to go on, either," he says slowly. He's about to launch into a story, one I couldn't care less about.

I let him talk, nodding when it seems appropriate, trying my best to appear interested, even as my mind wanders, replays those words—

Cy is silent, looking at me expectantly. I didn't hear the last thing he said.

"You've done some amazing work, Cy," I say.

His chest puffs out, the smallest bit.

I check my watch. "I'd love to hear more, but I better get ready for the first day of class.

"Of course, of course." He slides off the table. "Let's have lunch one of these days, shall we, Beth?"

"Sounds great."

"See you around." He tips an imaginary hat in my direction and leaves my office. He's barely a few feet down the hall when I hear him strike up a conversation with someone else.

I swivel back to my computer, look down at the folder on my desk. The Neighbor.

The Neighbor has found a new cul-de-sac.

My gaze drifts to the framed picture of the kids, the one on that hot summer day, with their flushed faces, their big smiles.

But it's not **them** I'm looking at.

It's the loop of pavement behind them.

FIVE

AUBREY AND AUSTIN MEET ME AT THE HOUSE
that night after work. I had asked if she wanted to
see it one last time; I figured she might. She's always
been the most sentimental of the three kids.

She and Austin each give me a quick hug as they
step through the front door.

"How are you doing, Beth?" Austin asks, his face
full of concern. He's sweet, that boy. He's Aubrey's
age, but looks even younger. A mop of blond curls,
blue eyes, soft features.

I smile at him. "I'm okay."

"I'm actually going to wait in the car," he says,
nodding toward the door behind him. "I've got
some calls to make. Just wanted to pop in and
say hi."

"Thanks, Austin." I don't know if he really has
calls to make, or just feels like this is a moment

that should be shared between the people who have memories here. I have a feeling it's the latter, and I appreciate the gesture.

He steps back outside and Aubrey and I walk around the house slowly, taking it all in. It's empty now, hollow. Dust bunnies congregate in the corners; a cleaning crew is coming first thing in the morning.

"Weird to see it like this," she says, standing in the middle of the great room.

"Sure is."

"Dad couldn't come?" she asks.

I examine the stone fireplace, avoid eye contact. "He was with the movers all day."

She turns and heads into the kitchen next. Stands in the open space where our table used to be, looks around.

"How's the house hunt?" I ask her. It's almost surreal to be saying goodbye to my empty home, closing such an important chapter of my life, while she's on the verge of starting her own.

Just like Madeline.

Only I'm **happy** for Aubrey.

Aubrey isn't taking my place.

"**Mom?**" She's staring at me, eyebrows raised, expectant, and I have the sense she answered me already, even though I didn't hear her.

"Sorry, what was that?"

She watches me, concern etched on her features.

I rack my brain, try to think of what I just asked her. "The house hunt—how's it going?"

"Good." She's still looking at me warily. "Saw a place we liked."

"You did? Where? Nearby?"

"Not really. In Maryland. Up near Fort Meade."

"Yeah?" I know the area; it's a good forty-five-minute drive, more with traffic. I had hoped she'd be closer. "Kind of far from work, isn't it?" The school where she teaches is in Northwest DC. Austin works on the other side of town.

"We can handle it."

I walk over to the desk area, adjust the bottle of cabernet sauvignon, the replacement I'd picked up on my way home from work, so that the label is facing straight out. Figured Madeline didn't need the cul-de-sac favorite pinot.

Then the envelope, so that it's straight, too. The card itself has a cheery **Welcome Home** printed on the front. Inside I'd written a short greeting, included my phone number in case they have any questions.

"What's the neighborhood like?" I ask, stepping into the empty living room.

"It's just a few years old. So there are lots of young families."

"That's nice." I feel a pang of sadness, even though I'm not sad. I'm **happy** for her. My gaze shifts to the bay window. Down the street, Jim's rolling his recycling bin to the bottom of his driveway. It looks heavy, and it's no doubt full; there's usually a deafening cascade of glass when it's emptied into the truck. **Jim with the Jim Beam**, Alice once called him.

"Is it a quiet street?" I ask.

"Yeah. Of course." She says it almost defensively.

I shift my focus back to her. She's looking out the window, too.

I turn and walk into the foyer, then start up the stairs. She falls into step behind me.

"And the house?" I ask as we walk. "It's what you want?"

"It's what we need. We don't need anything flashy like this."

I turn and cast her a sidelong glance. "Flashy?"

"Come on, Mom. Look at this place."

I continue walking up the stairs, feeling confused. Feeling **judged.**

I stop in the hall at the top, and she walks past me, toward her bedroom. I follow her in.

I should let this go, but I can't. "What do you mean, **flashy**?"

She stops in the middle of the empty room. "All I'm saying is we don't want to overextend ourselves." She gives me a pointed look.

Irritation bristles inside me. "Your father and I didn't overextend ourselves, Aubrey. We're doing just fine."

She shrugs noncommittally and walks into the bathroom, then through it to Caitlyn's room.

"We saved enough to pay for college for all three of you, didn't we?" I say, following her. I sound almost antagonistic. But really. Talk about looking a gift horse in the mouth.

She doesn't turn around.

The irritation is morphing into resentment.

It wasn't just college tuition we saved, either. **Times three**. It was enough for living expenses, too. Enough so they could focus on school instead of work, so they wouldn't have to take out a dime in student loans. That was a priority for Mike and me; my parents paid my way through school, and his parents mostly did. We wanted the same for our kids.

I give Caitlyn's room a once-over, then step out into the hallway. Blocking Aubrey's path, so that she has to look at me, has to acknowledge me.

"Yeah, this was more house than we needed," I say. "But we thought it would be the perfect place to raise you kids." My voice breaks, and I can see her face soften.

"It was," she says gently.

"You do what you need to for the people you love," I say. "If you have children someday, you'll understand."

"I don't need children to understand that," she says, this time with an edge to her voice, holding my gaze. "I already have people I love. People I'd do anything for."

I search her face, but can't read her expression.

"Is everything okay with you and Austin?" I ask. Because I know as well as anyone, marriages don't always work out. Although the thought that it might **not** work out between them is heartbreaking. They were college sweethearts, a perfect match. I couldn't have asked for a better partner for her.

Confusion clouds her features. "Of course."

Good. Just because Mike and I didn't work out doesn't mean **they** won't.

They probably **will,** just like Madeline and Josh. I find myself staring into Tyler's room. From this angle, in the hallway, it's the same vantage point captured by the home security camera. I can almost picture Madeline and Josh there, his arms around her, the way she arched her back—

"Mom?"

Aubrey's voice brings me back to the present. She's watching me, and there's a flash of fear on her face. **I'm worrying her**.

It's almost a relief to see that concern, after the cold conversation we just had. I can't have Aubrey slip away even more than she already has, not with everything else going on—

"Are you sure you're okay?" she asks.

"Yeah," I say, and force a smile.

But I can tell from the way she's looking at me that she doesn't believe it.

THE NEXT MORNING, I SIGN the closing documents at the law office. Alone, separate from Mike, because that was an option, because I didn't want the awkwardness of sitting in the same room as him if I didn't need to. He's coming in next, and the new owners are signing at a different office across town.

I head straight into work after I leave the law office. My class doesn't start until next week, and there's not much I need to do to prepare—the curriculum is easy and there's a handbook with lesson plans—so I'm basically twiddling my thumbs. My inbox is still mostly barren. I peruse the internal websites that are open to all analysts. The sanitized analytic articles, watered down for those with only minimal clearances, the ones that provide little more than judgments and supporting data sourced to a "clandestine source" or "signals intelligence." I miss knowing exactly who the sources are, exactly how and where the messages were intercepted.

I catch myself watching the clock. Ten A.M. That's the time the Sterlings are scheduled to close. I can picture them sitting at a long table, the kind I was just behind, only they're side by side, close. She's probably in more tailored clothes, another silk blouse, her hand resting lightly on his leg, smiling at him with those perfect lips.

At ten-thirty, I'm fairly confident the house is no longer ours. A sadness washes over me.

It's over.

The rest of the work day passes in a mindless blur. The dean of the Kent School shows me around, introduces me, gives me the code to the supply room. Each course has a bin, some of them big—like Cy's, full of spy equipment—some small, like mine. I bring my bin back to my office, look through it once I'm alone again. Just photocopied lesson plans and handouts, not much more. I wish again I were back in my office, doing real work.

When my eight hours are up, I drive to the rental. Step inside this place that's now mine, and mine alone, this version of home that isn't my home. There's nothing wrong with it. It's a nice townhouse, older, but well kept up. And it's got character: antique light fixtures, a claw-foot tub, a bronze mail slot in the front door. But it's not home.

I unpack a bit, but there isn't much to do. This is just short term; most everything's in storage. I stack some plates and bowls in the kitchen cabinets. Plug lights into smart plugs, set up the Echo Show on the counter. I've gotten used to relying on Alexa; it's a hard habit to break. Then I sit on the couch. Channel surf—nothing worth watching. Check my phone—

A new text, one I hadn't heard arrive. From a number that's not saved in my contacts, a Maryland area code.

Thank you so much for the lovely housewarming gift. How did you know Cab Sauv is our favorite? Hope you're settling in well to your new place. Cheers, Madeline

I realize part of me was hoping that something fell through with the closing.

But if she saw the bottle of wine, she's there.

I close the email, look around the rental. So empty, so quiet. Then, abruptly, I reach for my keys.

No harm in driving past. One more look at the house, now that it's no longer mine.

It only takes a few minutes to reach Langley Oaks, a few more to wind my way to the back of the neighborhood, turn onto my street—

There's a moving van in front of my house, blocking most of the cul-de-sac.

They're not wasting any time, are they? And there are the movers, bringing furniture into my house.

Their house.

I pull off on the side of the street, in front of Jim's house. Thankfully, his front porch is empty today. He's out there a lot, especially since Rose died, on one of the rocking chairs, a stiff drink by his side. Poor guy's closest companion now is the bottle.

From here it's a straight clear view down to the end of the cul-de-sac.

I watch the movers. One's at the rear of the truck, stacking cardboard boxes onto a hand truck. Another two are headed toward the house, carrying a couch wrapped in blankets and plastic—

A figure steps out the front door. Stands on the front porch—**my** front porch—observing the movers.

She steps to the side as the two men with the couch approach. Says something to them, a smile on her face.

Movement catches my eye. It's Alice, walking out of her house, toward my house. She gives a wave in Madeline's direction.

Madeline sees her. Hesitates momentarily, almost like she's not sure if the wave is directed at her. Then starts walking, down the porch steps, across the lawn, toward Alice.

They meet in the grass between the two homes, the spot where Alice and I always used to stand, used to chat. Now it's **them** standing together, talking together, outside **their** homes.

Madeline leans back and laughs at something Alice says. They look happy, both of them, and the conversation seems like it's flowing.

It hurts, looking at them. It feels like a betrayal. My best friend, and the woman who's taking my place.

I know I shouldn't feel that way. She's just moving into a new home, one that happened to be mine, and of course she's going to talk to Alice, because they're neighbors now.

It's just that she already has so much of what I used to have. The house, the adoring husband, the small children who need her.

Alice is **my** best friend.

She can't have **that,** too. It's just not fair.

I WATCH THEM UNTIL THEY drift apart, Alice back to her house, Madeline to mine. The moving van's still there, but it's clear they're just about done. A few of the movers are standing in the driveway, chatting, while the others are maneuvering a piece of furniture, something big and heavy, covered with one of those big moving blankets, up to the front door.

As they struggle to hoist it up the porch steps, the blanket slips, slides off. Underneath is a huge safe, tall and solid and heavy. Safes like this, they're designed for one thing.

Guns. Lots of guns.

Mike and I, we have a small safe, for my single handgun, something that's always seemed like a necessary precaution, given my line of work.

This one, though: this one's huge.

I start the engine and pull forward, drive in a

slow loop around the cul-de-sac, eyes on my house the whole time, softly lit, welcoming against the darkening sky.

I peer through the bay window into the house, trying to catch a glimpse of the woman inside, wondering what secrets she might be hiding.

I don't see her, but I see something else. A console table in front of the window, oddly placed, really, but they're only just moving everything in, so I'm sure they have some rearranging to do. It's what's on **top** of the table that catches my eye, that sends a cold shiver through me.

It's a vase filled with lush, red roses.

SIX

BACK IN THE RENTAL, I SIT DOWN AT THE kitchen table and open up my laptop, then google. Madeline Sterling. I can't get her out of my mind. Can't stop thinking about her. This woman, the one in **my** house. With a huge gun safe.

With **red roses** in the window.

A friend will make himself known by displaying red roses.

Still nothing, same as before—no Facebook, no LinkedIn, nothing—but this time I dig deeper. Add in Josh's name for good measure, and after scrolling through a few pages of results, I find something. An old wedding web page, one that listed their registries, now defunct, the links broken. Madeline Greene and Josh Sterling.

The wedding was seven years ago, in Richmond, and she was twenty-four at the time.

God, she's young.

I use the maiden name, the year of birth to keep searching, but I don't turn up anything else. No education, no career, nothing.

Frustrated, I close the laptop. The silence around me is thick, and feels suffocating. I stand abruptly and head to the counter, pour myself a glass of wine. A cab.

How did you know Cab Sauv is our favorite?

I sip it and reach for my phone. Pull up Annemarie's number, try her again. No answer.

Mike texted earlier, and I haven't responded. I look at the text again now. How are you?

Still I don't respond. Instead, I open up the chain with Tyler, type out a question of my own. How's everything going?

I wait for a response, but it doesn't come.

Then the text chain with Caitlyn. How are things across the pond?

I drain the rest of the glass as I watch the screen. No answer from either of them.

I open up another chain now, the one with Aubrey. Just thinking about you, kiddo.

The response comes immediately, and brings tears to my eyes. You okay, Mom?

I'm fine.

I set down the phone, and the silence again seems overwhelming. My thoughts turn to Madeline. In my house, surrounded by children and noise, and in my mind, I'm there, and Aubrey, Caitlyn, and Tyler are kids again, chattering and giggling and filling the home with such joy and love and **life**—

At once, the image vanishes, and I'm **here,** in the rental, alone.

I pad into the living room and turn on the television for some sound, some company. There's really only one thing I want to watch.

I open up the HomeWatch app, the saved videos. Warmth from the wine is spreading through me. I sink down into the couch cushions and press play.

I watch them walk through the house, the same thing I've watched before. This time, when they're in my bedroom, I turn up the volume, try to hear the conversation I missed the first time, make out the indistinct words from off-screen.

"Verizon's the internet service provider?" comes Josh's voice.

"I'd have to check," the Realtor says.

"No need," Madeline says, her voice the quietest of the three. She continues talking, but I only catch a couple of the words. **Lines run out here.**

"Yeah?" Josh says.

"Most of the—" Madeline says, and the next words are hard to hear.

"Cool. Reception seems strong," Josh says.

The three of them walk out of the bedroom, and I hit pause, rewind, listen again, closer this time, volume up higher.

"No need," Madeline says, her voice louder now. "Few different lines run out here. We have options."

"Yeah?" Josh says.

"Most of the neighbors use Verizon," she says. "Everyone except the Kanes, next door."

I listen to Josh answer, watch the three of them walk into the hallway.

Then I hit pause and stare at the screen, the frozen image of her. Rerun that conversation through my mind. This woman, the one with the guns, with the red roses, with the invisible past: She knows a lot about the neighborhood, doesn't she? About the internet. About my **neighbors**.

Much more than I knew when I moved in. More than most people would know, or **should** know.

Why?

WEEKS AFTER WE MOVED INTO the new house, the front porch lights went out.

It was a Saturday evening, and the kids were playing in the cul-de-sac. All the parents were out there, milling about: Mike and me, Alice and Charles, Des and Darryl. It was dusk, and the lights had been on, and all of a sudden, they shut off. It caught our attention, all of us.

"Uh-oh," Mike said.

"Should we go take a look?" Charles asked him.

"I guess we better."

Mike and Charles started up the front lawn toward the house.

Des gave Darryl a pointed look. "You gonna go help?"

"Honey, **you'd** have more luck figuring that out than I would."

"I don't know a **damn** thing about lighting," she said.

"Well, neither do I," he shot back. Alice and I exchanged a glance, and I could tell she was trying not to laugh, just like I was. Des and Darryl—and their constant ribbing—were nothing if not entertaining.

He turned to me, shrugged his shoulders. "Lights aren't my thing. Now, if it were a network issue, or your internet's down, I'm your man." He pointed a thumb toward his chest, flashed me a smile.

Des rolled her eyes theatrically.

I smiled. "I'll keep that in mind."

"It's not Charles's thing, either," Alice chimed in. "Something tells me those lights aren't coming back on tonight. Sorry, Beth."

I shrugged. "Oh well."

Movement caught my eye. It was Sean, approaching on the sidewalk, heading back home from a run. He slowed down to a walk as he neared his house.

"On second thought . . . ," Alice said. Then she cupped a hand around her mouth and yelled Sean's name.

He looked up, raised his hand in a wave, and started toward us.

"Hey," he said as he got closer. His face was glistening with sweat, and his breathing was fast.

"We've got a problem," Alice said. "And I think **you're** the one who can fix it."

He looked up at the front of my house, where Mike and Charles were staring at the unlit light fixtures, and suppressed a smile. "I'll see what I can do," he said, and headed up the lawn.

Ten minutes later, the lights were back on.

The three men made their way toward us.

"Nice work, fellas," Alice said.

"It was all Sean," Mike said.

"You don't say." Alice turned and grinned at me.

"You fixed that in no time," I said to Sean.

He shrugged. "It's what I do."

"Yeah?" I realized I didn't know **what** he did, actually. Something in the Directorate of Support. Facilities, Erin had said.

"Yeah."

There was an awkward beat of silence, and Alice jumped in to fill it. "Sean has a background in electrical engineering. He's responsible for the entire backup CIA power supply."

"Wow," I said, genuinely impressed. I wouldn't have guessed.

Sean shrugged, color rising to his cheeks, and gave me a sheepish smile. "I'm just the guy who keeps the lights on."

I watched him walk back to his house, chatter resuming around me. Watched a figure move past the bay window inside his house—Erin, no doubt, someone I hadn't talked to nearly as much as Alice and Des. Realized that I still had so much to learn about the people around me, so much that everyone else already seemed to know.

THE NEXT DAY DAWNS BRIGHT and sunny, one of those perfect early fall Saturdays. Before lunchtime I head out to Starbucks, pick up a venti latte through the drive-through, and then I'm driving back to the cul-de-sac, pulled there as if by some sort of magnetic force. My Nikon's on the passenger seat beside me, telephoto lens attached. Just in case I want to get a closer look.

The moment I turn down the street, I see it. Kids in the cul-de-sac. **Young** kids. It's been years since I've seen the sight.

I came to see **her**. I wasn't expecting to see **them**.

I park in front of Jim's house, and I watch. Two girls on bikes, one with training wheels, both of them in big helmets, the younger one struggling to keep up with the older one. They look the same ages as Aubrey and Caitlyn when we moved in, maybe a little younger.

And a little boy toddling around, dragging a brightly colored toy lawnmower behind him. That must be Theo. The one who's still in the crib, the one who still needs them.

My heart catches in my throat. It's like looking at my own kids, seventeen years ago.

Only there aren't parents there, keeping a watchful eye, the way Mike and I always used to—

There she is. She steps out the front door, stands on the porch between the stone planters, her phone held to her ear. Without taking my eyes off her, I reach for the camera. Lift it, find her again through the viewfinder. Zoom in.

She's carrying on a conversation and watching the children at the same time, a pleasant look on her face. Confident, and content. Infuriatingly so. I press down on the shutter release, almost instinctively. Then I lower the camera and watch her through the windshield.

I crack my windows open, and the girls' voices carry over. It's that sweet high-pitched chatter that I remember from so long ago. The occasional babble from Theo. And a laugh, from the porch, from Madeline. I wish I knew what she found funny, wish I could hear the conversation.

I switch to video mode on the Nikon, hit record.
I don't lift the camera, don't aim it at the cul-de-sac,
but I'm recording the audio, and I'm not even sure
if it's more because of her, or **them**, the kids. And
then there's a call, from the younger girl: "Look at
me, Mommy!" Instinctively I look—

But it's not me she's calling to. I'm not Mommy
anymore, I'm Mom, and she's not Caitlyn.

Madeline pulls the phone from her ear. "You're
doing great, sweetheart," she calls to the street, and
then she returns the phone to her ear, but I can't
make out the next words—

Theo trips, falls to the pavement. I see it out
of the corner of my eye, and Madeline's down
those steps in an instant, across the lawn, ending
her call, scooping him up, holding him against her
chest, soothing him, and in my mind that's
Tyler, and that should be **me**, and I'm filled with
anger, because this woman is in **my** place, and she
doesn't belong here—

She looks up, looks directly at me. Makes eye
contact with me, holds it, watches me over the
top of Theo's head, his body still held tight in
her arms. Doesn't smile, doesn't wave, doesn't do
anything neighborly like that. Just stares at me,
expressionless.

I shift into drive, pull forward, into Jim's driveway, then reverse, head back down the street in the
direction from which I came. I check the rearview

mirror; she's still watching me. Like she thinks I don't belong here, like this is **her** cul-de-sac.

It's true, though, isn't it? The thought runs through my head, echoes there, taunts me:

She **does** belong. She's the neighbor now.

I DROP OFF THE DRY cleaning, pick up a few groceries, and then I'm back in the rental—with nothing to do. It's clean. Laundry's done. There's no teenage boy mess, no teenage boy sound, no sound at all. Just me, and silence.

I pull out my phone, check the screen. No new texts, no new calls. I could try the kids, send a text just to check in, but I decide against it, put the phone away. They're busy with their own lives.

I reach for the camera next, hit the play button, look at the pictures I took of Madeline. This woman who barely exists on the internet, the one with the guns, the one who knew details about her neighbors before she moved in.

I press the button with the plus sign and zoom in, take a closer look at her face. Pretty, pleasant. Content.

Next image now. A black screen; it's the audio recording. I press play and listen again to the sweet sounds of the children in the cul-de-sac, the chatter, the toddler babble. The call: **Look at me, Mommy!**

There's that pull in my heart again; God, she sounds just like Caitlyn did.

And the response: **You're doing great, sweetheart.**

I close my eyes and continue to listen—

The cry, from Theo. In my mind I picture Madeline running toward him—

Another sound. Her voice, faint, saying something, ending the call. The words are indistinct—

Wait a second.

I rewind the video a few seconds, listen again. My pulse is starting to race.

The very last words she utters **are** distinct, just barely, at least I think they are.

And I recognize them.

Khoda hafez.

Goodbye.

In **Farsi**.

WEEKS AFTER WE GOT THAT first pull from Frozen Piranha, our first tipoff about The Neighbor, we intercepted another communication. A message from Reza Karimi to a high-ranking Iranian official in DC, a man with close ties to Quds Force but who was nonetheless untouchable due to his diplomatic immunity.

Pass The Neighbor the exact words I say, through means that I can't use.

I stared at the Farsi words on my screen, willing them to make sense. The **translation** did, in a literal sense. I understood the words. But the meaning wasn't clear, not by a long shot.

Of course, it didn't include the actual words he wanted passed along. **That** would have been useful. It was more a message about tactics. But it did tell me this:

Reza Karimi was directly running The Neighbor. There wasn't a middleman. Or there was, in a sense, but it was strictly for message conveyance.

The other targets I'd disrupted—The Jackal, The Goalkeeper, The Anchor—they'd all been run by middlemen. By globe-trotting Quds Force operatives, agents who ultimately reported to Karimi, but who had significant autonomy. Those middlemen were the key—I traced their IP addresses, then their movements, tracked new burner phones, waited until they made contact with their targets.

This was different.

And what **was** the way of conveying messages? What couldn't Karimi use?

We had been doing everything in our power to find The Neighbor. It's all I'd thought about for weeks. The Bureau put extra eyes on every U.S.-based Quds Force operative, watched everything they did, everyone they mct with, listened to everyone they spoke with.

There was nothing suspicious.

Because **they** weren't running The Neighbor. **Reza Karimi** was.

But **how**?

The Neighbor was recruiting other people. That was the whole point of an access agent. He—or she—was collecting information, and had to get that information back to handlers somehow. To **Karimi** somehow.

The Bureau might have been able to intercept a call straight back to Tehran, but Reza Karimi knew that. He was using email, I'd have been willing to bet. Anonymous, throwaway accounts, accessed from public IP addresses. Near impossible to trace.

But this message, this directive to pass Karimi's words to The Neighbor, by a method Karimi can't use . . .

What **was** that?

Maybe I'd been wrong about email.

But email had its advantages for Karimi. Because it wasn't like a face-to-face meeting, or a phone call. There was a written record of it, and would be, forever.

That meant **blackmail** forever. Karimi would have The Neighbor in his grasp for the rest of The Neighbor's life.

And I'd be willing to bet that was **exactly** what Reza Karimi wanted.

———

LATER THAT AFTERNOON I FIND my way back to Langley Oaks. I'm not going to turn down my street; I'm just going to drive down to it, see what's going on, turn the other way, turn around.

Only when I reach it, there's a white van in front of the house, the kind with a ladder on top, and I can't tell from here what kind of van it is, what business, and I need to know that. So I take the left, inch toward Jim's house, but Jim's outside today, in one of the rocking chairs on the front porch, and I can't exactly stop, so I keep driving, slowly, toward the end of the cul-de-sac.

There's no writing on the side of the van, no indication of what it is—

Movement near the house catches my eye. There's a man there, to the right of the front door, on a small ladder, installing a security camera.

A security camera. **Why?** And why so **soon?** They **just** moved in. There's no crime in our neighborhood, certainly not on our street. Seventeen years, and there was never a single incident on the cul-de-sac—

I'm nearly at the end of the loop when the Kanes' front door opens. Alice steps out, raises a hand, waves. **At me.**

Dammit.

I didn't want to stop. Didn't want to attract any attention. Just wanted to see what was going on at my house.

I pull closer to the edge of the street and begin to brake, then on second thought pull into Alice's driveway. There might already be cameras recording, or might be soon, and I'd rather not have an image of my car sitting outside my home. **Their** home. Her home.

I shift into park and turn off the engine. Turn and look again at my old house. The blinds are open, and I can see inside.

The roses are gone, the console table gone, too.

I step out of the car, and Alice gives me a quick, fierce hug. "I didn't know you were coming by," she says.

She thinks I'm here to see her. Good. That's my excuse. "I should have texted."

"Nah." She puts her arm around me, starts walking back toward the front door. "That would be weird, wouldn't it?"

"Well, things are different now."

"Isn't that the truth."

We walk inside, and I head straight for my usual stool at the island, slide into it.

"Can I get you something to drink?" she asks.

"Wine?"

She raises an eyebrow, just for an instant, and it's the sort of reaction I might miss if I didn't know her so well. "Sure."

She reaches for a bottle on the counter, open with a stopper in it. Pours two glasses, hands one to me. Then leans on the island, across from me, watches me closely. "So how are things?"

"They're . . . okay."

She smiles sympathetically. I take a sip of wine to avoid her gaze.

"How are things here? How's the new neighbor?"

She shoots me a quizzical look, and I catch myself.

"New **neighbors,** I mean."

"They're great. I mean, they're not **you guys,** but, you know, they're nice. They have young kids—it's nice to see kids playing in the cul-de-sac again, you know? And Maddy—she's funny. She'll fit in."

The words sting. I remember her saying that about me once.

"I don't know," I say. "Something's not right about her."

"What?" Her brow furrows. "What are you talking about?"

"I just . . . I don't trust her." I probably shouldn't have said that. But I did, and it's out there now.

"Yeah? Did something happen at closing?"

"No."

She looks at me expectantly. "What then? Dish."

"It's just . . . a feeling."

She gives me a funny look. "A feeling?"

"What does she do for work, anyway?" I take a sip of wine, try to act like it's just a conversational question, not like I care as much as I do.

Alice slides down into a bar stool. "She used to be a kindergarten teacher. Since their youngest was born, she's been a stay-at-home mom."

"See? How do they afford that house? You know what they paid for it."

"And you know he's a doctor."

"Still. They'd need another source of income."

She shrugs. "You don't know if they have family money or whatever."

"Do **you** know? I mean, now that you're such good friends." I sound petulant, jealous.

I can see in her eyes she heard it that way, too.

"She knew about you, before she moved in," I say. "Did she tell you? I heard her mention your name on the security footage."

"Google is a wonder." She smiles.

I take a sip of wine. I guess she has a point. But still. The red roses in the window—if only I could mention those. But I can't tell her the significance of them, not without disclosing classified information. "Have you heard her speak another language?"

Alice raises an eyebrow. "Nope."

"I have. Farsi."

"Okay." She draws out the word. Her brow is still raised. "And?"

"Isn't that unusual?"

She swirls the wine in her glass, watching me the whole time. "Beth, I'm worried about you."

"About **me**?"

"Yeah."

It's typical Alice. Blunt, to the point. It's one of the things I've always liked about her, really. I know she'll tell it to me straight. Mike told me once that her coworkers consider her abrasive. I just find her refreshingly **honest**.

"You're not acting like yourself. And I don't blame you. With Mike leaving, and selling the house, and Caitlyn and Tyler gone . . . God, Beth. I don't think I'd be keeping it together." Her eyes search mine. "But I worry that you're channeling those emotions the wrong way."

"Meaning?" The way I say it makes it sound like a challenge.

"Meaning you seem really focused on Madeline." She says it quietly.

"For good reason."

She looks down at her glass, like she's trying to figure out what to say next. "Beth . . ."

"Alice, if **anyone** should believe me, it's you."

"You know I'm always behind you, one hundred percent. It's just . . ." She shrugs, uncharacteristically at a loss for words.

She doesn't believe me. My own best friend. I dig in my heels. "They're putting up a security camera. Why? We don't have crime here."

"You had one, too."

"Yeah, but that's different. I'm CIA. I could have

been a target. And come on, it's one of the very first things they do? **Why?**"

"I don't know, maybe because of **you,** Beth."

I go still. "What?"

She looks like she wishes she could take that back.

"We all saw you here," she says, gently this time. "On the street. Watching them move." She leaves the rest of the thought unspoken. **It was creepy.**

I don't know what to say.

"I mean, I get it. It's hard to let go. You've got a lot going on right now. A lot of changes. I explained that to Maddy, but . . ." She shrugs. "She's got young kids and all. You understand."

Alice and Madeline were talking about me. Behind my back.

I look down at my glass, focus on that. The wine's almost gone; I didn't realize I'd nearly finished it.

"Another glass?" she asks gently.

"Better not. I'm driving."

"Oh yeah. That's right."

There's an awkward pause. I finish the last sip of wine.

"Things sure have changed, huh?" she says.

"Yeah."

I stand up, bring my glass to the sink. Rinse it, place it in the dishwasher. I've always been at home in Alice's kitchen. This is the first time I feel like I don't belong.

"Beth, you're welcome here anytime, you know. Just . . . just stop **watching**, okay?"

"Okay," I say.

But as I drive away, I can't help but watch the house as I pass. **My** house. The lights are off in the living room, but I think I see a shape, a person there, indistinct, watching me. Or maybe it's my imagination, and there's nothing there at all.

SEVEN

BACK IN THE RENTAL, I MAKE A CUP OF TEA and stand at the kitchen counter, waiting for it to steep. Everything is silent around me. Nothing but peace and quiet.

I stare out the kitchen window, a memory forming in my mind. I close my eyes and let it wash over me.

I'm back in our old kitchen, chopping vegetables for dinner. Aubrey's belting out a song, her fist held to her mouth like a microphone. Caitlyn's doing dance spins around the island, counting the beat aloud as she goes. Tyler's on his hands and knees, rolling a series of Matchbox cars, complete with sound effects.

"Caitlyn, you're going to hit the counter," Mike calls as he approaches the kitchen.

"What?" she yells back.

"Or slip on a Matchbox car," he says.

Aubrey sings louder, frustrated by the interruption.

"Aubrey, honey, can you keep it down?" I say. "Caitlyn, maybe take the ballet to another room?"

"It's **jazz,** Mom," Caitlyn says. She continues counting and turning.

I make eye contact with Mike as he heads to the kitchen sink. I roll my eyes, and he grins.

Down on the floor, Tyler begins pushing his cars into each other, screeching "Crash!" each time.

Mike washes his hands, dries them on the kitchen towel. "What can I do to help with dinner?"

"What?" I yell, theatrically loud, and he laughs. He comes up behind me, puts his arms around my waist, and kisses my cheek. "What do you need?"

"Peace and quiet," I say.

"Can't do that," he says. "But I can take over."

I hand him the knife, let him take my place at the cutting board.

"Who wants to play Candy Land while Dad finishes making dinner?" I say.

"Me, me!" Tyler calls, dropping the cars and scampering to his feet.

"Me, too," Caitlyn says, flashing me a big smile.

"And you?" I ask, looking at Aubrey.

"Of course," she says, and catches me by surprise by throwing her arms around me, hugging me tight—

The ring of my phone pulls me back to the present. The memory vanishes, replaced with silence. I open my eyes and check the screen: Mike. I debate whether to answer. The phone rings again. Finally, I do.

"Hi," I say.

"Hi."

Silence follows.

"Just wanted to make sure you're doing okay," he says.

"I'm fine. You?"

"Fine."

More silence.

"Anything new?" he asks.

"Nope." I think of our old house, the roses in the window. I can hear Alice's voice. **Just stop watching, okay?** "What about with you?"

"Same old same old."

This is so awkward it's almost painful.

"Well, just wanted to check in with you."

"Okay."

"I'll let you go then, I guess."

"Okay."

"Take care, Beth."

"You, too."

I set down the phone and look out the window. The last remnants of violet are fading from the sky, giving way to darkness. That conversation was stilted, awkward, loveless. But there's no sense of sadness, no sense of longing, nothing like that.

Maybe because I'm not thinking of him. I'm thinking of **her**.

This person who must have **everything** she wants.

THE SUNSET THAT EVENING LONG ago had left the sky streaked with brilliant pinks and oranges. It was unseasonably warm out, and our wineglasses—filled, as always, with cold pinot grigio—were sweating. I was in the lawn chair in the center that day, Alice on one side, Des on the other.

"I unpacked the last of the moving boxes today," I said.

Alice turned toward me and snickered. "You've been here more than a year now, haven't you?"

"I consider it an accomplishment that it didn't take longer," I say with a smile.

"Hear, hear," Des said, lifting her glass. And then to Alice, "I **may** still have some unpacked boxes of my own."

I took a sip of wine and watched the kids play. Aubrey and Caitlyn were on their scooters today, rolling in endless circles around the loop, Caitlyn trying hard to keep up with Aubrey's pace.

As they passed by the O'Malleys' house, I caught sight of Erin at her bay window, watching from inside.

"There's Erin," I said, nodding toward the house. "How come she never joins us out here anymore?"

She was never out here as often as Alice and Des and me, but she'd join us here and there. A few times a week in those early days, gradually less. It'd been a month, at least, since she brought out a chair.

"I think it's too hard," Des said. "Seeing all the kids out here. And we talk about nothing but parenting."

"We **complain** about parenting," Alice said.

"And she wants nothing more than to be a parent," Des said.

"Oh, crap," I muttered. I hadn't looked at it that way. I mean, I knew they wanted kids, but they were also younger than the rest of us. "Have they been trying?"

Des gave me a confused look. "For years."

The words make me go quiet. "I didn't realize," I finally said.

"Maybe they should consider IVF," Alice said.

"They've done it," Des said. "Five times."

"What?" I said. Alice and I gaped at her. "Why'd you never tell us?"

"She never told **me**. Until about a week ago. Said it was their fifth try, and maybe their last."

I felt overcome with guilt. All this time I'd been complaining about Tyler's tantrums or Caitlyn's moodiness or Aubrey's troublemaking friends at school—

"Damn," Alice said. "That's a pretty penny. IVF ain't cheap."

"It's a fortune," Des said. "My sister and brother-in-law went through it. More than fifteen grand. For **one** cycle." She shook her head. "Can't even imagine five."

"Ugh. Last time we saw her, I was complaining about the cost of the kids' lessons," Alice said. I remembered the conversation. Charles had scheduled it so that each child—two-year-old Preston included—had some sort of activity every day. Violin and chess and tennis and even some sort of toddler brain-building class. And Alice was detailing just how much it cost them. It still surprised me how open she was about her finances. Maybe it's just that I **wasn't**. It wasn't something my family ever really talked about, or Mike and me, until we had to. The **CIA** knew more about his finances than I did before we were married and merged accounts.

"Guess it goes to show you never really know what's going on behind closed doors," Alice added quietly.

"Have they considered adoption?" I asked.

"Not possible," Des said. "Something to do with Sean's past."

"Yeah?" I said, surprised. "I wonder what that's all about."

"DUI," Alice said.

Des and I both looked at her. She shrugged. "Criminal records search."

"Uh, **why**?" Des asked.

"Because it's important to know who your neighbors are."

"Have you run them on **us**?" I asked.

"Of course." She said it like it was the most natural thing in the world.

Des and I exchanged a glance. There was a beat of awkward silence.

"Well," Des finally said. "What'd you dig up?"

"Y'all are clean." Alice raised an eyebrow at Des and grinned. "Unless there's something you're hiding."

"Sounds like I've hid it well," Des said with a wink, and Alice and I laughed.

I took another sip of wine and watched the girls. They'd hopped off their scooters, left them on their sides in the street. Joined Piper and Jasmine at the base of the Johnsons' driveway, coloring an elaborate scene with sidewalk chalk.

"I didn't even think Sean drank," Des said.

"Maybe he doesn't anymore," Alice said. "It was a long time ago."

I looked back over at the bay window of Erin's house. Looked for this woman whom I thought I was getting to know, who I now realized was harboring secrets, and secret heartbreak.

There was no one at the window. She was gone.

EIGHT

I'M ONE OF THE FIRST TO ARRIVE AT THE KENT School Monday morning. I skim the few new messages in my inbox, log on to the internal Agency messenger application. Look for Annemarie online, but she's not there.

I run a search on The Neighbor, just for the heck of it. Frozen Piranha, too. Nothing, as expected.

I spend the hour before class begins studying the roster. Twenty new analysts, all with just a few months on the job. From all different parts of the Agency, with different backgrounds, and one thing in common: incredibly impressive résumés.

And they're **young**. Aubrey's age, or a little older. Some fresh out of graduate school, some with a few years' work experience under their belts.

They're an attentive bunch, and I present the established Kent School curriculum. It really doesn't take a lot of thought or effort. A job anyone could do. Designed that way intentionally, I'm sure. And it gives my mind plenty of time to wander. Back to **her,** to Madeline. A teacher herself, once. At least that's what she told Alice—

What she told Alice.

I glance at the screen at the front of the classroom, the PowerPoint presentation slide. **Corroborating Information.**

Always corroborate. That's what I just told these students. And that's a message I need to take to heart.

At lunch, I sit in my office with the door closed. Run a Google search on the unclassified system, print the results. Fold the printout, tuck it into my pants pocket.

I teach the rest of the class, more hurriedly this time, let the students go early, at around two. I'm out the door just after them, into my car. I turn on my cellphone, then pull the piece of paper from my pocket, unfold it, dial the first number on the list.

"Abraham Lincoln Elementary," comes the voice in my ear.

"Hello," I say. "I'm doing a reference check on a teacher who used to work at your school. Madeline Sterling. She taught kindergarten."

"Hmm. That name doesn't ring a bell, I'm afraid."

"She may have left two or three years ago. Could have gone by her maiden name, Madeline Greene?"

"Greene? I don't remember anyone with that name either, but let me take a quick look."

I can hear the clack of keys in the background, then a pause.

"Nope. I'm sorry. I'm afraid you have the wrong school."

"Thank you," I say. I reach for a pen from my purse, draw a line through the first school on the list. A **long** list, all the elementary schools in the DC metro area.

Then I start tapping out the digits for the next.

THE CALLS TAKE ALL AFTERNOON, and turn up nothing. Not a single school has any record of a Madeline Sterling—or a Madeline Greene—who taught kindergarten.

Just as I thought. Just as I **knew**.

She lied to Alice.

I'm back in Langley Oaks that evening. On Hunter Court, the next street over. There's a stretch of pavement where I can park and catch a glimpse of the cul-de-sac, and of the front of my home. It's not perfect, not by a long shot, but it's a way to keep an eye on activity at the house. The Nikon's on the passenger seat beside me.

The silver Audi's in the driveway. The street is empty and the house is softly lit, and I imagine they're inside, eating dinner, giving the kids baths, getting them ready for bed.

I don't expect to see anything, not really, not at this hour. We rarely ventured out after dinner on a school night, not when the kids were so young. But there's no real reason to head back to the rental, nothing I'd be doing there. Might as well be here.

And so I stay, even as the streetlights come on, as the last bit of light fades from the sky, as night settles over the cul-de-sac.

I focus in on the light from the dining room window, faint, because it's coming from the kitchen. That was the heart of our home, and I wonder if it is for them, as well. If they sat around the table earlier, all five of them. If Theo was in a highchair, if he was using a little baby spoon or just his fingers. If the girls were drinking milk from brightly colored plastic cups, if Madeline and Josh reminded them to use good manners. If the two of them exchanged a smile at something cute one of the kids said—

Headlights wash over the cul-de-sac, the front of my house. There's a car driving down Riverview. I reach for my camera, focus in.

It's a black sedan, and it slows in front of my house. Brakes, idles there, on the street.

Another light now. The motion-detecting floodlight mounted above the garage. There's Madeline, walking down the driveway, quickly, head bowed.

She looks around, almost furtively, then opens the passenger-side door, filling the inside of the car with light. As she does I catch a glimpse of the driver. A man, around Josh's age but most certainly **not** Josh, and not someone I've seen before. I press down on the shutter release, a quick flutter of shots.

He smiles at her, says something as she slides in—

And then the door shuts, and I lose sight of them both.

The car pulls around the rest of the loop and accelerates back down Riverview, past Jim's house, past the Patels'.

I drop the camera on the passenger seat and start the engine. Then I pull a U-turn, and just as I do, I see the black sedan drive past, onto Oaks Drive.

I take a right now, onto Oaks. The taillights of the black sedan are in front of me, not too close, and I don't **want** to be too close. But I have to see where she goes.

The sedan winds its way out of the neighborhood, traveling the speed limit, or maybe a touch above. I follow behind, keeping a safe distance, my eyes on the taillights.

It's approaching the exit to the neighborhood now, slowing to a stop, left blinker illuminated. Full stop, and then a slow turn onto the main road.

I take my time coming up to the stop sign,

look to the left, look for the sedan a short distance away—

It's way down the road, practically out of sight. Gunning it, going full speed—

Brake lights.

I catch sight of them just in time. A moment later and I'd have missed them entirely, wouldn't have seen the car pull a right. It would have just disappeared.

Which may have been exactly what they wanted.

I pull out onto the main road and press my foot down hard on the gas. The engine roars in response.

I'm going fast, too fast, but the road is nearly empty. I'm almost at the turn now. I slam on my brakes, pull the wheel hard to the right, take the turn—

I don't see anything. No cars, no sign of taillights, nothing. Just a handful of traffic lights dotting the road in the distance, marking a web of cross streets. "Dammit," I say aloud, and I press down on the gas nonetheless, because they have to be somewhere.

The first traffic light's green, but I slow anyway, look left and right. A smattering of cars, nothing easily distinguishable as the black sedan, but certainly a possibility. I hesitate, because if I turn here and it's the wrong choice, the wrong street or the wrong direction, I've lost them completely.

I jerk the wheel hard to the right. It'd be the quickest way to disappear from sight, and my gut tells me that was their goal. Press down on the gas again, speed up, check each car on the road, on the side of the road. Nothing.

I reach another intersection, a red light this time. I slow to a stop, look all around. No sign of the black sedan. And no way to find them now. Too many possible routes it could have taken. Once I lost sight of it, that was it.

And they knew it, didn't they?

They knew they were being followed, and they set out to lose me.

They **did** lose me.

And they did it well. The way I've been trained to do it. The way **any** spy has been trained to do it.

They knew **exactly** what they were doing.

IT HAD BEEN A YEAR since we first learned of The Neighbor. A **year.** And I was getting desperate. We had tried everything. Increased real-time monitoring of the encrypted line, sought out **other** encrypted lines. Developed a list of targets, anyone and everyone who might have access to Reza Karimi, dug into them, narrowed that list to those with the best chance of access, and with the greatest likelihood of working with us. Tried to lure them out of Tehran so we could approach them. Tried to lure Karimi himself out. But nothing worked. We couldn't get close.

But we needed to do **something**. I identified an existing asset of ours who could potentially be redirected toward Karimi. A source we called Bronco, an oil tycoon with access to senior Iranian political figures. **No way,** I was told. He was too well positioned, and the information he was giving us was too valuable. We couldn't risk a redirect.

I argued that **this** was just as critical, because if Karimi hacked into our network, they would have **everything**. The powers that be finally agreed, allowed us to redirect Bronco. We built his access slowly, inched him ever closer to Karimi, took our time, made it look natural. Finally, Bronco had plans for a face-to-face with Karimi.

And they **talked**. Karimi was cagey, of course, as we would have expected. But he bragged about having a source in the U.S., one who was doing recruiting on his behalf. Bronco didn't press for details, per our instructions. There'd be time in the future for that; we didn't want to raise any red flags.

You must be worried about losing such an important source, Bronco had said, conversationally.

No, Karimi had replied, surprising Bronco, surprising us. **There's always another plan. If this network were to fail, we would salvage what we can and leverage it into something new.**

Bronco went on his way, and we celebrated. Made plans to send him back for another face-to-face, this time with a tracking device, one he'd covertly place on Karimi's belongings, so we could watch his movement.

And when the day finally came—

Karimi refused to meet with him.

We didn't know why. **Bronco** didn't know why.

We had Bronco attempt to set up a new meeting, but Karimi refused again, through intermediaries. He didn't give Bronco a reason, but the message was clear, both to Bronco and to us: he didn't trust our source.

We could never figure out why, what had possibly happened between that first meeting and the second to tip off Karimi about our true intentions.

And, to make matters worse, the next time Bronco tried to contact the Iranian officials he had previously been close to, he was denied. **They** wouldn't have any contact with him, either. He had lost access.

Karimi must have intervened.

We had no choice but to exfiltrate the source, get him out of there. If Karimi and the Iranian officials somehow knew he was working for a foreign service, that he was a traitor, his life was in danger. And we had to protect him.

I knew then and there that we'd never get another

asset redirected toward Karimi. The powers that be would never approve it.

Karimi was too good. He knew too much. And we didn't even know **how** he knew so much.

But we did know this:

He was always one step ahead.

NINE

AFTER LOSING SIGHT OF MADELINE, I DRIVE straight back to the cul-de-sac, pull into Alice's driveway. Floodlights illuminate the area, the same motion detection ones we have. I walk to her front door, rap my knuckles against it.

Nothing.

I knock again, louder this time. It's after ten; they might already be in bed.

Light flickers on inside. A moment later Charles opens the door, in a T-shirt and plaid flannel pants, blinking back sleep. Alice is right behind him, in her pajamas, too. She squints at me. "Beth?"

Then to Charles, "I've got this, honey."

He gives me another look, one of confusion, or maybe sympathy, then turns, heads back upstairs.

"Is everything okay?" Alice asks me.

When I don't answer right away, she opens the door wider, gestures for me to come in.

I step inside, then into the kitchen, but this time I don't sit. I'm too wound up to even stand still, let alone sit.

"Beth, what's going on?" she asks. She's standing near the refrigerator, watching me pace.

"It's Madeline."

Alice crosses her arms across her chest. "What about Madeline?"

A laugh escapes me, because I almost don't know where to begin. "Well, she wasn't a kindergarten teacher, for starters."

"What? What are you talking about, Beth?"

"I called every school in the DC metro area. Public and private. Not one of them had a Madeline Sterling who worked there."

She looks befuddled. "You **did**? Seriously, Beth?"

"Yeah, I did. She **lied** to you."

"Beth—"

I come to a stop in front of her. "Do you believe me now?"

She watches me in silence. "**No,**" she finally says. "Maybe she used her maiden name. Maybe she taught **online**. I have no idea. But I doubt she lied."

For the first time, I think that maybe Alice **is** too blunt, that she **should** soften the blow. "You've got to be kidding me."

"Even if she **did,** Beth, so what?"

"What do you mean, **so what?**"

"I mean, what does it matter? She's a nice woman. They're a nice family."

"But she's not!"

The kitchen falls silent. Upstairs I hear a faint creak of springs, probably Charles getting back into bed.

"And I saw her get into a car just now," I say, more quietly, more measured. "With a man. One who **isn't** Josh. All covert-like. And then they sped away."

She's looking at me like I'm crazy. But I'm not crazy.

"How do you explain that?"

"Beth, I don't know. I don't know who her friends are. Her colleagues—"

"She doesn't **have** colleagues, remember? She's a stay-at-home mom. Or so she says."

Alice stares at me.

"Well, how do you explain it?" I press.

"What do you want me to say, Beth? That maybe she's having an affair? Fine. **Maybe she's having an affair.** It wouldn't be the first time it's happened on the cul-de-sac, would it?"

"That she's not who she says she is. That she has secrets."

Alice gives me a long look. "Don't we all?"

CAITLYN HAD WOKEN UP THAT morning with a temperature of 102. Mike had a full day of meetings and my own schedule was light, so I was the one who stayed home. Caitlyn was on the couch under a blanket, entranced by some kids' cartoon on the TV, while I was picking up the house.

It was an impossible task when the kids were young, keeping the house clean. Seemed like no matter how much Mike and I picked up, we were never on top of it, probably because there was always someone right behind us, making another mess.

I was sweeping the hardwood floors, assembling a mound of crumbs and dirt, shocked—as always—by the amount of it. The floors never looked that dirty, but boy, were they.

Vinnie, the lawn guy, was out mowing, like he was every Wednesday morning. I wasn't sure which yard—we all used him, everyone on the cul-de-sac. His rates were cheap, and in our calculation at least, it was worth it to take one lengthy chore off our already overly full plate, while at the same time helping support a friendly college student's side business. Win-win.

The sound of his mower mixed with the strains of the kids' cartoon, a disjointed chorus, until all of a sudden it cut out, and there was silence outside.

I was just starting in on the dining room floors—a thankfully light task, since we only used the room a few times a year on holidays—and movement outside the window caught my eye. It was Vinnie, walking to the Johnsons' front door.

I lingered by the window out of curiosity. Vinnie always left an invoice in the mailbox at the end of the month. I don't think he'd ever rung my doorbell. I wondered what was going on, what he needed to say to the Johnsons—or maybe to all of us—in person.

In any case, he wasn't going to have any luck at the Johnsons' door. Darryl was out of town, and Des was at work—

The door opened from the inside before he could ring the bell, and I caught a glimpse of Des. What was she doing home from work? Was one of her kids sick, too?

She opened the door wider, and Vinnie stepped inside. She quickly shut the door behind him.

I stared. What just happened?

I walked into the living room, stood near the bay window to get a better view, but not directly in front of it, sort of off to the side, out of sight. It's like I knew I'd just seen something I wasn't supposed to see. That I shouldn't be looking. But I couldn't look away.

I watched the house, waited for him to come back out—

Movement, upstairs. At one of the windows. The blinds, closing.

I knew that house. It was the same floor plan as ours. I knew those windows. Those were her bedroom windows.

"Oh, Des," I murmured. "What are you doing?"

I couldn't pull myself away from the window. Just stood there, broom in hand, watching the front of the Johnsons' house, as the landscaping truck sat idle in the cul-de-sac, as the strains of the kids' cartoon from the other room reached my ears.

Twenty-seven minutes. That's how long he was inside.

He left with his head bowed, walked quickly back to his truck. Started up the engine, drove in a slow loop around the cul-de-sac, then off down the street.

I watched the Johnsons' home a moment longer, then reached for the phone, dialed Alice at work.

"Des is having an affair with Vinnie," I said when she picked up. It was sort of an urgent whisper; I didn't want Caitlyn to hear.

"Vinnie?"

"The lawn guy."

"**What?**"

"He just spent **twenty-seven** minutes inside her house."

"You're kidding."

"I'm not."

"Just now?"

"Yeah. Caitlyn's sick, so I'm home. I don't know why **she's** home."

"I do." Alice snickered at her own joke.

"This is serious."

"I know," she said, sounding chagrined.

"What do we do?"

"Nothing."

"**Nothing?**"

"I mean, what **can** we do? It's her business."

"And Darryl's."

"Well . . . yeah." She sounded uncertain. "But she's our friend. And maybe there's a perfectly good explanation for it, anyway. I mean, she always goes in late on Wednesdays."

"Since when?"

"Since . . . a month ago, maybe?"

"This has been going on for **a month**?" I'm speechless.

"There might be nothing going on."

"Really? So why was he there?"

"I don't know, doing some handyman work?"

"In her **bedroom**? With the blinds closed?"

"Damn. Really?"

"Really."

She's quiet on the other end of the line. Then, "I still think it could be something else."

"We'll see, I guess."

I bit my tongue around Des that week and took

a personal day the following Wednesday. Stayed home, waited for Vinnie to arrive. Watched him get started on the O'Malleys' lawn, listened as he made his way to the Kanes', and then to ours, and then to the Johnsons'.

The mower stopped, and silence descended. I took up a spot near the dining room window, waited—and watched.

Sure enough, there he was, walking up Des's driveway, to the front door—

The door opened, he walked in, and the door closed.

"Dammit, Des," I said under my breath, my mind on Darryl, and the girls.

I couldn't sleep that night.

"What's wrong?" Mike asked that evening, as soon as he got home from work and saw the look on my face. I told him about Des. Told him I didn't know whether to tell Darryl.

"You shouldn't," he said matter-of-factly.

"But wouldn't you want to know?"

"Well, I wouldn't want you to **do** something like that in the first place."

"I wouldn't. We're better than that," I say.

"I know we are. And yes, if I were Darryl I'd want to know. But I'd be willing to bet he'll find out eventually. Don't be the messenger. They'll **both** blame you."

I took his advice. Never said a word to her,

and she never said a word to any of us. Then one Tuesday evening, months later, we were all out in lawn chairs in the street, watching the older kids play, passing Erin's new twins between us, marveling at how small, how perfect they were, when a new landscaping company showed up to mow Des's lawn.

She watched them quietly, didn't say a word.

"No more Vinnie?" Alice finally asked, because it needed to be said, needed to be acknowledged.

"Time for a change," Des said, avoiding eye contact with all of us.

In the silence that followed, she took a long sip of wine.

"Change is good," Alice said.

Des nodded. Her eyes looked glassy.

"Why don't you text me the info for this company," I said gently. "Maybe I'll switch, too."

"Same," Alice said.

Erin looked from one of us to the other, her gaze resting the longest on Des. "I'm not totally sure what's going on, but I can switch, too."

Des nodded, still not making eye contact. "Thanks."

I didn't know what happened. Did Vinnie end things? Did **she**? Did Darryl find out?

I'd never know, would I?

"No problem," Erin said quietly. "We neighbors stick together, right?"

TEN

I LEAVE ALICE'S HOUSE, DRIVE DOWN THE street, away from her house, and my house, and I know I can't go back to the rental. I need to watch for Madeline to return. Need to get the plates on the car, or see where it goes, or something.

So I turn down Hunter Court again, pull over on the side of the road where I can see through the trees to the cul-de-sac, turn off the engine, wait.

It's dark and still, the streetlights casting a soft glow, along with the porch lights of the houses around me. Through the trees, there's faint light coming from Tyler's room, and Caitlyn's. Night-lights, probably. In my mind I picture the way their rooms used to look when they were young, when we first moved in. That soft light that staved off nightmares, that let us peek in and see their sweet features, sleeping peacefully, tucked in tight—

A knock at the passenger-side window makes me jump. I spin toward the sound, heart thumping, because it's **late,** the middle of the night, and I thought I was alone. There's a man there, one I don't recognize, standing in the darkened street. He takes a step back and motions for me to roll the window down. He's on the short side, and slight, and doesn't look like a threat. I keep the doors locked and roll the window partway, enough to hear him, enough for us to converse, not enough for him to get into my car.

"What are you doing out here?" he asks, his voice unfriendly.

"I'm sorry?" I say, stalling for time.

"I asked what you're doing out here."

Behind him, on one of the front porches, I see a woman in a robe, arms folded across her chest, watching us.

And at the house next door, a man in sweatpants, also watching.

"We've all seen you. Just sitting here. None of us know who you are or why you're here."

I could say I used to live on Riverview Drive. But then I'd be telling these people exactly who I am, and I can't do that. I've attracted enough attention as it is.

"Sorry. I'll go," I say.

"Yeah you will," he says. "And you won't come

back, either. If we see you loitering here again, we're calling the cops."

I start the engine, pull forward, around the loop, feeling eyes on me, from him, from the people on the front porches, and from other houses, too, no doubt peering through their windows. They must have all been texting each other, calling each other.

I turn back onto Oaks and drive slowly, eyeing the other darkened side streets in the neighborhood, wondering if I could pull onto one of them. Nothing gives me the view of Riverview I need, though. I could sit by one of the entrances to the neighborhood, but what if they use the other?

This is a lost cause, isn't it?

There's nowhere to sit and watch. Everyone's banded together here, neighbors who text and talk, who know who belongs and who doesn't, and I don't belong here anymore.

It's her neighborhood now. Riverview is her cul-de-sac—

I stare at the darkened road in front of me, empty now, a thought from the back of my mind clawing its way to the front.

The traffic light ahead turns yellow. There's no one around, but I brake hard. As soon as the car comes to a full stop, I open up my email on my phone, pull up our contract.

There it is, right beside their names. Their old address.

I'd looked up the property records, but I never looked it up on a map, never looked up the exact location.

Now I do. Now I type the address into Google Maps, and I watch the screen zero in on a single house, one that's on a cul-de-sac.

The light turns from red to green; I know even without looking up, from the glow that's made its way into the car. But I ignore it. I can't take my eyes off the screen.

They lived in a house on a cul-de-sac before. Now they do again.

The Neighbor has found a new cul-de-sac.

ELEVEN

I FINALLY PRESS DOWN ON THE GAS, ACCELERATE through the empty intersection.

Cul-de-sac's a code word, a way for Iranian intelligence to discuss the case on an encrypted line. It's not literal. It's not **actually** a cul-de-sac.

Is it?

My cul-de-sac's filled with CIA. Charles is head of CTC, Des is a senior polygraph examiner, Erin is a team chief in the Middle East division, Sean keeps things running behind the scenes.

I'm speeding now, driving too fast, mind racing.

It would explain why Madeline bought my house, sight unseen. Why she has the gun safe. Speaks Farsi. Why she doesn't seem to have a past.

Why she had those roses in the window.

And if it's true, she's coming after my neighbors. My **friends**.

I'm just admiring the view. You can see everything from here. Those words run through my mind, the ones Madeline spoke when she was seeing my house for the first time. Standing at the bay window, transfixed. I thought she was focusing on the street, thinking about watching her kids play. But the street isn't all you can see from that window. You can see every single house on the cul-de-sac.

She wasn't speaking like a mom; she was speaking like a spy.

Another yellow light ahead. This time I gun it, cross through before it turns red.

Is it really this obvious? Is The Neighbor a **neighbor,** recruiting people that live nearby? On a **cul-de-sac?**

Cyrus thought The Neighbor was targeting a new agency.

If it's NSA they've penetrated, they're moving on to CIA.

Maybe he's right. Madeline lived in Maryland. Not Fort Meade, but still. Bethesda's not far. And she lived on a cul-de-sac. Was she targeting her neighbors? Neighbors who worked for NSA?

Maybe she's about to target her **new** neighbors. The ones who work for CIA.

What do I do next? Where do I go from here?

Agency security, maybe, or Dale, and work my way up my own chain of command. My **old** chain of command.

Or do they already know? Does **Annemarie** know?

Let it go, Beth.

Those words she spoke in the parking lot ring in my head. That look on her face, almost like a warning, like I was too close to something. Something **dangerous**.

Maybe they already suspect Madeline. Maybe Annemarie knew Madeline bought my house, that we're in the same orbit.

I reach for my phone and dial her number, but she doesn't answer.

I'd drive to her home if I could, but I don't know her address.

Dale. I need to start with him. We need to keep this in house, within CIC, to the greatest extent possible. The information's too sensitive, too compartmented, to go straight to Agency security. My chain of command can get the information into the right hands, **cleared** hands. I trust Dale to do it.

I have **his** address; I've been to his home for his annual holiday party. I eye the phone on the passenger seat. I could call, but he might decline it, and it's not like I can speak freely on the phone, anyway. Or I could just wait until tomorrow. I **should** just wait until tomorrow. But this is **The Neighbor** we're talking about. **I've found The Neighbor.**

I pull a U-turn and head for his house.

———

I RING THE DOORBELL AND wait. Nothing happens. I ring it again. Maybe too soon, too persistent, too impatient, but he'll understand when—

The door opens, and Dale stands in front of me, shorts and a T-shirt, bare feet, mussed hair. He squints at me, a quizzical expression on his face.

"Beth? Is everything okay?"

"We need to talk."

"At this hour?" His gaze shifts behind me to where my car is parked, then lands back to me. He doesn't make any move to let me in.

"It's about The Neighbor."

"**Beth**," he says with a tone of warning.

"I wouldn't come if it wasn't an emergency."

His gaze flickers to the street, then he opens the door wider, lets me in without a word.

I step inside, and he closes the door behind me. Stays standing in the foyer, doesn't make any move to walk deeper into the house, to sit down.

"What is it?" he asks.

"I found The Neighbor."

He eyes me wordlessly. I can't read his expression. "Who is he?"

"**She**," I correct. "And she's the person who bought my house."

His jaw tightens. His eyes never leave mine. "The person who bought your house," he repeats, his voice devoid of inflection.

"Yes. On a **cul-de-sac.** And she's moving from

another cul-de-sac. **The Neighbor has found a new cul-de-sac.**"

I realize too late that I'm not supposed to have that information. But whatever. If I **didn't** have it, I wouldn't have just found The Neighbor, so they'll be glad I **did** have that information, won't they?

"Why do you think she's The Neighbor?" he asks.

"Because she moved from one cul-de-sac to another. To a cul-de-sac **filled with CIA**. They didn't even see the house before they made an offer. And they can't afford it. I mean, they **can**, somehow—"

Now I can read the expression on his face. He doesn't believe me.

"I saw them moving in a huge gun safe," I say.

He gives me a long look, impassive. "So they have guns. Lots of people do."

"Doctors and stay-at-home moms?"

"Some people like their weapons." Another long look, one I can't read. "**That's** why you think she's The Neighbor?"

"I heard her speaking Farsi. On the phone."

He opens his mouth to speak, closes it.

"Even if she was, that doesn't mean she's an Iranian spy, Beth."

"I know." The words come out high-pitched. Defensive. "But she lied. Said she was a teacher, and she's **not**. And the internet, too. She knew all about the internet when she moved in. All the lines that run to the house."

Dale just stares at me, doesn't say a word.

There's Annemarie's warning, too. **Let it go, Beth.** But I don't want to say that, don't want to throw her under the bus like that, not when I sense she was doing me a favor.

But how does **she** know something about Madeline and Dale doesn't? None of this makes sense.

I lower my voice. "She had **red roses** in the window. The day she moved in."

He says nothing. Maybe he doesn't remember that intel—

"Gift from the previous owner?"

"**I'm** the previous owner!"

"Or the real estate agent?"

What am I supposed to say? Sure, it's possible. But it's too much of a coincidence. **All of this** is too much of a coincidence. We stand there in awkward silence.

He starts to speak, his eyes never leaving mine. "Beth, you've been a great employee for many, many years. I'd hate to see you ruin things now, like this."

I stare at him.

"You know you can't talk about this here."

"Yes, but—"

"And what you're saying, this **claim,** with no proof—"

"The proof is everything I just told you! All these

things. They add up. And it's my **instinct**. You've always said I have good instincts."

"You did. But right now . . . Beth, you're seeing something that isn't there."

A sick feeling is settling into my stomach.

"Why don't you go home, get some rest. We'll pretend this never happened, okay?"

I nod, because what else am I supposed to do?

"Do you need a ride home?"

"No. I told you, I'm fine."

I reach for the handle, open the door, step outside. He doesn't stop me, doesn't say a word. I turn around at the bottom of the steps, and he's standing in the open doorway, just staring at me.

I TRY TO SLEEP WHEN I get home, but I can't. I'm too wound up. Dale doesn't believe me. And I don't have proof to convince him.

Finally I get out of bed, head to the kitchen. Pour myself a glass of wine to relax. Then a second, because the first didn't do a thing.

Madeline's The Neighbor. The person I've been searching for all these years is in **my** house, on **my** cul-de-sac, living beside **my** friends.

Trying to **recruit** my friends.

I make my way into the living room, glass and the rest of the bottle in hand. The room's spinning a bit, fuzzy at the edges. I wrap a blanket over myself and pull up HomeWatch on the TV. Navigate to the old videos—

There's nothing there.

The screen is blank, except for three words: **No saved items**.

Sure, the cameras are long gone, but the old videos, the ones I recorded, they're saved on **my** account, and they're supposed to be there until I erase them. They've **been** there, up until now.

I restart the app, then the system.

Still nothing.

My account's been reset.

It could be a glitch. But it doesn't feel accidental, not in the slightest. It feels intentional. The work of someone—or some service—that's technically sophisticated, and that wants to send me a message.

They know I'm watching Madeline, and they want me to stop.

In my mind I hear Annemarie's voice, the words she spoke when I followed her out to her car that day. **Let it go, Beth.**

Maybe I should.

But I'm not going to.

I OVERSLEEP THE NEXT MORNING and wake up with a dry mouth and pounding headache. By the time I get to work, most of the offices in the hall leading to my own are lit, the doors open—including, I realize, **my own**.

There's a person sitting in the chair opposite my desk, her back to me. She turns as I approach.

It's Annemarie.

"Hope you don't mind," she says with a smile. "I let myself in to wait."

"Of course not." I step inside the office and shut the door. "I've been trying to get in touch with you."

"I know."

I walk around to the other side of the desk, slide into my chair. She's watching me, silent.

"Do you have a class here today?" I ask.

"No. I'm here to see you."

I nod. I feel wary in a way I can't quite place.

"Dale told me you visited him—"

So much for pretending it never happened. I say nothing.

"—and that you think you found The Neighbor. Do you **still** think that? Or was it just, you know . . ."

"What?"

"**The alcohol.**"

"What alcohol?"

She raises an eyebrow. "Beth, I can smell it on your breath."

Shit. I feel my jaw clench. "You **know** it's her."

Her brows knit together, leaving creases across her forehead. "Who?"

"The woman who bought my house. She's The Neighbor."

"I don't know that."

"You know **something**. What you said, in the parking lot . . ."

"I didn't say anything."

"You told me to let it go."

She nods slowly. "You should. They took you off the case—"

"The way you said it. Like I need to, like it's for my own good."

She gives me a long look, then sighs. "Look, at the time, I just thought . . . it's weird that they took you off the case the way they did. So abruptly. Made me think . . . I don't know. That there was some **connection** to you. You know?"

"And you're **right**. So help me. It's **her**. I'm sure of it."

She watches me, silent. Then, finally, "What do you know about her?"

"She's . . . like me. Like I **was**. She has what looks like this perfect life. Perfect husband, perfect little children, now the perfect house—"

I can see her gaze shift behind me, to my desk, settle on something. I know instantly what it is. It's that crayon drawing of our home, Tyler's name scrawled at the bottom. "So she's young?"

"Yeah. Your age. Early thirties." Thirty-one to be exact. But I don't have to admit I know that.

"Early thirties." She repeats the words, her tone flat. Her gaze flickers again to that crayon drawing. Then her mouth turns down into a frown, one that looks condescending. "Beth."

"What?"

"How many years have you been tracking The Neighbor?"

The question feels like a blow, one I should have seen coming, and somehow missed. "Fifteen."

"Right."

I don't know what to say. The math doesn't add up; I get it. **But she's The Neighbor**. I know she is.

"So, since she was a teenager?" Annemarie presses.

"Maybe she's older," I say. But it sounds feeble. She's thirty-one. And that means she's been working as The Neighbor since she was sixteen.

"Beth—"

"It's possible."

"Sure." She says it gently, and that's almost worse than sarcasm.

I can feel my cheeks growing hot.

"Look, she knows Farsi," I say. "She put red roses in her window. She has guns. She knows too much about the neighbors, and she's watching them—"

Annemarie gives me an impassive look. She doesn't believe me, not at all.

"Don't you **want** to find our target?" I ask, incredulous. And then, "Why are you here, anyway? Did Dale send you?"

"Dale didn't send me. I just want to make sure you're okay—"

"Tell me what's going on in the case."

She almost recoils. "You know I can't do that."

"We're friends, aren't we?"

"You know it doesn't work that way. Mission comes first. I'm just asking you again to stop—"

"She knows I'm watching her," I say. "I have a video of her. And she **erased** it."

Annemarie stares at me. "What are you talking about, Beth?"

I wish I hadn't just said that. "Home security footage. From inside my house, her walk-through. It was saved. Until yesterday. It just disappeared."

"Disappeared?"

"The account was reset."

She nods slowly. "Those things happen, Beth. My Netflix account—"

"It's not like that." I shake my head. "It was **her**. Or **them**. Quds Force. Reza Karimi."

Annemarie gives me an even gaze. "Look, I was wrong," she finally says. She's speaking very clearly, very deliberately, almost like she's speaking to a child. "I don't think there's any more to the story. I think they just took you off the case because it's time."

"You don't believe me."

"No, Beth, I don't. I don't think the woman who bought your house is The Neighbor." She opens her mouth like she's going to continue, then presses her lips together.

"Okay," I finally say. Because what else **can** I say?

Behind her, through the windows of my office, I can see a few of my students heading toward the classroom.

"I need to be getting to class," I say.

"Right." She pushes back her chair and stands. Heads to the door, then hesitates. Looks at me with sympathy written all over her features.

"Beth, I do think it's time for you to let it go," she says gently. "To move on."

I say nothing, and she lets herself out, leaves the door open behind her. I watch her walk down the hall, disappear from sight. Watch more of my students heading toward the classroom, the place I should be.

It's going to take every ounce of strength to go in there and teach today.

The last thing I want to do is move on.

I MAKE IT THROUGH THE rest of the day and back to the rental to watch her. To find proof for Dale, for Annemarie. For **myself**. But I can't, not from my street. Not from the street over, either. I'm shut out of my own neighborhood.

I dig through a moving box labeled **Electronics** and pull out our photo printer. Attach the Nikon, select two photos: one of **her**, on my front porch, between the stone planters, looking out at the cul-de-sac. And one of him, the man in the car, through the open passenger-side door.

I make myself dinner. Salmon; Mike always hated salmon, so we never had it. I thought it would be satisfying, but it's not.

Then I call the kids. A quick conversation with Tyler, who's as uncommunicative as ever. It's like pulling teeth, talking to him.

A call to Caitlyn goes unanswered, as it should, since it's late in London, but she's a night owl, and it's not unheard of for her still to be awake. Still, though, it fills me with that old familiar feeling of helplessness, that fear of not knowing exactly where my kids are. It's worst with Caitlyn, always has been, ever since she wandered off one day when she was young.

Aubrey next. "You sound terrible," she tells me, toward the end of the small talk. "Are you going to tell me what's going on?"

"It's work," I say.

"What about it?"

I shouldn't say anything. But I **want** to. "My case. The one I've worked forever. I'm close to finding my target, Aubrey. I can feel it. And no one believes me."

There's silence on the other end of the line. "Why does no one believe you?"

"Because . . ." Now it's my turn to go quiet. Because The Neighbor is in **my** house. Trying to recruit **my** neighbors. "It's a little too close to home."

"Yeah?"

"Yeah. And it just . . . it sounds a little crazy."

More silence.

"What are you thinking?" I ask.

"Honestly, Mom?"

"Yeah."

"That you're dealing with a lot right now. Tyler going off to school. Caitlyn moving away. Me getting married . . ."

"And?" I press.

"And maybe if your coworkers think it's crazy, it is."

The words feel like a blow. Of all people, I was hoping Aubrey would believe me.

My gaze rests on the television. "They hacked in here, Aubrey."

Another beat of silence. "What do you mean?"

"Our old security system. All the saved videos. They're gone."

"Okay." She says it slowly, like she doesn't know what to make of what I'm saying. "Maybe they just expired or something?"

"No. It said . . ." What **did** it say? Account reset? Something like that. I had too much wine to remember clearly. "Let me pull it up." I reach for the remote, turn on the TV, open the HomeWatch app. Navigate to saved videos—

There they are. All the old videos. **Madeline's** included.

"Mom?"

"Well, it's here now. It's back." I'm still staring at the screen. Wine or no wine, I know it didn't look like this the other night. "They must have put it back."

There's an awkward pause.

Annmarie's voice rings in my head. **Those things happen, Beth. My Netflix account . . .**

"Mom, where's Dad?" Aubrey asks gently.

Not **this** now, too. "Not here right now."

"He's been gone an awful lot lately, hasn't he?"

She's fishing. She knows.

There's a beep on the line. I lift the phone away from my ear. Caitlyn, calling back. "Aubrey, I need to go," I say.

"Mom, wait—"

"I'll talk to you later, okay?"

A pause. And then, "Okay."

Relieved, I switch to the new call. More small talk, and I know I'm distracted, only half listening, my mind still on the conversation with Aubrey, on the HomeWatch app—

"Mom, is everything okay?" Caitlyn asks. It's uncharacteristic of her, and I immediately wonder if Mike's said something about our split.

"Yeah, why?" I sound defensive.

"You sound . . . sad."

I look down at the pictures I printed earlier. Focus in on the one of Madeline. I'm not **sad**. I'm frustrated.

Am I sad? Sure. Anyone would be if they were in my shoes. Nothing's working out the way I want it to. But most of it I can't say to Caitlyn. So I settle for what I **can** say.

"A lot's changing right now, you know? And talking with all of you, hearing about what's going on in your lives, it really drives that home."

It's what Aubrey thought was going on. And there's some truth to it, sure. There's a lot of change right now. Tyler starting college; Caitlyn jumping into her career; Aubrey, newly married, about to settle into a new home.

"You're all **beginning** things," I say. "My life feels like a series of endings. Of doors shutting."

"Mom, you're not having a midlife crisis, are you?" Caitlyn laughs, but it's that high-pitched laugh she does sometimes when she tries to make a joke out of something she believes is the truth.

"Of course not."

"Okay." She sounds unsure.

Awkward silence follows. I said too much. I shouldn't be laying this on her.

"It doesn't have to be a bunch of doors shutting, you know," she says. "Just . . . be bold. That's what you used to tell us when we younger. Do you remember?"

Be bold. I haven't thought of that in ages. I said it to the kids all the time.

"Yeah," I say. "Good advice."

"Look, I gotta go, but you take care of yourself, okay, Mom?"

"You, too, honey. Love you."

"Love you, too."

The line disconnects, and I slowly lower the phone. I look back down at the picture of Madeline.

Be bold.

Dale thinks I need to let it go. Annemarie does, too. And Aubrey. But Caitlyn—Caitlyn's **right**.

I need to be bold. That's the only way I'm going to find the truth.

MINE IS ONE OF ONLY two cars in the lot at Langley Park. The fields are empty except for a father and daughter playing catch in the distance, savoring those last minutes of fading daylight before darkness descends.

I pull on the hooded sweatshirt I grabbed on my way out. Sling on my crossbody camera bag, Nikon safety tucked inside, and slide a flashlight into the back pocket of my jeans. Then I start off on the trail.

It's silent, except for my footsteps, the sound

of hiking boots on packed dirt, leaves crunching underfoot, as I approach the river.

I stop at the bank and watch the water run over the rocks, then turn and head upstream. I walk until the worn path ends, until I'm trekking through overgrown grass, ducking under and swerving around the occasional tree branch.

Langley Oaks is off to my left, in the distance, and I can see faint light from the houses, through the trees. The woods are quickly darkening.

There's a noise up ahead, the crackle of branches, twigs snapping, something moving through the woods, and it sends my pulse racing. Deer, probably. **Hopefully**.

I reach the bend in the river, the clearing with the boulders, and change direction, head into the woods, toward the neighborhood. I step carefully, quietly. My house is a straight shot, and I don't want anyone to hear me approach.

I'm about halfway there when the sound of a voice drifts toward me, from a distance. I go still and listen. **Two** voices. A conversation. It's got to be coming from one of the houses on my cul-de-sac.

I start walking again, as silently as possible. I need to get closer, need to figure out who's talking, if it's her, and what she's saying.

I'm close enough now to see a light through the trees, the one from my back deck. The voices are coming from there. This is exactly what I was

hoping for. Mike and I were out on the deck constantly that first year, enjoying the quiet nights, the
solitude of the woods.

I can't get too close. Can't risk that they'll hear
me. I have no reason to be here. But I need to be
close enough to hear more than vague strains of
conversation.

One step, then another, softly, quietly—

Snap.

A branch underfoot, broken in two, and the
crunch of leaves. **Dammit.**

I go still.

"What was that?" comes Madeline's voice,
the one I recognize from the home security footage,
her words clear.

"Deer," Josh says matter-of-factly. "Did I tell you
I saw three of them yesterday?"

"You told me." She sounds unconvinced. I
can picture her staring off into the woods, in my
direction.

But it's too dark out here to see anything. I know
it is, from all the times I stared into the woods,
looking for the source of other sounds.

I wait for them to speak again, but they don't.
It's quiet. And I start to panic. Did they head back
inside? Did I spook them into leaving?

I crane my neck, ever so slightly, to find a clear
line of sight to the patio. The pair of lights flanking

the back door are illuminated, and so is the string of lights overhead.

I unzip my camera bag, slowly, silently, and pull out the Nikon. Uncap the lens, zoom in as far as I can—

There. Clearer now. Madeline and Josh are sitting in wicker chairs that are unfamiliar, probably brought from their other house, a small table between them, with two wineglasses on top. I click the shutter release, capture the scene, and continue watching through the telephoto lens.

"We have to get past it," Madeline says. Quietly, but her voice carries clearly.

The houses on either side of them are dark, no one outside. They must feel confident no one can hear them. **They're wrong**.

"You weren't honest with me," Josh says.

"I know. But I was doing what I had to do."

They fall silent. My heart is beating so loud I can practically hear it. **What are they talking about?**

"If it was just **you**, fine," Josh says. "But you brought the kids into it. And me. We made a major life **decision** because of this."

"I had to. This was the only way."

"No. This was taking things too far."

"I needed to, to blend in." She's speaking even more quietly now, but I can still hear her clearly. "Look, we shouldn't be discussing this out here."

"We shouldn't be discussing it **at all**. Because it never should have happened." Josh's anger comes through, loud and clear. "**They** matter more than your family."

"I'm **doing** this for our family."

"Bullshit. You're doing it for **you**."

"Yeah? Is **your** salary enough to pay for all of these kids to go to college? In addition to the house and our student loans and the cars and the food and clothes and toys and God knows what else?"

"The **house** is the whole problem, Maddy!"

"House or no house, we'd be **drowning** with just your salary."

"At least we wouldn't be living a lie."

More silence. I'm holding my breath, waiting for more—

"You're blowing this entirely out of proportion," Madeline says, her voice calm, and cool.

"I'm done with this." Josh stands, the chair scraping the wood as he pushes it back. He storms into the house, slamming the door behind himself.

Madeline continues to sit quietly, expressionless. She picks up her wineglass, drains the rest of the wine. Then she stands up, picks up the other wineglass, too, and follows Josh inside, shutting the door gently behind herself.

A moment later, the patio lights shut off, and darkness descends.

I lower the camera and stare at my house, dark now, barely visible.

It's like it was all a dream, like it never happened. But it **did** happen.

They're living a lie. **Making money** living a lie. **Just like I thought.**

TWELVE

I ARRIVE AT WORK THE NEXT MORNING FEELING energized, feeling **justified**. The conversation I overheard last night, that proves it. She's not who she says she is.

Only problem is, that conversation's not **enough.** She'd deny it, or come up with some other explanation, and I'd have to admit to trespassing, or eavesdropping at the least.

I need more.

I shut the door to my office and turn to the classified system. Bring up Alpha, type in her name, hit search.

No results.

Not surprising. It's not like Iranian intelligence is going to mention her by name and we'd be lucky enough to pick up the details.

I close Alpha and stare at the blank screen, thinking. Then, abruptly, I open my lower desk drawer and pull out the file folder at the bottom.

I open it up, and my gaze settles again on that very first report. New Target: The Neighbor. I flip to the second page, and zero in on that phrase that I've never been able to decipher. Use the children.

I think of it now in the context of Madeline. How Madeline could be using the children. **Her** children? She used them as an excuse to move into the neighborhood, didn't she? As cover for getting to know the neighbors.

But those kids weren't even **born** when that message was intercepted.

She's too young. The thought hits me again, gnaws at me. She'd have been a teenager when she was recruited.

It's possible. I don't know her past. Don't know her parents, her family. What if they were involved?

I flip to the next report, another pull from Frozen Piranha. Karimi had switched to a new encrypted line just before this transmission, probably for operational security, but he did it in a way that left behind signatures of the old line, that let our tech gurus know exactly how to break the new encryption.

The Neighbor wants us to provide payments, Reza Karimi had said.

Why? replied the official in DC.

Personal reasons related to The Neighbor's past.

That was another one that ate away at me. I

consider the words now with Madeline as The Neighbor. What are the personal reasons she'd want to provide payments?

What's in her past?

I turn that page over, and the next bunch, until I'm at the end. The last report in my folder, the most recent, but still several years old. Another intercept, from Reza Karimi:

When the Americans see the light, it will all be over.

I reread the words, but they're no clearer now than they've ever been, and certainly no less ominous.

But the previous report, the one about the payments, that one's sticking in my mind. It makes me think of last night's conversation, the one I overheard, the one that revolved around money. **She's making money.** If I can find proof of that, I have what I need.

But how?

I can guarantee she didn't receive a giant deposit into her checking account. The money's probably sitting in some offshore account. And she's probably smart enough not to have withdrawn too much. I know from the closing paperwork that they put twenty percent down on the house, have a mortgage for the rest.

Surely they **have** more, but they're not spending it. Not right now, anyway. They're being strategic.

How can I possibly find the account, or proof of the account?

My eyes drift to the crayon drawing tacked to the corkboard behind my computer, the one of our house.

That's where the proof is.

I need to get into that house.

THE MORNING PASSES IN A blur. All I can think about is getting into that house.

They have security cameras out front. They might have an alarm system.

Then again, they don't have any little stakes in the landscaping by the front door with the name of a security company. No stickers on the windows. The van that was there the day of the installation was unmarked. Maybe it's just a self-contained camera system, like HomeWatch. Maybe there's no alarm.

And I have a key.

We turned over a few at closing, but there was a spare set in the junk drawer that I'd already packed up with the kitchen stuff. Found it when I unpacked in the rental.

They might have changed the locks. **Should** have changed the locks, if Alice was right, and they were concerned enough about **me** to install cameras.

But they may not have.

I'll go when no one's home. I'll try my key in the lock. If it works, and there's no alarm, I'm in. Free and clear.

If anything happens, if the key doesn't work, if an alarm goes off, whatever, I can play it off. **I wasn't thinking. Seventeen years walking through this door. I did it by rote.** A simple misunderstanding.

That should work, should get me off the hook. It's not like I'm a hardened criminal. I've never been in trouble with the law. I hold a top secret security clearance. They'll have to believe it's an honest mistake.

But I'll have to make sure no one's home.

In my mind I can see those movers again. That huge safe.

These people have guns.

And I'd bet anything that Madeline, at least, knows how to use them.

I CAN'T RUSH THIS. I need to take my time. Need to figure out their schedules.

I need to be damn sure there's no one in the house when I get there.

I can't sit on Riverview and watch. Can't sit on Hunter, either. They're watching for me. Waiting for me.

I look out my office window. There's Cyrus,

walking past, the bin of his class's technical equipment in hand, headed back to the supply closet.

A smile crosses my lips.

I turn back to my computer, the unclassified system. Open up Amazon. Search for items with same-day delivery. Click on something at random, doesn't even really matter what it is. Printer ink; why not?

I hit the checkout button, select my old address. I'm not sure it'll work, but I'm hopeful. I complete the transaction and submit the payment.

Then I head back to class. Rush through the day's lessons. I don't want to be here, and let's be honest—they don't, either.

I send them home early. There's one stop I have to make before I leave.

I head for the supply closet.

BACK IN THE RENTAL, I track the package, refreshing the Amazon page constantly, until finally it happens:

Status: Delivered.

There's a picture, too, of a padded envelope sitting outside my front door, between the stone planters.

It worked.

I stare at my phone and wait for Madeline to get

in touch, to tell me a package has been misdelivered. Seconds pass, and then minutes.

This might be the wrong course of action. She might not **want** to get in touch with me. She might contact the shipping company, ask that the package be picked up, redelivered. I can't risk that.

I reach for my phone, find the text she sent me the day she moved in, the one thanking me for the wine. Type out a new text.

> Madeline, it seems a package of mine was mistakenly delivered to your house. I'll swing by and pick it up, if that's okay. Best, Beth

I wait, watch the phone—
A response, from Madeline.

> Sure thing.

A smile pulls at my lips. A rush of anticipation runs through me.

I reach for my work bag, double-check that what I need is inside, and I leave the rental, head toward my house.

I DRIVE SLOWLY THROUGH LANGLEY Oaks, all the way to the back of the neighborhood. Left on Riverview, down to the end of the cul-de-sac. I pull into my old driveway, feeling smug, almost, because I'm **supposed** to be here this time.

I get out of the car and walk up to the front door, my focus first on the locks. I don't remember exactly what the old ones looked like, but nothing about these scream that they've been recently changed.

And there's no security system sign in the landscaping, no stickers on the windows. Nothing to indicate that the camera above the front door is being monitored in real time, that police would be alerted to a break-in.

The envelope's sitting there, just as it was in the picture. The flowers in the stone pots on either side are wilted, which sends a surge of anger through me. How hard would it be to water them, honestly?

I reach for the envelope, pick it up, place it under my arm. Then I stand on the porch, look out at the cul-de-sac, at all the neighbors' houses, their perfect front yards. It's so quiet here, so peaceful. It feels like coming home. It **is** coming home.

I take a deep breath, transport myself back in time to when I could step out here anytime, and enjoy this view, this air, this peace and quiet—

Movement catches my eye. From the O'Malleys' house. A figure in the bay window, but off to the side, like they're trying to stay hidden. Someone's watching me.

I walk down the steps, then back along the path toward the driveway. I open my shoulder bag as

I walk, drop the Amazon envelope in, and at the same time reach for something small, clasp it in my fist, keep walking.

There's a tree there, where the sidewalk meets the driveway. A dogwood tree, one that the kids used to climb. I walk up to it, my back to the front of the house, to the security camera. I glance over at the O'Malleys'. I don't see anyone at the window, but I have to imagine they're still there, still watching.

I reach up and place my clasped fist on the trunk of the tree. Like I'm remembering, or saying good-bye, or something.

Then I open my hand. There's a camera in my palm, tiny, smaller than anything on the market. Weatherproof, wireless, Wi-Fi enabled. With a sharp spike on the end, one that I press into the bark of the tree. If anyone's watching, hopefully it looks like nothing more than a pat.

I take a step back and blow the tree a kiss. Let them think I'm crazy, anyone who's watching. They already do, don't they? But they'll know the truth eventually.

I look at the spot on the trunk where I planted the camera. I don't see a thing.

This always **was** a good tree, wasn't it?

I smile and head back to my car.

THIRTEEN

I SET UP AN ANONYMOUS ACCOUNT, LINK THE camera, then let it do its work. Now instead of curling up at night after work and watching the old HomeWatch video, I'm watching this. I can view in real time or recorded, and I'll wipe it all clean when I'm done. No one will ever know.

Really, there isn't a whole lot to see. The camera's pointed at the exterior of the house, aimed at the garage and the driveway, capturing the front door and a sliver of the street at the edges of the frame. I need to see when they're there, when they leave.

And if I can catch Madeline heading off for another nighttime rendezvous, all the better.

I force myself to wait a full week, and it's tough, because Madeline's there, doing God knows what as The Neighbor, and we're **letting her**. But it's necessary. I need proof to stop her. The proof is in that house, and the only way to get in that house without getting killed is to know their schedules, precisely.

The footage makes it clear: Josh leaves for work every day at seven, arrives home around four-thirty, sometimes earlier. Madeline is gone each day reliably from eight to nine—school drop-offs, I imagine, because she leaves with all the kids and returns with just the baby—and then again from three to four for pick-ups. She sometimes leaves at other times during the day—running errands, I'd imagine—but doesn't have a set schedule.

My best bet is between eight and nine in the morning.

Once the full week is up, once I've watched them each day of the week, I'm ready.

Thursday morning I park on the side of Oaks Drive near the entrance to the neighborhood. Put up a sunshade on the front dash, watch footage from the camera in real time.

I know the order in which everyone leaves. I focus on the sliver of street at the edge of the frame and check everyone off in my head, one by one. The twins first, off to the bus stop. Then Sean and Erin, together, in Sean's car. Charles and Alice next, same time, different cars.

Josh leaves the house at seven, slides into his car.

Starts the engine, backs down the driveway, then heads down the street.

Darryl leaves. Then Des.

I wait, and I watch my house.

The front door opens and two girls step out, backpacks on, head to the car. Madeline walks out a moment later, Theo on her hip.

She gets Theo buckled into his car seat, then climbs into the driver's seat. The engine starts, and the Audi backs down the driveway, then speeds off down the street.

I put down the phone and look out the windshield—the small section of glass that's not obscured by the sunshade—at Oaks Drive. There it is. The Audi, approaching. It speeds past my car, and I watch in the rearview mirror as it leaves the neighborhood, heads right, toward the schools.

I force myself to stay put for another minute, then two. For good measure, just to make sure they haven't forgotten anything, turned around. It hasn't happened yet, not since I planted that camera, but there's a first time for anything, and I sure don't want it to be today.

I shift the car into drive and pull forward. Slowly head down Oaks to Riverview, then turn left.

I slow as I approach the end of the cul-de-sac, then pull into my driveway.

Live your cover.

Sure, I'd rather park in front of Alice's, or Erin's. Draw less attention. But my cover story's that I made a mistake. Entered the wrong house without thinking. So it has to be **my** driveway.

Sweat is tickling my forehead. I pull all the way to the top, shift into park, turn off the engine. Deep breath, then I step out of the car. Walk, purposefully, toward the front door.

It's broad daylight. I wish it were night, that I were doing this under the cover of darkness, but that would be more dangerous. The neighbors might be watching, and the house would be occupied. This is the only option.

And everyone on the end of the cul-de-sac is gone; I saw them leave.

I'm at the door now, keys in hand. I find the key I need, the one that opens this door, or used to, at least. If it doesn't anymore, I could jimmy it. I know how, learned on the job years ago. But it's one thing to try my own key in my old lock, play it off as a mistake. It's another to forcibly break in. That I can't play off.

I slide the key into the lock—

It fits.

I turn it, easily. They haven't changed the locks.

The door's unlocked now, and I hesitate. If I open this door and they **do** have an alarm system, it's over. I'll have to play out my cover, stay here until the police arrive, pretend I made a mistake, and I don't know if anyone will believe me, not when I've been hanging around the way I have.

But I've come this far. I have to try.

Another deep breath. I turn the handle, push the door open—

Silence.

Complete and utter silence.

I step inside and close the door behind me. I'm trembling, whether from excitement or fear, I don't know. Maybe both.

I look around. It feels surreal. I'm in my house but it doesn't look like mine. There's a coat rack by the door, with a diaper bag hanging there, and a purse that isn't mine. Two child-sized raincoats, and two pairs of tiny rain boots below.

I look up at the ceiling, where our camera used to be. Nothing. I don't see any, anywhere. Maybe the one by the front door is all they have. Maybe it **was** just to keep an eye on me.

Or maybe they're better hidden, more covert, the kind provided by Quds Force. Maybe there's even a silent alarm, and they already know I'm here.

But it's a risk I'm willing to take, because this is the way to get what I need, to get that proof. And once I have it, **we** can come after **them,** and we can put an end to all of this.

Ahead, in the great room, there's a leather sectional against the wall, kids' toys scattered on a plush rug. No entertainment center, just a large TV mounted to the wall, bigger and sleeker than the one we had.

I walk into the room, then head left, into my kitchen. Same gray granite countertops, same dark cabinets. But there's a drying rack on the counter, filled with brightly colored plastic cups and bowls. A different coffeemaker, one of those fancy ones. A box of sugary cereal left out on the island.

And the table, it's different. Round, instead of rectangular, with a high chair pulled up to it. A brightly colored rug underneath.

But it doesn't matter what it looks like, what they've done to my house, how they've changed it. What matters is what's **here**, what I can find to prove Madeline's The Neighbor.

I pull latex gloves from my back pocket, slide them on. My prints will still be on the front door, but they'll have footage of me there, anyway. There will be no denying I walked into the house. If I wear gloves now, at least there won't be proof that I was snooping around inside.

Unless there **are** cameras inside. Unless they're watching me right now, recording me.

But it's worth the risk. I need this proof.

I scan for any electronic devices—laptops, phones, tablets. Don't see a thing. I head to the desk area, start opening drawers. Maybe there's a burner phone stashed away somewhere, or some covert communications equipment. The contents are sparse; they haven't been here long enough to accumulate too much junk. There's a small stack of bills in the middle drawer, and I thumb through it, looking in vain for a bank statement, something, **anything**.

Nothing. I close the drawers and head for the stairs. If they're hiding something—and I **know** they're hiding something—there's a good chance it's in the master bedroom. In that safe.

I get to the top of the stairs, turn left toward the master—

When I reach the doorway to Tyler's room, my breath catches. There's a crib against the wall, white, same style as the one I remember. I can almost picture Tyler as a baby standing in that crib. A big smile on his face. Reaching out his arms to me—

I force myself to continue on. Into the master bedroom, one that now looks nothing like before. Everything's sleek and modern, minimalist and dark.

I head to one of the nightstands first, open the drawer. Empty.

The other nightstand next. Also empty.

Panic is starting to creep through me. I've been in here too long. If I'd truly entered the house by accident, I'd have noticed immediately, made a hasty retreat. I wouldn't have stayed.

But I'm here now. The damage is done. I need to get what I came for.

I pull open the dresser drawers one by one, quickly, rummaging through each one, looking for anything hidden beneath the clothes—

A faint noise, downstairs. I pause and listen, pulse racing, but there's nothing, no other sound. It must have been my imagination, or something outside.

I go back to rifling, make my way through each of the drawers.

Nothing.

Into the closet now—

There's a safe in one corner. Midsized, not that huge gun safe I saw the movers bringing in. I head straight for that. Crouch in front of it, try to open it, but it's locked. There's an electronic keypad, and I briefly consider trying to enter code after code until something works, but it would be futile to even try—

"Hands up or I'll shoot."

A voice, from behind me. A **woman's** voice.

I go still, fear coursing through me.

Then I turn, rising slowly to my feet, palms extended—

It's Madeline, in the doorway of my bedroom. And she's pointing a gun directly at me.

FOURTEEN

THE WAY SHE'S HOLDING THAT GUN, SHE ISN'T a stay-at-home mom. She isn't a kindergarten teacher. This is someone who's been trained to shoot. Someone who's done it before, done it often. And **recently**.

The gun's steady, the barrel pointed directly at me. She doesn't look the least bit afraid. She's completely confident.

"Down on your knees," she says.

I don't move.

"On your knees."

She levels the gun, eyes me through the sights, and I know she isn't messing around. I drop down slowly to my knees, one at a time, hands still up, palms extended toward her.

"What are you doing in my home?"

"It's **my** home," I say. It's the first thought that

enters my mind. I say it impulsively, but then I realize it's the right thing to say. **Live your cover**. "I mean, it **was**. I'm Beth Bradford. The former owner."

"I know who you are."

The words sound chilling.

"Look, I made a mistake—"

"Bullshit."

She's right. It's bullshit, and we both know it. I've walked all the way through the house, all the way upstairs, into the master bedroom, and now I'm caught, red-handed, **in gloves,** in front of her locked safe.

I need something else—

"I can't let go," I say. Because that's what Alice told her, right?

She watches me impassively, the gun still pointed directly at me.

"I'm having a hard time. This was where I raised my kids. Where my husband and I— We've split up, you know."

"I know. And I know that's not why you're here."

"Then why am I here?"

"You tell me."

My gaze flits to the barrel of the gun. I'm still on my knees, completely vulnerable.

"What are you looking for?" she asks.

"Nothing. I just . . . I wanted to look around."

"Who sent you?"

"What? No one."

She takes a step closer. "Stop lying to me."

"I'm not. I—"

"You **are**."

I can see fire in her eyes.

"I'm going to ask you one more time," she says slowly, moving even closer to me. "**Why are you here?**"

She could shoot. There's nothing stopping her. I'm in **her** house. An intruder. She could tell the police that I threatened her. She could say whatever she wants.

She shrugs. "Suit yourself." And then she aims. **Really** aims this time, and I see her finger wrap around the trigger—

"Because you're The Neighbor!" I blurt it out and cringe, eyes scrunched close, **waiting**.

There's silence. I open my eyes the smallest bit, peek through half-shut lids, because maybe she's just waiting for me to open my eyes. Maybe she wants me to see her press that trigger—

She's watching me, over the sights again, but her grip has eased on the gun. I open my eyes more fully, cognizant for the first time of what I just said.

She looks like she's trying to make sense of something, figure something out.

"The Neighbor has found a new cul-de-sac," she finally says, expressionless.

"Yes."

"You think it's me, and it's this cul-de-sac."

"Yes."

She gives a half laugh, then lowers the gun, holsters it. Reaches into her back pocket, pulls something out. Credentials. She opens them up, extends them toward me. "Madeline Sterling, FBI."

I force myself to take my eyes off her, to focus on the creds. They look real.

"You can stand up," she says. She extends a hand, which I ignore. I get to my feet on my own.

"I'm not The Neighbor," she says. "But someone on this cul-de-sac is."

FIFTEEN

SHE CLOSES HER CREDS, SLIDES THEM BACK into her pocket. "How do you know about that intercept?"

I'm so caught off guard by what just happened, by what she just **said,** it's like I can't even think straight.

But I have to. I didn't have access to that intel. If she's really FBI, I could get into some serious trouble right now.

"Someone mentioned it offhand," I say. "Someone who didn't know I'd been taken off the case."

Does **she** know I've been taken off the case? She must, if she's wondering how I knew about the intercept. She knows far more about me than I know about her.

She's watching me intently, like she's trying to determine if I'm lying.

"Come on," she finally says. "Let's talk downstairs."

She turns and starts walking away, and I follow, numb.

"Silent alarm," she says as she walks down the stairs. "Knew the instant you opened the door. Dropped off the kids with a sitter at the front of the neighborhood."

I know who she's talking about. Friendly woman who runs a small home daycare, advertises babysitting services on the neighborhood message boards all the time.

She stops abruptly at the bottom of the stairs, turns to face me. Looks me straight in the eye, dead serious. "Don't do it again."

I nod, and she turns, continues on to the kitchen.

"You're lucky it was me and not some trigger-happy hotshot agent," she says, sliding into one of the chairs at the kitchen table, nodding for me to do the same.

I pull out a chair across from her and sit, my eyes on her the whole time.

She knows about The Neighbor. She knows about **the intercept,** the one even **I** wasn't allowed to see.

"You work The Neighbor?" I ask.

"I do. **Did.** Still do." She seems unsure. "You'd know that, if you worked with us."

It's a dig, but I can't focus on it right now. I'm still trying to make sense of everything.

"What do you mean, it's someone on the cul-de-sac?" I ask.

"What part of that is unclear?"

"Who is it?"

She gives me an even stare. "That's what I'm trying to figure out."

"Then how do you know it's **this** cul-de-sac?"

"I have my ways."

I wait for more, but she says nothing. In the silence, I can hear the faint ticking of a clock from somewhere in the house, and it's unsettling, because it doesn't belong here.

It doesn't make sense, that it would be someone on this cul-de-sac besides her. I know this cul-de-sac. These are my friends.

She's wrong.

"So the **Bureau** bought my house?" I finally say.

"**I** bought the house."

More silence. My gaze shifts behind her to the kitchen, settles on the things that look out of place. That coffeemaker. Those children's cups and bowls.

"We got something that convinced me The Neighbor was **here.** On this street."

"What?"

She shakes her head. "I can't say."

"And you kept it within the Bureau?" I sound incredulous. I **am**. I should have known about this, whatever it was.

"It's strictly about U.S. citizens. It's outside CIA's purview. And besides, it's not like **you've** ever shared with **us**." She sounds defensive. "But we did share it. Weeks ago."

That interagency meeting.

"Anyway, early on, the Bureau didn't believe it. I couldn't convince them to open a case. So when your house came on the market . . ." She shrugs. "No open case. No problem, right? And Josh had been wanting to move for a while. I was the one holding back."

I think back to the conversation I overheard, the one on the patio. "You didn't tell him **why** you wanted this house, did you?"

"I couldn't. It was classified."

She doesn't look sorry. She looks defensive again.

"But that intercept—**The Neighbor has found a new cul-de-sac**—that was the first time anyone in the Bureau really seriously considered I was onto something. They still don't believe me. But it was enough to get you moved off the case."

That's why I was moved off the case. Because the Bureau had some sort of intel that pointed to **my** neighborhood, **my** cul-de-sac.

"You didn't think it was a coincidence, did you? The timing?"

Frustration boils up inside me. **Annemarie was right.** "So, what, I'm a suspect?"

"Nah." She waves a hand dismissively. "Nothing about this case has ever been leaked. You never attempted to access information you weren't authorized to have—well, not until two weeks ago, anyway."

She's been watching me. Monitoring what I've accessed. I've always known there's a record of everything I do online at work, but I didn't know **she** was looking at it in real time.

"You and your husband are both off the hook. This thing we have . . . well, you couldn't have done it. Either of you."

"What **is** it?"

"I told you, that's not for you to know."

Frustration is bubbling up inside me. "**Why** can't I know? **Why** am I off the case, if I'm not a suspect?"

"Because your friends are." She says it evenly. "Because we don't know if your loyalty would be to the Agency or to **them**."

"That's bullshit." **Of course** it would be to the Agency. "I've been searching for The Neighbor for fifteen years."

"And you've been friends with these neighbors for seventeen."

My frustration's at a boiling point now.

"So, what, this is all an undercover op?" I ask.

"No."

"You're pretending to be an Iranian intelligence agent, or a sympathizer or something?"

"Of course not." She eyes me evenly. "I'm just working from home at the moment. Getting to know the neighbors."

"Didn't you **lie** to the neighbors?"

"Everyone lies, Beth."

The room falls silent again, except for the tick of the clock.

"I think you've got the wrong cul-de-sac," I say. "I **know** these people."

"Do you, though?"

"Of course I do."

She leans forward, arms resting on the table. "I'm going to crack this case. It's going to make my career. **Inshallah.**"

Inshallah. God willing.

She **was** speaking Farsi that day.

She leans back in her chair. "You should probably get out of here. That car's been in the driveway long enough."

I nod. I want nothing more right now than to leave this house, process everything I've learned.

"If anyone says anything, you came over to show me how the appliances work," she says matter-of-factly, rising from the table.

I stand up, too. "Okay."

She starts walking toward the front door, and I follow. She reaches for the handle, turns and faces me. "Everything I told you is just between us. It's so you'll leave me alone, give me space to work. So you don't make the neighbors suspicious of me."

Her expression hardens. "If you tip anyone off about this, so help me God, there will be hell to pay."

I hold her gaze and say nothing.

She pulls the door open, stands aside. I step out onto the porch. "Thanks for coming over," she says, her voice higher pitched, fake cheery. She smiles at me, a hollow smile. "You're a lifesaver."

I stare at her, a chill running through me. I force myself to raise a hand in farewell, but it's a moment too late—the door is already shut. I turn, walk to my car.

As I drive away from the cul-de-sac, my thoughts are in a jumble.

She's FBI. She's not a stay-at-home mom, not a kindergarten teacher. I was right.

What I didn't see coming is that she's looking for The Neighbor, just like I am.

I leave the neighborhood, a strange feeling of apprehension bubbling up inside me. Something doesn't sit right.

I try to put my finger on what it is, and finally, as I approach the rental, it hits me:

The red roses.

She said this wasn't an undercover op. That she wasn't pretending to be an Iranian spy, or a sympathizer.

So why the roses in the window?

Sure, she had the FBI creds. She knew about The Neighbor moving to a new cul-de-sac.

But she also lied to Alice. She lied to **her husband.**

How do I know she didn't just lie to **me?**

SIXTEEN

I BARELY SLEEP THAT NIGHT, AND THE NEXT
morning I'm back at work bright and early. First
thing I do is dial FBI headquarters, ask to be connected to Madeline Sterling.

"I'm afraid we can't connect calls," the reception-
ist replies. "If there's a Madeline Sterling who works
here, you would have to dial her direct line."

"What do you mean, if?"

"It's our standard response. We can't confirm or
deny the employment status of any particular individual. It's a security precaution."

"I'm a colleague, though. I'm calling from CIA."

"Then you'll have to go through one of the FBI
liaisons at Langley to find her contact information."

"Okay."

That won't work. Any liaison would log the
request. Would probably notify Madeline herself.

Considering she told me to stay away—and I **did** just break into her house—I shouldn't risk it. I'm not even sure they'd give me the information I want. I'm probably on some sort of do-not-assist list.

"Thanks for your help," I say.

I hang up the phone and think. Then I log on to the messenger app and wait for Cyrus's name to change from black to green. As soon as it does, I lock my computer and head down the hall to his office.

"Morning, Cy," I say, rapping my knuckles lightly against his half-open office door.

He swivels toward me, a smile spreading across his face. "Beth! Top o' the morning to you." He tips an imaginary hat in my direction and crosses one leg over the other. "What can I do for you?"

"Just walking by, thought I'd say hello," I lie.

"Well, isn't that a lovely surprise. Come on in, let's chat."

I step all the way into his office, and he motions to the chair opposite his desk. I take a seat.

"How's your class treating you?"

"Oh, it's fine."

"Are you enjoying it?"

"I guess."

"**I guess**? Well, **that's** an enthusiastic response if I've ever heard one." He chuckles at his own joke.

"It's just . . . an adjustment, you know?"

"I know." He reaches for his mug and pulls it

closer to himself. "You miss CIC, I'd be willing to bet."

"I do. I miss my target."

He wags a finger at me. "Knew it." He takes a sip from the mug. "It's tough, at first. Our targets, they're like relationships, in a way. And when you have to leave a target . . . it's like a breakup."

"Yeah, I guess it is."

Someone catches Cy's eye through the window behind me. His raises a hand in greeting. I don't turn.

"Listen, Cy. Question for you. Do you have access to any FBI databases?"

"Sure do." He wags a finger at me again. "That's what happens when you're a senior analyst. I have a feeling you might get there someday, Beth."

I smile pleasantly, because I know that's what he's looking for. "Well, I'm wondering if you could look something up for me. Some**one**. There's a person who claims to work The Neighbor for the Bureau, and I just want to verify."

"**Trust but verify**, am I right, Beth?"

"Exactly."

He swivels back to his computer, opens up a database. "What's the name?" he asks without turning around.

"Madeline Sterling."

He types, then stops and watches the screen. "Yep. There's a Madeline Sterling assigned to the

Washington Field Office." He turns back toward me. "Counterintel."

"Wonderful. Thanks, Cy."

"My pleasure, Beth."

Someone else outside walking by his window catches his attention. He waves again.

"Well, I'm sure you need to get back to things," I say, standing. "I don't want to keep you. Like I said, just wanted to chat. And I appreciate the help."

"Always happy to help, Beth. You have a good day, now."

"You, too, Cy."

I head back to my office, deep in thought.

So she's FBI, fine. Counterintelligence, so it's certainly plausible she's assigned to Reza Karimi, and to The Neighbor.

But there's just something about her that's not right. Something I don't trust.

I sit down at my computer and stare at the blank screen.

If she truly thought The Neighbor was on my cul-de-sac, why wouldn't she ask me about the neighbors? I've known all of them for seventeen years.

Why wouldn't she want my help?

And she's being so evasive. Hiding so much.

I don't know what this mystery information is that led her to my neighborhood, my cul-de-sac.

She didn't give me any details. Maybe it was all made up.

Maybe it was all a lie.

I should be getting ready for class, but honestly, there's no need. Today's topic is databases. A refresher, at most, because all of these analysts have been on the job for months anyway, using databases.

I need to know what led her to my cul-de-sac. I need to know what they talked about during that interagency meeting.

I can't ask Cy, not again. I don't want him to get suspicious. There's no good reason why I **wouldn't** have access to the readout, unless I was blocked from the case. I doubt the information's that highly classified—it's from the Bureau, after all, and they tend to underclassify rather than overclassify. It should be easily accessible—just not to **me**.

I can't ask Annemarie, can't ask **any** old colleagues, because they all know what happened to me, that I was forced out, that my access was removed. I could ask a friend outside CIC, but again, how would that look? What possible reason would I have to ask someone to access information about **my** case?

It shouldn't be this hard to find readily available information. I'm a CI analyst, for God's sake. This is like CIC 101.

CIC 101.

I look up, out the office window, at my classroom, down the hall. My class is starting to arrive. Those twenty students, bright and talented, all from different walks of the Agency.

And then I have an idea.

"CLASS IS GOING TO BE a bit different today," I say, standing at the front of the room, looking out at the attentive faces staring back. "You've all learned on the job how to use different databases. Now we're going to put that knowledge to the test with a little competition."

A few of the students exchange smiles. I've seen their résumés; they're a competitive bunch.

"As most of you know, I'm a CI analyst. For years, I've worked a Quds Force target known as The Neighbor. Now, two weeks ago there was an interagency meeting at headquarters on The Neighbor. Your mission is to find a readout of that meeting, using only the databases available to you."

"But what if we don't work counterintelligence?" one of the analysts in the front row asks. The one who never fails to mention he went to Princeton.

"Doesn't matter," I say. "It was interagency. Chances are high there's a noncompartmented summary readout. You all should have access." **Unless you've been blocked from the case,** I think.

Some of the other analysts are already focused on their laptops, already typing. Princeton notices, and immediately focuses on his own laptop.

I eye the door. This is dangerous. Madeline essentially told me they're monitoring my searches. Would they catch any unusual search activity on The Neighbor?

Probably eventually. But I can't imagine anyone's monitoring it in real time. Certainly not monitoring a bunch of new analysts' activity—

"Got it," comes a voice from the back of the room. The CTC analyst. She stands, walks over to the printer.

"You found a readout?" I ask.

"Sure did. And even better, I found you the slides they used during the presentation."

The printer goes quiet. She takes the papers from the tray, organizes them into a neat stack, hands them to me, a satisfied smile on her face.

"Nice work," I say. I eye the first slide. FBI Updates on The Neighbor. "Why don't you all take a quick break. We'll resume in fifteen."

I SHUT THE DOOR TO my office and start skimming. The slides begin with an overview of the case, facts I already know.

A few pages in, there's finally something new. A sanitized description of a key FBI source: a U.S.

citizen with close access to a senior Iranian intelligence official in Tehran.

The next slide is gold. A year ago, the U.S. citizen downloaded the contents of the intel agent's computer. One of the items captured was a screen grab of Google Maps, with a pin dropped—right on my street.

I reread that slide, just to be sure.

How is this **possible**? How did the Bureau obtain this information **a year ago** and never tell us?

And who's the intel agent, the one whose computer held this information? Is it someone reputable, someone with proven access?

If so, **why** did an Iranian intel agent have **my** street marked on a computer? Shouldn't I have been notified?

I turn to the next page. Another new piece of information. Three weeks ago, a U.S. citizen with a security clearance was pitched. Attempted blackmail. Fortunately, the man reported the pitch to the authorities.

The slides don't name him, but one bullet in particular draws my attention, holds it:

He lives in Langley Oaks, on a cul-de-sac street.

I flip to the next slide. My pulse is beginning to race.

This one is analysis: The FBI judges with high confidence this individual is the latest target of The Neighbor.

So **this** is the second piece of information Madeline referenced. The one that got me removed from the case.

I reach the last slide. It's one of those catch-all slides, the ones that a presenter throws together at the last minute. Key words to jog their memory, remind them of what they plan to say. Target's vulnerabilities, it reads.

Loneliness.

Dependence on alcohol.

And then:

Tactic: Blackmail.

I turn the page over, lay it facedown on my desk.

I know exactly who was pitched.

SEVENTEEN

IT'S JIM.

Madeline said the FBI's intel led her to **my** cul-de-sac. Jim's on my cul-de-sac. Jim has a security clearance, and a dependence on alcohol, and he lost Rose a few years ago—of course he's lonely.

These slides—maybe Madeline's telling the truth. This intel seems **real.** The pin drop on Google Maps. Jim, being pitched.

Jim.

Jim with the Jim Beam.

A knock at my door. "Come in," I call.

It opens, and Princeton's there in the doorway. "Um, Beth?"

"Yeah?"

"It's been more than fifteen minutes."

Has it really? "I'll be right there."

He nods, drifts back toward the classroom, leaving the door open behind him.

I make no move to leave.

There's a strange feeling swirling inside me, almost a nagging sensation that something isn't right.

The FBI judges with high confidence this individual is the latest target of The Neighbor.

Sure, drinking's a vulnerability. It leads to loose lips, impairs judgment. And he's lonely, and there was some sort of blackmail involved.

But these slides say Jim reported the pitch to the authorities. In all the years I've been working Reza Karimi, in all the years I've been searching for The Neighbor, not one target has **ever** gone to the authorities.

If Jim's really part of this, then The Neighbor misjudged the situation.

And The Neighbor has **never** misjudged the situation.

AS SOON AS CLASS IS done for the day and I'm back in my car, I reach for my phone and pull up Madeline's number from my text messages, place the call.

"Hello?" she answers. Her voice is tense.

"Hi. It's Beth."

"I know. What do you want?"

She couldn't sound less friendly if she tried.

"I want to get back on the case," I say. I **need** to get back on the case. I think they're barking up the wrong tree with Jim. I don't think The Neighbor was behind his pitch. But I need to understand why they feel so confident it was The Neighbor.

I need to know what **they** know. Who's this source of theirs with access to Iranian intelligence? What else do they **have**? Maybe **I** could connect the dots, if they haven't been able to.

And Jim. Somehow Jim's caught up in the middle of all of this. Poor Jim, who's battling addiction, who's **alone,** who tried to do the right thing by going to the authorities.

"No," she says.

"Please. I'm begging you. If one of my friends were The Neighbor, I would **never** cover it up. You have to believe me. I've spent fifteen years of my **life** focused on finding The Neighbor."

"The decision's made."

"Please, Madeline. Do what you can to change their minds, whoever's behind this. I think together we could solve this."

She said it would make her career. I could tell how important that was to her.

"You can get all the credit," I add. "You and the Bureau. Honest. I don't care. I just want to find

The Neighbor. Please. There has to be someone you can talk to."

"It was **my** decision to take you off the case. I was the one behind it. And I'm not changing my mind."

There's a click, and the call disconnects.

I pull the phone away from my ear and stare at it.

Madeline's the reason I'm off the case?

I know this case better than anyone. Whatever information they have, keeping it from me will only make it **less** likely we'll ever find The Neighbor.

And then another thought hits, sends a cold chill running through me.

Maybe that's the point.

EIGHTEEN

I NEED TO TALK TO JIM.

I need to find out what he knows.

I can't go to his home—Madeline could see me. She warned me to stay away. And I'm not supposed to know who he is.

I can't talk to him at work, either. I've **never** talked to him at work, don't even know **where** he works, and I'm not about to send him a message, not when they're monitoring my activity.

I need to talk to him **outside** work, **outside** his home—

And then it hits me. Today's Friday. I know exactly where to find him.

"LOOK OUTSIDE," ALICE HAD SAID, as soon as I picked up the phone. I stopped what I was doing—reading Tyler's final freshman-year report card—and walked to the bay window, phone held to my ear with my shoulder.

Flashing lights. An ambulance, parked in front of Jim and Rose's house.

"Oh no," I said. "What's going on?"

"I don't know. I looked out and saw it. Didn't hear any sirens."

"I didn't, either."

Apprehension crept through me. Flashing lights and no sirens usually meant one of two things: something minor that was already resolved, or something major, that wouldn't be. "How long has it been there?"

"No idea."

I stayed at the window and watched, the phone still held to my ear. I had a feeling Alice was doing the same.

Moments later, the front door to the house opened. Two paramedics maneuvered out a stretcher, on which lay a person—

"Oh shit," Alice said, and I saw it just as she did. The sheet covering the person was pulled up high, covering the face.

This was a **body**.

Jim stepped out of the house behind the paramedics.

"Oh, poor Rose," Alice murmured.

"Was she ill?" I asked.

"Not that I know of."

Jim climbed into the back of the ambulance. Eventually the flashing lights powered off, and the ambulance headed down the street slowly.

"What do you think **happened**?" I asked.

"No idea."

There was no sign of Jim that night or the next day, and none of us—Des and Erin included—felt we knew him well enough to knock on his door and check on him. "Let's just watch the house," Alice said. "Anyone sees him grab his mail, get out there immediately and talk to him." We all agreed.

It was Des who saw him walk out to the mailbox, that Wednesday evening. Des who made a beeline for her own mail, waved him down. I watched from the window as they had a short conversation. As soon as she stepped foot back in her house, I called her.

"Stroke," she said. "Out of the blue. She died, like we thought."

"Oh God. How's Jim holding up?"

"Well, he was drunk, if that's any indication."

"Oh no."

We didn't know what to do. What **could** we do? We sent flowers to his house, signed **Your neighbors on the cul-de-sac.** And I found myself drifting to the bay window more often, peering down at his house. Hoping he was okay. Wishing I knew him better.

One day I was getting my mail at the same time as Alice. The next day was trash day, and Jim's can was already by the street, along with several cardboard boxes from the liquor store, stacked beside it.

Alice nodded toward his house. "He's just sitting around drinking, by the looks of it."

"So sad."

"He's jeopardizing his clearance. He's a liability now, with the drinking."

"I'm sure it'll be short-lived. And I don't think he's gone back to work yet. Haven't seen him leaving."

"Doesn't matter if he's at work or not. Think how much classified information is in his head."

"I'm sure Jim would never betray his country."

"Jim under the influence might. That's the problem."

I stared at those boxes stacked by the trash can. "Let's bring him dinner," I said impulsively. "Show him we care, you know?"

Alice shrugged. "Okay."

That Friday I stopped on the way home from work and picked up a lasagna from Antonio's. Alice met me in the driveway as I was getting out of my car, and the two of us walked down to his house.

I was fully expecting to see Jim stumbling around in sweatpants, reeking of alcohol. But when he opened the door, he seemed completely sober, dressed in pressed pants and a button-down. "Well, hello, neighbors," he said.

"Hi, Jim," I said. "We just wanted to let you know we're thinking of you." I extended the bag from Antonio's. "We brought you dinner."

He looked down at the bag, then back at me. "Well, isn't that nice. I'll pop it in the fridge for tomorrow night. I'm just headed out now, actually."

"Yeah?" Alice said.

"Friday's our night for the Golden Diner."

"**Our** night? You and . . ." Alice said. I was thinking it, but she was the one nosy enough to ask.

"Rose."

We just stared at him.

"Oh, don't worry," he said, smiling sadly. "I know she's gone. I'm not losing it. But we used to go every Friday night. Barely ever missed a week. I figure I can still go, can't I?"

"Of course," I said. And then, more hesitantly, "Do you want company?"

"I do. But not yours. No offense."

I smiled. "None taken. You want Rose's."

"Yes. I'm fine eating alone. She'll be there in spirit."

"I'm sure she will," I said. I handed him the bag of food. "For tomorrow, then."

He took it from me. "For tomorrow. And thank you. This means a lot."

"How about we bring dinner next Friday?" Alice asked, just before he closed the door.

He smiled at us. "Next Friday I'll be out, too."

THE GOLDEN DINER IS A popular place in McLean, retro fifties theme and local farm-fresh ingredients, lines practically around the block on weekend mornings. Outside, the building's rather nondescript, long and low. Inside there's black-and-white-checkered tile and jukeboxes playing oldies, a long counter with stools, red vinyl booths along the windows, Formica tables.

I get there early, back into a spot with a good view of the lot. A half hour later, his Buick turns in, parks near the front. I watch him get out of his car and walk inside. Watch through the windows as a hostess leads him to a booth. He slides into it, picks up a menu.

I stay in the car until his meal's over. Seems only fair to let him enjoy his tradition in peace. But as soon as I see him stand and head for the exit, I get out of my car, walk toward the entrance. Just as expected, our paths cross. He's looking straight ahead at his car, doesn't notice me at first.

"Hi, Jim," I say.

He focuses on me. "Beth! Well, hello, neighbor. Heading in for some dinner?"

"Jim, there's something I want to talk with you about."

"Yeah?"

"Yeah." I glance around. We're alone here, no one within earshot. "I need you to tell me about being pitched."

A shadow crosses his face. "I don't know what you're talking about." He lowers his head and starts walking past me toward his car.

I turn and follow him. "Yes, you do."

He keeps walking.

"I work CI, Jim." I leave it at that, hope he takes it as meaning I know more than I really do.

He stops near the Buick, his back still to me. Almost like he's thinking. Finally, he turns to face me. "Are you in on it?"

"Of course not."

"Are your friends?"

What's he talking about? "I need you to tell me everything."

"I told the Bureau everything."

"The Bureau's the problem. Tell **me**."

He watches me evenly. "What do you mean **the Bureau's the problem**?"

"Someone there . . . I think they're involved. Let me help you."

He shakes his head.

"If you've told the Bureau, there's no harm in telling me, too, is there?"

A van drives past, behind us. Jim's gaze flickers there, then back to me. "You don't trust the Bureau. Well, I don't trust **you**, Beth. I don't trust any of my neighbors."

He takes the last remaining steps toward his car, reaches for the driver's-side door—

"Jim, wait—"

He doesn't look at me, doesn't stop. Opens the door, slides into the car.

"Jim—"

"Don't bring this up again, Beth."

The door slams shut, and the engine starts. I step back and watch as he backs out of the parking space, then pulls forward. He never casts another look in my direction.

I stand still and watch as his car leaves the lot, disappears from sight. He's going to report this, that I approached him. Just like he reported the pitch.

Worse, I didn't get what I came for. Didn't get the answers I need.

And the things he said have left me completely unsettled.

Are you in on it? Are your friends?

I don't trust any of my neighbors.

It's like he thinks the pitch came from someone in the neighborhood.

Why does he think that?

What does he know?

NINETEEN

I CAN'T SLEEP THAT NIGHT, OR THE ONE after. I toss and turn, mind racing.

Sunday evening, I call each of the kids.

"Mom, where's Dad?" Aubrey asks.

"He's out, honey."

There's silence on her end of the line.

"Okay, Mom," she finally says.

When that call ends, I dial Mike.

"We need to tell the kids, sooner or later," I say.

"I know."

"I think Aubrey knows something's up."

"I've been getting that feeling, too. She's been . . . off."

"So . . . when do we do it?" I ask.

"I don't know. I mean, we could make plans to see her in person, together. But obviously with Caitlyn it'll have to be on the phone. And probably Tyler, too, unless we're both going to drive to UVA."

"Yeah."

"Next weekend?" he says. "Why don't we make plans to have dinner with Aubrey. Then we can call Caitlyn and Tyler, together."

"Okay."

There's a sound in the background. A voice. A woman's voice.

"Where are you?" I ask. I figured he was in his apartment. Alone, like me.

"Just . . . home."

Home. Home is in Langley Oaks.

"You know, the new place," he corrects himself.

He's at the new place on a Sunday night, and there's a woman there.

"Who's there with you?" I can't help myself.

There's no response. I listen for the woman's voice, but it's gone silent. I wonder if they're exchanging a look, if he's put a finger to his lips. **Quiet. It's the soon-to-be ex-wife.**

"Who, Mike?"

"Britt."

Britt. The secretary at his firm. The peppy, pretty, thirty-something-year-old secretary. The kind of woman I might have been threatened by if Mike were the cheating type—but I never in a million years thought he was. She's a single mom with a young son, a boy who can't be more than four or five. Is **he** there, too, at Mike's apartment?

Or is Mike at **her** place?

"We're just going over a case." It sounds like a feeble excuse. It's a **lie,** is what it is. He's **never** gone over a case with Britt, not out of the office, not after hours.

He's a cliché. **I'm** a cliché. Wife gets dumped, husband takes up with secretary.

"Want me to make dinner plans with Aubrey?" he says. "Maybe next Saturday?" He's clearly anxious to end the call. I can't blame him.

"Sure," I say.

"Okay, sounds good."

"Talk to you later, Mike."

I end the call and set down the phone. There's silence around me, and I can't help but think of Mike, of what's happening on his end of the line. Is she talking again? Is her son there, chattering away? Does Mike get down on the floor and play with him, the way he used to with our own kids, so many years before?

The thought hurts.

The Mike I knew wouldn't do this. Leave his wife of twenty-five years and immediately jump into a fling—**a relationship?**—with his secretary. Or maybe it started **before** he left me.

One thing's certain: he isn't the person I thought he was.

People aren't always who they seem.

———

MONDAY MORNING I GET TO work, skim the sparse contents of my inbox. Then I watch the messenger app, wait for Dale's name to change from black to green.

Green. He's in his office.

I pick up the phone and dial his number.

"Hello?" he answers.

"Hey, Dale, it's Beth."

There's a brief pause. "Beth. Hi."

"Listen, Dale, I need to get back on the case. There's something going on, and I—"

"Beth, stop."

His tone makes me go quiet. I can feel my heart rate pick up.

"I know you approached Jim. We all do. He reported it."

Of course he did. He didn't waste any time, either.

"I don't know how you found out about him, but I know this: you need to stop. Stop trying to access information you're not authorized to have. And for God's sake, Beth, stop interfering in an active FBI investigation."

"That's just it, Dale. The FBI's just throwing up roadblocks. Madeline Sterling, one of the agents—"

"**Enough**, Beth."

I go quiet again. My heart is thumping now.

"I know you broke into her house. She filed a report."

I'm not surprised, but I'm disappointed nonetheless. She obviously understood **why** I broke into her house. Couldn't she have let it go?

"You're damn lucky she's not pressing charges. She wants you to have a psych evaluation instead."

A psych evaluation. No worse career killer in the intelligence community than a psych evaluation.

"Beth, for God's sake. You're one wrong move away from making **yourself** a primary suspect in this case. From getting your clearances revoked, from losing your job. I'd advise you **strongly** to let this go."

I don't know what to say. Then there's a click, and a dial tone.

I stare at the receiver in my hand, and slowly lower it back onto its base.

Madeline knows I don't need a psych eval. She **wants** me to lose my clearance, doesn't she?

She wants me to look crazy. She wants to make sure no one will believe me.

Why?

IF THEY'RE NOT GOING TO put me back on the case, I need to do this on my own.

Letting it go isn't an option.

And my first step is to learn the details of Jim's pitch.

Cyrus would have the information. He'd have access to the FBI case file. Approaching him again, asking him for it, it's a risk. He might already know I've been taken off the case. That Jim filed a report on me, and Madeline did, too.

But if it's the only way I can get the information I need, it's a risk worth taking.

I look back at the messenger app. His name is green.

I lock my computer, stand, head down the hall before I can change my mind.

His blinds are closed today, but the light's on and his door's ajar. I give the door a knock. No answer. Strange. I take another step, peer through the opening—

He's not there. The office is empty.

And his computer's still on.

It's open, unlocked. A violation of Agency policy, one I've seen time and time again here.

There's a peal of laughter from down the hall, from the break room. **Cyrus's** laughter.

This could be fast. I saw him open the FBI database the other day. Saw where he entered the search term. It would take seconds to search for Jim's name, print off what I find.

If Cy comes back, catches me at his computer, I'd

be done. My security clearance would be gone. I'd be fired.

But I'd have that report in my hands. I'd know exactly what Jim knows. How he was pitched. I might be able to figure out if Madeline was behind it.

I'm going to do it.

I throw one last glance down the hall, toward the break room. No one around. I can still hear the din of chatter.

I step into the office, heart pounding. Pull the door mostly closed. This way I'm shielded from passersby. From Cy, if he's on his way back from the break room—

I double-click the Bureau database. Type the name. Jim Brewer. I don't know if I'll need to use a full name, or add in The Neighbor as a search term—

Results populate. I skim the list—

Attempted blackmail of CIA employee Jim Brewer—full report.

Bingo.

I double-click. Hit the print button—

Close the search results, close the database—

Control-alt-delete.

I stand up so quickly from the chair it almost tips. Walk to the printer. It's still working, still spitting out page after page—

The office door opens, and there's Cy.

TWENTY

"HI, CY," I SAY. I TRY TO KEEP MY VOICE relaxed, try desperately not to look as guilty as I feel. That damn printer is **still** printing.

"Hello, Beth." He's still in the doorway. Just looking at me, with a question on his face.

Think, Beth.

"My printer quit on me," I say, giving my shoulders a shrug. "Hope you don't mind I used yours." They're all remote, the printers. As long as it's in range, I can print to it. Only trouble is, there'd be no reason I'd have the serial number of his printer—

"How on earth did you know which was mine?" He says it like an innocent question, but is it?

"I came in and checked."

The printer stops, and silence takes its place. Cy is still watching me, giving me a searching look. My heart is pounding.

If he asks to see what printed out, he'll know. Everything prints with a cover page attached, one that lists a name and a classification. This one will have **his** name on it, not mine, because it was printed from his account.

"You know, Cy, I was hoping we could do that lunch we talked about sooner rather than later. I wanted to pick your brain about some potential career moves. Get your advice about a few things." I fight to keep my voice steady, and light.

And then I practically hold my breath, hope he won't ask any follow-up questions, because I have no idea what I'll say. I'm speaking completely off the cuff.

"Well, of course, Beth." He brightens, and that searching look he had been giving me vanishes. "Nothing I enjoy more than giving advice." He tips his head to the side, looks thoughtful. "Doesn't happen much anymore."

"It should."

Pulse still racing, I lift the printed sheets from the tray and tuck them under my arm. He barely seems to notice.

"Gotta get back to work," I say, giving him a smile. He offers me a weak smile back.

I head toward him, toward the door, wait for him to stop me, to ask to see the papers I just printed.

He doesn't, just moves aside to let me pass.

I pause at the door. "You know, Cy, I think anyone who's **not** asking for your advice is really missing out."

"Yeah?" he says hopefully.

"Yeah," I say, and then add the honest truth: "I don't know what I would have done without you."

MY FIRST STOP IS THE shredder in the hallway. I drop in the cover sheet, watch as Cy's name disappears into thin ribbons of paper.

Into my office next. I close the door and start reading.

It was a video. That was the blackmail. Jim received a large manila envelope in the mail, postmarked from the Langley area. Inside was a DVD, with a video recording.

The report includes a handful of screenshots from the video, and that plus the description paints a clear picture in my mind.

It was footage of Jim, in his garage, empty bottles around him. He was stumbling around drunk, apparently. And it was filmed by someone passing by. Jim catches sight of the person filming the video, raises a hand in a wave, says in slurred speech, "Well, hello, neighbor."

There was also a note in the envelope. White copy paper, black marker, block letters. YOU'LL lose your job if this comes out. If you want it to remain hidden, agree to do us a favor. It then provided an email address.

The note was right: that kind of behavior, and the frequency with which it was happening, **would** be enough to jeopardize Jim's security clearance, and in turn his job. Alcohol abuse leads to impaired judgment, loose lips—and neither of those things mixes well with access to the government's most sensitive information.

Jim went straight to Agency security nonetheless, handed over the contents of the envelope. The Agency then turned the case over to the FBI.

All of this happened when I was off work, vacationing and packing and getting Tyler ready to head to college. The video was shot and left in Jim's mailbox while Tyler and Mike and I—and Aubrey and Austin—were at the beach in Ocean City; by the time I got back to work and saw my belongings packed up for the Kent School, there was an open investigation and my access had been removed.

That's why Madeline said Mike and I weren't suspects. We weren't in the neighborhood when it happened.

Neither was Madeline.

The thought hits me like a slap. She and Josh were on vacation; that's why they didn't see our house until two days before closing. And Jim wouldn't have known her yet, anyway.

I feel like everything's up in the air again. Completely unclear.

A **neighbor** shot that video.

Could it be one of my **friends**?

I'm not sure I actually entertained the idea until now.

It's what Madeline thinks, isn't it?

Could she be right?

Could The Neighbor really be one of my friends?

TWENTY-ONE

I SIT AT MY DESK AND FORCE MYSELF TO consider the possibility, painful as it is. That one of my **friends** is a traitor.

It would be consistent with that Google Maps pin drop on our street.

But who would it be?

We were out of town. The Patels were, too; they spend every August and September in India. But the others, they all would have been there.

I think about the latest intercept. **The Neighbor has found a new cul-de-sac.**

Des and Darryl are looking at new construction. Erin and Sean are planning to move in the spring. Have any of them found a new house already?

Is it on a cul-de-sac?

And Alice and Charles—they're staying put. Alice was adamant. Seems like they're out.

Of course they're out. Alice is my best friend. How am I even considering the possibility that it could be her? **Or** Charles.

But how can I be thinking it could be one of the Johnsons or O'Malleys, either? None of this seems possible.

So why don't I just rule it out?

I pick up the phone, dial Alice at work. She answers on the second ring.

"It's me," I say.

"Hey, Beth. What's going on?"

"Question for you. Des and Erin—have either of them found new houses yet?"

There's a beat of silence. "I have no idea."

"They haven't said anything to you?"

"I know as much as you do. Just from that conversation we had right before you moved."

"Okay."

There's more silence on the other end of the line. I'm sure she's wondering why I'm asking. "Is that all, Beth?"

I'm about to say yes, but I stop myself. "You and Charles—you're definitely staying put?"

"Yeah."

"Looking at any second properties? Vacation homes, anything like that?" I don't think it's in the cards for them financially, but I could be wrong.

"I wish. A kid at Yale, remember? And two more who just graduated."

"Right. Okay, thanks. I'll talk to you later."

There's a pause. "Talk to you later."

Of course it's not Alice, or Charles. I feel guilty for even thinking it.

Let's just rule out the others, and be done with this.

I look at my messenger app, the friends list. Des and Erin are near the top, two of my most frequent contacts. I'll chat with each of them at least a few times a week, have for years. We'll trade neighborhood gossip, discuss the kids' activities, make plans to meet for lunch. Des is yellow, away from her computer, but Erin's green. I open a window and type.

Hey Erin. Just curious: have you and Sean found a house yet? I know you said you were listing in the spring, but I never asked if you'd already started looking.

I hit send, then reread the words I just typed. Too direct? Too nosy?

I wait for a reply—

Hi Beth. No, it's a little too early.

Of course it's too early. It's not them—

Another message:

But our Realtor has a client who's planning to list in January, and the house hits a lot of what we want. So that might work.

I stare at the words. A lot of what they want?

That's wonderful, I type. And then, Like what?

I keep my eyes on the screen and wait. Seems to be taking a long time for her to respond.

You know, like what we have now. Space, good schools, quiet street.

Quiet street.

A cul-de-sac?

I can feel my pulse starting to quicken.

I reread the chat, and my eyes focus in on a single word. **January.**

Would you move that soon? I type.

Not till summer. We'd just own both houses for a little while.

Own both houses. Exactly the situation Mike and I had tried to avoid.

Obviously they're doing better than I thought. I've always assumed they had to pinch pennies a bit more than we did. All those rounds of IVF, and two government salaries, and this expensive house—

And now **another** house. Possibly on a new cul-de-sac.

In Maryland, too. That's what she had said. I can't help but think of Cyrus's words. **If it's NSA they've penetrated, they're moving on to CIA.**

Or vice versa.

There's a sick feeling settling into my stomach.

In my mind I can see Erin through her bay

window, watching us, back when the kids were young, before she had the twins. When she and Sean couldn't afford another round of IVF, couldn't have the baby they so desperately wanted—

Oh God. Is it **Erin**?

TWENTY-TWO

I TEACH THE CLASS, MY MIND ELSEWHERE, basically just reading the prepared slides. Quick lessons, quick assignments. The bare minimum, so I can send the students home and have some time to think.

Once they've been dismissed for the day, I sit in my office, alone, and read that report again, the one from the FBI. I try to imagine if Erin really **was** The Neighbor. If she really **did** attempt to recruit Jim.

A note in the mail, followed by email communication.

It actually seems like something she'd do. Avoid face-to-face contact. It seems fitting.

Is that how she's communicated with others? Is that how she's stayed under the radar for so long?

Is that how she communicates with **her** handlers, too?

It can't **really** be Erin, can it?

Abruptly I head to the supply closet down the hall. Pull out a box of manila envelopes, bring them back to my office.

I carefully open the box, pull out the first envelope using just my fingernails, careful not to leave any prints on it. Do the same with a sheet of copy paper.

I open up the FBI report again, turn to the picture of the letter that Jim received.

Then I open a black Sharpie and write.

We need to talk. Email me, or I'll reveal what you've done.

I try to match the handwriting on Jim's letter as closely as possible. Block letters. Try not to touch the paper with any of my fingertips. Hold it down with a closed fist, write with the other hand.

I add an email address, a long random array of letters and numbers. I jot the same string down on a Post-it for myself. I'll set up an account later, anonymously, from a different IP address.

Then the envelope next: Erin O'Malley, her address, two numbers away from mine. The same block lettering.

No return address.

I dig into my desk drawer for stamps, attach them. Use a tissue over my fingers to place the letter into the envelope. Tape it closed; don't want to leave any DNA behind on the seal.

Then I tuck it in my bag, along with the Post-it.

I drive to the lot at Langley Park. There's a big blue mailbox at the far end, and never anyone around it.

I take a deep breath and drop the envelope into the slot.

As I drive away I have the distinct sense I just set something into motion, and it's something I won't be able to control.

I DRIVE BACK TO THE rental, deep in thought.

Two days. That's how long it should take for the envelope to make its way to Erin's house.

She's usually the one who picks up the mail. She and Sean arrive home together; he usually unlocks the front door while she walks down the driveway to get the mail.

She doesn't do it every day. Not like Des, who does it almost religiously; I'm not sure I've **ever** seen Darryl pick up the mail, and I've certainly seen Sean do it. But it's **usually** Erin.

And she usually flips through the stack on the way back up her driveway, same as we all do. This envelope ought to catch her attention, especially if she's sent ones just like it, with the block lettering, with no return address. There ought to be some kind of reaction, and I want to see it.

I can't sit on the street, can't risk that she'll see

me, connect me in any way to the envelope. If I'm wrong and she goes to Agency security, and they go to the FBI, the last thing I want is for Madeline to review her security footage, see my car, think I had something to do with it.

The camera's still on the tree in front of Madeline's house, but the battery's dead. It'll probably fall off the tree eventually, disappear into the mulch and leaves. It's that small; it doesn't have to be recovered.

And I don't want to try Hunter Court again, don't want to risk those neighbors calling the police.

I'm almost at the rental now. I slow to a stop at a red light. There are no other cars around, no movement. My gaze drifts to the sky. A plane is passing by overhead, in the distance, almost invisible, except for a thin trail of exhaust in its wake.

As the light turns green and I press down on the gas, a smile spreads across my face.

I have an idea.

ONE STOP AND TOO MUCH money later, I'm the proud owner of a mini drone, complete with HD video and live streaming. It's the smallest, quietest one I could find, and it's supposed to be nearly undetectable.

Monday night I spend reading manuals; Tuesday after work I head to a park near the rental and test it out, then make another stop at the public library in McLean, set up a new Gmail account using the string of digits jotted down on the Post-it.

On the way home, I stop and buy a couple of cheap phones. Burners, just in case.

Wednesday I'm ready to go.

I finish class at three, let the students leave early.

Erin and Sean always arrive home around four-thirty. Creatures of habit. That'll work to my advantage right now.

I'm at Langley Park by three-thirty, hike along the river until I get to the clearing. Then I force myself to wait. Thirty-minute battery life. I'll launch at four-fifteen and hope for the best.

At four-fifteen on the dot, I send the drone up. I watch it hover, lift into the air, then I use the remote control to guide it toward the cul-de-sac. I watch on the app on my phone as it reaches a position near their house, one with a clear view of the street. I let the drone hover there in the distance, watch for their car, and wait.

At 4:28, the red SUV drives slowly down the street.

I inch the drone closer to the house.

The SUV comes to a stop in the driveway. The driver's-side door opens, then the passenger side, and both Erin and Sean step out.

Erin reaches for the back door of the SUV and opens it.

Sean starts walking down the driveway.

"Dammit," I murmur, watching the screen.

Erin pulls out two soccer balls, balances them in one arm while shutting the door with the other, then walks to the front door.

Sean's at the mailbox now.

I move the drone closer. There's no indication he sees it or hears it.

Hopefully I can at least make sure the envelope's there.

He opens the mailbox, removes a stack of mail. Starts walking back up the driveway, flipping through it.

I zoom in as much as I can—

There it is. The envelope, the one with Erin's name.

Sean stops dead in his tracks.

I send the drone in a wide arc so that I can zero in on his face.

It's ashen. He's standing stock-still, staring at the envelope.

Then he glances around furtively, like he's trying to see if anyone's watching.

All of a sudden he looks up, quickly slams shut the pile of mail so the envelope's in the center, not visible. I move the drone's camera up to see what drew his attention.

There's Erin, walking back down the driveway.

Sean tucks the mail under his arm.

Erin's pointing to the bushes and saying something to him, and he's responding. Some sort of conversation about the landscaping.

Then she starts back up the driveway. He follows, albeit a few paces behind. While she's examining the landscaping, he discreetly pulls the manila envelope from the pile of mail, tucks it into the waistband of his pants, flat against his back, pulls his shirt down over it. Hidden from view.

Hidden from **Erin's** view.

Then he catches up to her and they disappear into the house together.

I let the drone hover there for a few seconds longer, camera focused on the closed front door.

I'm stunned by what I just saw.

Sean recognized the handwriting on the envelope.

And he didn't want Erin to see it.

It's not Erin I should be worried about.

It's Sean.

TWENTY-THREE

I HIKE BACK TO MY CAR, ENERGIZED, AND drive to the public library in the center of McLean. It's a big building, full of light, with a huge wall of windows overlooking serene woods. I make my way past well-kept rows of books to a bank of public computers in the back, mostly vacant, only a few in use.

I sit down at a computer in an empty row, open a browser window, navigate to Gmail. I glance around, but don't see anyone looking my way. It's quiet, except for a kids' story time taking place in the corner of the room, preschoolers and parents sitting cross-legged on the floor, facing a librarian in a chair, one who holds a book open so they can see the pictures as she reads. I log in to the account I set up last night.

One new message, from an unfamiliar email

address, another random string of letters and numbers.

Why are you contacting my wife? What do you want?

It must be from Sean. A throwaway email account, like the one I'm using. He obviously didn't want Erin to see that envelope. And if he'd gone to the authorities, to Agency security or to the FBI, there's no way there'd be a response this quickly. There's too much red tape.

I could go to the authorities right now, tell them it's Sean. But **is** it Sean?

Could **Sean** really be The Neighbor?

Mild-mannered, quiet Sean. The guy who runs the church youth group. Helps coach his kids' soccer teams.

It doesn't seem possible.

I look at the screen, fingers poised over the keys, considering what to say—

Why are you contacting my wife?

That's his first thought, his first question. He doesn't want her involved.

What do you want?

And those words. They don't sound like the words that come from the boss, someone doling out taskings.

Sean recognized that envelope. But maybe it's not because he's sent one.

Maybe it's because he's **received** one.

We need something from you, I type. A shot in the dark. We'll see if it works.

A new message appears.

Leave Erin out of it.

And then, a moment later:

Can it wait until next time?

I stare at the screen. **Next time.** Like there are regularly scheduled meetings, or communications of some sort. Between Sean and The Neighbor.

"They got to you, didn't they?" I murmur. Then I lift my hands to the keyboard: No.

Fine. When? And where?

I glance at my watch. One wrong move here and I could extinguish this lead. But if I play my cards right, I could get the answers I need.

Seven tonight, I write. Same place as last time.

Then I log out of the account and head for my car.

I GET ON THE TOLL road and follow the signs out to Dulles Airport, then take the exit for the rental car companies. Twenty minutes later, my car's left in the lot and I'm driving back on the toll road in a silver Hyundai Elantra. The same model car that Mrs. Patel drives.

I head into Langley Oaks, to the back of the neighborhood, then onto Riverview. Pull into the Patels' driveway, park there, sink down into the driver's seat, wait. If anyone notices the car, they should assume the Patels came home early.

I'd considered doing this before, using their driveway, a car that looks like theirs, but here's the problem with it: it's a onetime deal. Too risky to come and go. I wouldn't do it if there were any other option. But I have to be able to see Sean leave. I have to follow him.

I'm glad I got here early, because Sean leaves earlier than I expected. Six-fifteen. I wait until his car turns onto Oaks, then I start my own engine and pull out of the Patels' driveway, follow a safe distance behind.

He turns in to a strip mall off of Chain Bridge Road, parks in front of the liquor store. I park several storefronts away and watch as he gets out of his car, walks into the store, head bowed.

This can't be where he's meeting his handler. And it's too early. He's got to be running a surveillance detection route. Classic spy technique. Make a few stops on the way to a destination, check to see if any of the same cars follow from point to point.

I've been trained to run SDRs. But I've been trained to evade them, too.

It's easier to avoid detection when there's more than one person, more than one car. But it's just me, and I'm doing the best I can.

Sean walks out a few minutes later, paper bag in hand. He doesn't look around as he slides back into his car.

I reach for the Nikon and zoom in. He's sitting in the driver's seat, unmoving, staring straight ahead. Then there's movement. He reaches over to the passenger seat for the paper bag. Twists the cap off whatever's inside, takes a long swig without removing it from the bag.

Sean, the onetime alcoholic, who's been sober as long as I've known him. At least I **thought** he had been.

I didn't know him nearly as well as I thought I did.

He starts his engine and pulls out of the parking space. I follow again, at a distance. He's heading back toward the neighborhood. **Into** the neighborhood.

I feel myself tense. He's supposed to be heading somewhere else. Not back home.

Was that **it**? Maybe seven didn't mean seven to him. Maybe they use a code for a different time. T minus thirty minutes or something. Maybe the liquor store was the meeting point, and when he didn't see his handler there, he left.

Maybe I've blown this lead.

I pull onto Hunter Court because I can't risk the Patels' driveway again. And I can't leave, either, because I need to see if he heads out again, closer to seven.

I park between two houses and turn off the engine. Sink low into my seat and watch my cul-de-sac, through the trees. Wait for Sean's car to appear again.

A porch light flickers on, the house just up ahead. There's movement in front of the blinds in the bay window.

Dammit.

I check my watch. It's just minutes until seven now. Still no car.

This didn't work.

A woman steps out of the house with the illuminated porch. She crosses her arms over her chest and watches me.

My hands ball into fists. This is **not** working out the way I want it to.

I start the engine and pull away, casting one last glance at the O'Malleys' house—

It's **Sean**. Walking down his driveway in workout gear, breaking into a jog.

TWENTY-FOUR

IT'S A SIGHT I'VE SEEN COUNTLESS TIMES over the past seventeen years. Sean, out for a run through the neighborhood.

I inch down Hunter Court, don't approach the stop sign until he passes by on Oaks Drive, his pace steady, his gaze straight ahead. He doesn't look in my direction.

I turn onto Oaks, catch sight of him again, up ahead. I pull to the side of the road and watch as he winds his way through the neighborhood, try to figure out which way he's going. Toward the pond, by the looks of it.

I turn down Orchard Street and circle back onto Meadow Lane, park on the side of the street. He's on the paved trail around the pond now.

I take out my camera and watch him through the zoom lens. Steady pace, eyes forward.

He's nearing the part of the trail where it dips closer to the pond. His pace slows to a walk as he approaches the bench there. He sits down on it, all the way on the right side.

Looks around, like he's waiting for someone.

I look, too, but don't see anyone. Glance at my watch: 7:02.

Then I focus in on him again—

There it is.

If I didn't have the zoom lens, if I wasn't watching so intently, I never would have seen it. Almost imperceptible.

Reaching down with his right hand, touching the underside of the bench, feeling for something he expects to be there.

I press down on the shutter release, snap a flurry of shots.

He thinks there's a **message** waiting for him.

This is a dead drop.

He's not meeting his handler face-to-face. They're leaving messages for each other. In our neighborhood.

In plain sight.

Everyone uses this bench. Runners taking a breather. Dog walkers resting their feet. Parents taking a break while their kids explore the edges of the pond, throw bread to the ducks. I used to bring the kids down here when they were young. We all did. We've all sat on this bench.

And someone was leaving messages here.

Sean straightens again, places both hands in his lap. **Empty** hands. He looks around again, his expression nervous. **Suspicious.**

I lower the camera and watch him from a distance. He pulls his phone from his pocket, types something with his thumbs.

I reach for my own phone, the burner. Search for Wi-Fi, find an unsecured network nearby, connect. Then I pull up the throwaway Gmail account. Sure enough, there's a new message.

It's not here.

I smile and set down my phone.

He stares at his screen, waiting for a response that doesn't come. Then he looks around again, quickly. Shoves the phone back into his pocket and stands, starts off toward home, faster this time, almost like he knows someone's after him.

TWENTY-FIVE

I'M BACK IN THE APARTMENT, AND I'M PACING, trying to figure out what to do next.

Sean's a recruit. He recognized that envelope because he's received his own. Some sort of blackmail, just like Jim, but instead of going to security, he followed their demands. He's been passing information to The Neighbor.

I could take this to the authorities. Agency security, or FBI. I have pictures of him on that bench, reaching under it, coming up empty-handed. Emailing the person he thinks is his handler. **It's not here.**

But would it be as clear to **them** as it is to me? Or would they doubt me, like they've doubted me all along?

And if they **did** believe me, what would they do? Cut me out, that's the first thing. Turn everything over to the FBI. To **Madeline**.

If I can just figure out **who** Sean's communicating with, what Sean knows, then I find my target.

I need to keep going.

I can't confront Sean, not directly. I can't risk being reported a third time. Besides, I don't know how he'd react, what he'd do. He has everything to lose, and I don't want him to know it's **me** digging around.

But I need to know. I need to run down this lead.

I open up my laptop, then the Gmail account. Connect to an unsecured Wi-Fi network. Attach a picture of Sean on that bench, reaching down. And a message:

I don't think you want this to end up in the wrong hands.

The response comes an instant later, like he's there, waiting.

Who are you? What do you want?

I smile.

I'm a neighbor. And I want to make a deal.

WHICH NEIGHBOR? HE TYPES.

Doesn't matter.

I wait for him to respond.

This isn't secure.

I roll my eyes. Of course it's not. But he has bigger concerns.

Another message:

Let's meet in person.

"I don't think so," I murmur. Then I type:

I'll call you.

I close the browser window, then the laptop, and pull out a burner phone, a good one. It takes me a few minutes to find and download a voice-changing app—I choose a generic female voice—and an anonymizer that promises to scramble the cell tower location.

Then I look up his cell number from my own phone, and I call him from the burner.

"Who are you?" he asks when he picks up.

"I told you. A neighbor." I like the sound of the voice. It doesn't sound like me.

"Who?"

"Tell me the truth, Sean. From the beginning."

"Why should I?"

"Because if you don't, those pictures and those emails find their way into the hands of the authorities."

"And if I do?"

"You're in a better position."

"How can you guarantee that?"

I think back to those words Madeline spoke to me, that day she caught me in her house.

Everyone lies, Beth.

"Because I'm FBI. And it's your handler I'm after."

TWENTY-SIX

TECHNICALLY, I SHOULDN'T BE IMPERSONATING a law enforcement officer. But if it's what I need to do to get a confession from Sean, to find The Neighbor, so be it.

The ends justify the means.

Everyone lies.

I unlock my own phone with my thumb. Tap the audio recording app, then press the round red button. Set the phone down in front of me.

"Who's tasking you?" I ask into the burner phone.

"I don't know."

"The pictures, Sean. The emails. I can send those out with one click."

"I don't **know**. I don't know who it is." He sounds desperate. He sounds like someone who's telling the truth.

"What **do** you know? How'd they get to you?"

The question is met with silence.

"So help me God, Sean, I will send this—"

"It was after our fifth round of IVF," he says.

I go quiet, waiting for more.

He's quiet, too, like he knows he said too much.

"Go on," I say.

"We were out of money. Worse than that. Mortgaged to the hilt, so far in debt I didn't know if we'd be able to claw our way out. My wife—all she wanted was a baby, and it was my fault we couldn't adopt—" His voice breaks.

"What happened, Sean?"

"I can't do this," he pleads. "I can't tell you this."

"You either tell me, or you tell the agents who are going to be on your doorstep as soon as I make a call."

"Okay! Okay, I'm talking, aren't I?"

His voice sounds unnaturally high-pitched. I wonder where he is right now. I can picture his house. I don't know it as well as the Kanes', or the Johnsons', but I know it. I've had dinner there. Wine, around the kitchen island. My kids have played there—

"I got an envelope in the mail. The person who wrote it knew about our situation. Said they'd fund additional rounds—as many as we needed—if I did something for them. Something small."

"What was it?"

"Whatever it **was** isn't going to help you find my handler." His voice has an edge. "That's what you want, isn't it?"

He knows what he's doing. He's being careful. He's been careful for fourteen years now, hasn't he?

"And you did it?"

"Again, let's focus on what you need."

Now I'm annoyed. "Watch it, Sean. I'm the one calling the shots here."

He doesn't respond right away. Then, in a more chagrined tone: "If I **did** do it, I was supposed to send an email. New account, different IP address."

"Okay." Now we're getting somewhere.

"I should have gone to security. For anything else, I would have, I swear. But this . . . this was like my Kryptonite. Seeing my wife every day like that. **Depressed**. And every month, every negative test, it was worse."

There's a clink on his end of the line. Glass against glass. He's drinking whatever's in that bottle. He's refilling.

Dammit, Sean.

Has he always been a drinker? Did he hide **that**, too? Or maybe this is driving him to drink. But at the same time, maybe it's driving him to **talk**. To come clean. To confess.

"She wanted this so badly. I mean, I did, too, but not like her. This was all she wanted. And I couldn't give it to her. And then that letter arrived, and suddenly I **could**."

I nod slowly, even though he can't see me. In my mind I picture Erin, watching us from the window.

"It wasn't something that would hurt anyone. I swear to God. If it had been something terrible, I wouldn't have done it. No one got hurt. They didn't get classified information. I don't **have** classified information. I'm just the guy who keeps the lights on, for God's sake." He slurs the last words.

I glance at my phone. Still recording. That was about as close to a confession as I might get.

"So you gave them information about the backup power supply?"

The question is met with silence.

"Was it enough to let them hack into the network?"

"No. God, no. Not possible. There's no way to access classified information from the power supply. Swear to you. I run that system. I **know**."

Now it's my turn to go quiet.

"Look, I knew I was making a deal with the devil," he says. "I knew they might be back. Might ask for more. But I figured I could say no. If they asked for too much, I'd turn myself in then. At least I'd have given Erin another shot at a baby."

There's silence on the line, and I wonder if he's throwing back more of whatever he's drinking.

"What happened next?" I ask.

"The very next day, I got a call from the clinic. Our balance was paid, and so was the fee for the next cycle. They were calling to schedule our next appointment."

I nod again.

"That's the cycle that worked. Erin was pregnant."

"And then?" I ask.

No response.

"They came back?" I prompt.

Still nothing.

"Let's talk hypothetically. If they came back, if they asked for more, what do you think would have happened?"

"I'd have said no," he says quietly.

I'm losing him. He's realized he's said too much. He's going to stop talking—

"And then they'd have threatened my family."

I close my eyes and breathe deeply.

"They'd have sent me proof of what I did. Proof that'd get me locked away, you know? And a note. **We'd hate to see anything happen to the babies when you're in jail.**"

He's slurring his words again.

"It wasn't the only time. They've known everything about my kids, all these years. They've sent pictures. Notes. Things like **we like Shannon's new backpack.** Things that scared the shit out of me."

"And you were in deep at that point. So you just went deeper."

He doesn't say anything.

"Did you ever meet the person who was doing this?"

"Never."

"Did you always use that bench?"

"Nah. Not very often. Usually taskings came through the mail. Sometimes they'd give me an email address to send things to. Sometimes it'd be a physical location."

I'm racking my brain, trying to think of some angle to follow up on, something that could lead me to The Neighbor.

Mail, throwaway email accounts, dead drops— it's all **good**. It's all hard to trace.

"What's the name of the IVF clinic?"

"No use," he says. "They went out of business years ago. I tried to trace the payment and it was all backstopped. Same with—"

He stops himself.

"Was there another payment?"

There's a sound on his end of the line, like he was about to say something and changed his mind. "No," he says.

"You hesitated."

"I never asked for anything else."

"Dammit, Sean, one call is all it will take—"

"Fine. Yes. There was another."

I wait.

He takes a deep breath. "After the twins were born, they set up accounts. College savings, 529s. One for each kid. Made deposits, sent me a printout in the mail showing me the accounts and balances. It was like a thank-you. One that wouldn't raise any alarm bells on financial disclosure forms, you know?"

It was more than a thank-you. It was a way to force him to accept payment in exchange for the information he provided, which changed the nature of the crime. And he's probably right: I doubt Agency investigators paid as much attention to 529 accounts. "So your wife knows?"

"No. You mean because of the accounts?"

"Yeah." **I'd** know, if someone had added money to **my** kids' accounts. I'd watched those numbers grow—too slowly, it often seemed—from the very first deposits.

"No. I manage them. I make the deposits from our accounts. Erin's never realized the balances are too high."

I'm quiet, thinking. Money trail seems like a lost cause. He's never met his handler.

"Any idea who it is?" I ask. "Who's behind this?"

He goes quiet. A ripple of anticipation runs through me.

"No. But I always sort of wondered if it was

someone close by. Those dead drops, they were usually in the neighborhood. I don't know . . . I always wondered if maybe it was a neighbor."

"Any idea **who**?"

He hesitates. "No."

"Who?" I ask again, because I can tell he's lying. I can tell he knows something.

"I don't know. Honest. It's just a guess."

"Tell me."

He sighs. "One time I was getting the mail, and someone else was getting the mail at the same time. We each flipped through our stacks, and then we looked up and locked eyes, and it's like . . . she knew. She knew what I was looking for. And then she just turned around and walked back inside, without saying a word."

There's only a few houses with mailboxes close enough for that—

"Plus Erin told her about the IVF. She's the **only** neighbor Erin told. The only one who knew."

She wasn't the only one who knew, not by a long shot. We all knew.

But we learned it from one person.

Des.

TWENTY-SEVEN

SURE ENOUGH, SEAN SAYS HER NAME. I TELL him I'll be back in touch and I end the call, then stare at the phone.

Either Des is The Neighbor or she was recruited by The Neighbor. My **friend** Des.

And Sean. **Sean** is a recruit. A spy. Sean's been passing information to The Neighbor for years.

I'm still reeling from the conversation.

He did it at first for money, and for the promise of a future that was just out of his grasp. Did something he knew he shouldn't have done, but that he thought was small, insignificant.

Then they had him.

They threatened his family. If he went to the authorities for help, he'd be guaranteeing himself prison time. And they made him fear that his family would pay the price.

So he spiraled further into a web of deceit.

I consider calling Dale, telling him what I know. But if I do, all bets are off. Agency security will turn the case over to the Bureau. They'll go in and arrest Sean. And then what? It'll spook The Neighbor, for sure.

The Neighbor's within my reach now. It's Des, or Des knows something. Either way, I need to figure that out.

But Sean is guilty. He gave them information. He insists it wasn't something that would hurt someone. That it wasn't classified information. But it was **something**.

And I can't sit on that.

I reach for my phone, dial Annemarie.

"Beth?" she says when she picks up. Her voice sounds heavy with sleep—which might explain why she answered this time. She might think it's an emergency if I'm calling this late at night. "Is everything okay?"

"I need you to do something for me."

"Yeah?"

"Talk to IT security. Make sure there's no way into JWICS through the backup power supply."

"What?" She sounds confused. "Why?"

"Please just do it. But do it quietly."

There's silence on the other end of the line.

"Make sure there's no way in through the generators."

"Why are you wondering?" she asks. She sounds more alert now, more awake.

"I'll tell you soon," I say, and I end the call.

I **will** tell her soon. I'll tell everyone. I have the audio recording. I'll turn it over eventually. **After** I find The Neighbor.

I try to relax. Try to **sleep**. But I can't stop thinking. About Sean, about Erin, the fact that the life she's leading is built on a lie. Sean thought he was giving her what she wanted. Now it's all about to come crashing down.

I'm finally starting to drift off, in that place between wakefulness and sleep, and there's one final string of thoughts floating through my mind.

It was too easy. The confession. He said too much.

Maybe because he was drunk. Maybe he just needed to get it off his chest, after all these years.

Or maybe he thought, for some reason, that no one else would ever hear the truth he'd just revealed.

NEXT THING I KNOW, MY phone's vibrating on the nightstand. Disoriented, pulled from slumber, I reach for it, squint at the screen.

Madeline.

I fumble to answer. "Hello?" My voice sounds scratchy with sleep.

"Is there a **reason** you're trying to get me killed?"

She ends the call without another word.

Confused, I pull the phone from my ear and look at the screen.

A string of new texts, from Alice.

You'll never believe what's happening.

Police all over the cul-de-sac.

I sit up straight and unlock the phone, touch Alice's name in my contacts. She answers on the first ring.

"What's going on?"

"**Sean** barged into your old house. In the middle of the night. **Drunk** and confused."

"You're kidding." Panic is racing through me.

"I wish I was. God, he's been sober all these years."

"What **happened**? Why?" I feel like I'm sputtering. I never **said** I was Madeline. But somehow he assumed it was her. Does he know she's FBI? How did I find out?

"He must have been so drunk he thought it was his own house. Erin's a mess, as you can imagine."

"I'm sure," I murmur. My mind is still racing. I told him I was a neighbor. I told him I was FBI. Maybe he has access to the same database as Cy, was able to start searching for anyone who lives nearby. "Is Madeline okay? And her family?"

"I guess. I'm sure they're pretty freaked out."

"Where is he now?"

"Jail. They **arrested** him."

"For that?"

"What do you mean **for that**? Of course."

"I just mean, if it was an accident . . ."

"Couldn't they have let it go?" she finishes for me.

"Yeah."

"Well, here's the thing. I was talking with one of the cops outside, trying to get the whole story. And **apparently**"—she lowers her voice, takes on that conspiratorial tone she always uses when she's gossiping—"apparently there was **theft** involved. He was trying to steal a **phone**. And when he broke in, he had a **gun** on him."

TWENTY-EIGHT

MY MIND IS RACING. SEAN WAS TRYING TO steal Madeline's phone. He thought he was erasing proof of the conversation he had with her.

The one he actually had with **me**.

Did he say something to Madeline about me? Is that why she thinks I'm behind this?

Or is she just guessing?

Her words ring in my head. **If you tip anyone off about this, so help me God, there will be hell to pay.**

And Sean had a gun.

Why did he have a gun?

Would he have hurt her if he had the chance?

Would he hurt **me**?

I text Erin: I'm here if you need anything.

Thanks, she replies.

Now there's only one woman on that cul-de-sac

I haven't talked to tonight. The one who might be behind it all.

If Des is The Neighbor, she must be panicking right now, with a cul-de-sac full of police, with Sean being led away in handcuffs.

I think of what Sean said about the two of them making eye contact over the mail.

If she's **not** The Neighbor, if she's a recruit, does she suspect that Sean is, too?

She must be panicking either way.

And it's only going to get worse.

SLEEP DOESN'T COME THE REST of the night; I knew it wouldn't. I go into work early the next morning, watch the messenger app. Des's name appears, green. Erin's never does.

I need a different approach for Des. She's not going to spill everything the same way Sean did. She's stronger. More cautious.

Annemarie calls, and I press her for details on the power supply. "IT security's adamant there's no way in," she says.

"There's got to be something we're missing."

"There's not, Beth. Now are you going to tell me what's going on?"

I notice she doesn't mention Sean. Security **must** know he's been arrested. Word didn't get back to her, I take it.

"Not yet," I say. "But soon."

I teach my class, go through the motions, my mind elsewhere.

At lunch I call Alice at work. "What's the latest on Sean?" I ask. If anyone knows, it's her.

"Out on bail this morning," she answers. A ripple of apprehension runs through me. I had hoped he'd be locked away for longer. I wouldn't have expected him to come clean about anything, but this makes it clear he didn't.

My eyes land on Des's name again, green on the messenger app. She's been awfully quiet.

After I end the call with Alice, I send Des a message, because that's what I'd do if everything were normal, and I need to **act** like everything's normal.

I hear there was some excitement on the cul-de-sac last night.

Isn't that the truth. Poor Erin.

My fingers hover over the keyboard, but I don't know what else to say. And she doesn't send anything else, either.

Des tends to go quiet when she doesn't want to talk about something.

What's she thinking right now? What's she **doing**?

Is she getting ready to run, to disappear?

Is Quds Force going to step in and protect her? Exfiltrate her, get her out of here, keep whatever she knows out of our hands?

The thought sticks in my head the rest of the day. Churns there, haunting me.

I finish the day's lessons, let the students go early. Stop on the way home, pick up more burner phones.

Then to the rental. A quick dinner in the microwave. No wine tonight; I need my mind clear.

At six, I pick up one of the new burners. Find Des's number in my own phone, transfer it to the new one, send a message.

Network has been compromised. We need to discuss exfiltration.

I watch the phone, wait for a response.

Nothing.

Each passing minute feels excruciating.

Was Sean wrong?

Am I wrong?

Then an incoming text. From a different number.

No exfil. Need other protection.

A smile creeps to my lips. That's the Des I know. Using a burner of her own. Making **demands** of her own.

I consider what to say.

No protection plan. Only exfil.

I need to lure her somewhere in person. Snap a picture. Prove she **thinks** she's being exfiltrated, and she's agreeing to it.

Her response comes an instant later.

I'm not leaving. My family is here.

I chew my bottom lip and think. I could promise to exfil her whole family. But things would get complicated. The timeline would be stretched.

A better idea dawns on me.

Will develop protection plan, I text. Need to confirm details of case.

I hold my breath and wait. She **could** see this as a red flag, someone soliciting information. But she's stressed, and probably feeling desperate, and she might assume that the person communicating with her right now is a backup handler, one not completely familiar with the case but trying to meet her demand for a protection plan on short notice.

Please let it be the latter.

Finally, a response.

What do you need to know?

TWENTY-NINE

WHAT DO I NEED TO KNOW? EVERYTHING.

But I need to temper it with what I could plausibly ask. Need to pretend I'm some sort of Quds Force spy who isn't familiar with the details of the case, but who needs to come up with a plan to protect her. And I have to pretend there's some sort of file I'm looking at.

The file would begin with **how** they got her in their grasp.

How **did** they get her in their grasp?

And then it hits me.

Vinnie. I bet they had proof of her dalliance with Vinnie, compromising photos and video, and I'd be willing to bet they threatened to send them to Darryl, or make them public.

I know Darryl. If he'd seen something like that,

he'd have left. And he'd have made damn sure he got custody of the girls.

I know Des, too. And I know she wouldn't have been able to bear the thought of losing them. **Or** him.

Initial outreach involved an affair? I text. That's a nice way to put it, I guess. What I'm talking about is blackmail, plain and simple. I hold my breath and wait for a response—

Yes.

I exhale slowly. Method of communication with handler, I text. Mail?

Yes. And dead drops.

Dead drops were local?

Yes.

In the neighborhood, probably. The bench, maybe. Doesn't really matter. What matters is that it's somewhere nearby.

You do not know the identity of your handler, is that correct? I type.

Correct.

You provided sensitive information related to your position at work?

There's a pause.

Yes, comes the reply.

I wait for her to offer more, but she doesn't. And I don't want to press it. What reason would I have to ask for details? How would that affect our protection plan?

Sean was drinking, loose with his words, tried to cover it up. She's cautious.

Right now I'm getting what I want, and I don't want to raise any red flags.

And besides, it's obvious, isn't it? She's a senior polygraph examiner. She played a role in getting someone—or more than one person—cleared for employment. Turned a blind eye to lies on a poly-graph, probably, or coached someone into passing. It doesn't have anything to do with the backup power supply, after all. Maybe that was an angle they pursued, and came to the same conclusion as IT security: no way in.

You have never approached U.S. authorities, correct? I type.

Of course not. I'd never risk my kids' safety like that.

I lean back in my chair and reread those words. I bet they got to her like they got to Sean. Something small in the beginning, something she could justify to herself. Then threats involving her children. To keep her quiet, keep her active.

Use the children.

The parallels to Sean's case are striking.

A thought occurs to me.

I'm not seeing notes in the file—was there any payment? I text.

The response doesn't come immediately. And as I wait, a memory takes hold, and I know the answer.

———

IT WAS THE FRIDAY OF the first week of school, the year Aubrey was in fourth grade. We were at the bus stop in the afternoon. Alice, Des, and me, waiting for our older kids to arrive home, Tyler and Preston—the preschoolers—rolling Matchbox cars on the sidewalk around our feet. Erin was there, too, out for a walk, the twins asleep in their double stroller. She was pushing it back and forth as we talked, a rocking motion to keep them asleep. The rest of us barely even noticed the motion; we'd all been there.

"I can't believe this is Piper's last year of elementary school," I said.

"I know," Alice said.

"Then middle school."

She groaned.

"And **high** school," Des chimed in.

"**College** is only eight years away," Alice said. "How's **that** for a scary fact?"

"Not going to think about it," Des said, shaking her head.

"You're only a year behind," Alice said to her. "You, too, Beth. And you—" She turned to Erin. "It'll be here before you know it."

"I'm with Des," I said. "Not going to think about it."

There was a pause in the conversation, all of us

wrapped up in our thoughts, I'd imagine, about how quickly these years were passing, about how soon the next stage would arrive.

Then Alice spoke again. "Y'all saving for it?"

I exchanged a glance with Des, then Erin. Alice had always been the most open about finances. I still felt awkward talking about the subject.

"We are," I say, when no one else answered. "We have 529 accounts for all the kids. Put in what we can." I had opened them years ago. Watched them grow from those first dollars to a more sizable sum, though not nearly as quickly as I'd like.

"We do, too," Erin chimed in.

"Already?" Alice asked.

Erin shrugged. "Not much in them, I'm sure. We're still paying down IVF bills. Sean's the one who set everything up."

"You don't look at them?" Alice asked.

"Nah. It's Sean's domain. We've got time, anyway."

I snuck a glance at Des, who still hadn't said anything. She was staring at Erin.

Alice shook her head. "I look at our balances way too much. Charles does, too. And of course he's got his heart set on the kids going to Yale, like we did."

"Scholarships?" Erin said, in her usual cheerful tone.

"Let's hope so," Alice said.

Des was still quiet. I glanced over at her again.

They probably didn't have anything set up. This was probably making her uncomfortable.

"What about you, Des?" Alice asked.

I shot Alice an annoyed look. Sometimes she didn't know when to stop talking.

"We've got accounts," Des said. Rather shortly, tersely.

"Does Darryl handle them?" Erin asked quickly. She could tell Des didn't want to talk about it. She was giving her an out.

"I do," Des said.

"Yeah? Are they in good shape?" Alice asked.

Honestly. Alice needed to shut up.

Des gave her a cool look. "They're fine."

The tone, this time, was clear, even to Alice. Des didn't want to talk about it.

We all fell silent, and waited for the bus to arrive.

NEVER ASKED FOR ANY PAYMENT, comes the reply, pulling me back to the present. But yes.

Describe, please.

I send the text, even though I already know what she's going to say.

Deposits into my kids' college savings accounts.

I'll be back in touch with a plan, I text.

Then I put the phone down, mind racing.

The same thing happened to Sean. Payments into college savings accounts. Money that could be withdrawn by the account holder for any reason, less taxes, or could be used for the account's intended purpose: paying for education.

One of the old intercepts from Frozen Piranha floats through my mind. One of the messages I'd never been able to figure out, one that I'd printed and placed in that folder for reference.

The Neighbor wants us to provide payments.

Why?

Personal reasons related to The Neighbor's past.

A sick feeling is forming in my stomach. Because I remember who I called that day, when I saw Des and Vinnie together.

Someone who knew about Erin and Sean's failed rounds of IVF.

And about Jim's drinking problem.

Someone who's in the neighborhood, close to the dead drops.

I feel like all the pieces are clicking into place. And one big one, in particular. One mystery, that now seems solved.

Personal reasons related to The Neighbor's past.

Alice had student loans. She said they were astronomical. Or rather, Charles did. It was a topic of conversation the very first time we met. I remember it clearly: Charles asking Mike if his loans were as high as Alice's, me jumping in and saying he was lucky that his parents had paid his way. **Lucky is an understatement,** Alice had said.

Maybe the payments into the college savings accounts weren't just a form of entrapment.

Maybe it was a way to help out the neighbors. To try to right the wrongs she knew she was committing.

Maybe **Alice Kane** is The Neighbor.

THIRTY

ALICE IS MY CLOSEST FRIEND. MY NEXT-DOOR neighbor of seventeen years.

It doesn't seem possible.

But the signs are all there. She knows everyone's secrets. She always has.

And now she's becoming friends with her **new** neighbor. The FBI agent searching for her.

Keep your friends close, and your enemies closer.

And then another thought hits. Sends a cold chill running through my veins.

Is that why she was friends with **me**?

I PACE THE RENTAL, DEEP in thought. I need to figure out how to approach her. How to get a confession.

Maybe the answer is **I don't**. Maybe I just turn her in. But what if I'm wrong? I would destroy my friendship with my best friend.

And good God, I hope I'm wrong.

Right or wrong, I don't have proof. I need that confession.

And in the meantime, I need to do something about Des. Warn someone. Because someone she cleared—or coached—might have access to our systems right now.

I dial Annemarie—no answer.

I consider calling Dale, but I don't know whether he'd go straight to the FBI, and I'm not ready for the Bureau to swarm my cul-de-sac, take Des into custody. Not until I get what I need from Alice.

I continue to look at the screen of my phone, wheels turning in my brain.

The Bureau. **Madeline.**

She wouldn't insist on following protocol. Especially if it means cracking the case that'll make her career.

There's really no reason anymore not to trust her, is there? **She's** not The Neighbor. **Alice** is.

Abruptly I reach for my phone, dial her number. She answers on the first ring. "Hello?"

"Hey. It's Beth."

"I know."

Her voice sounds tense. Unfriendly.

"Look, you need to check out everyone that Des

Johnson has cleared for employment. Any polygraph that she's touched."

There's a beat of silence. "Why?"

"Just—"

"**Why,** Beth? What do you know?"

"You're gonna have to trust me on this one. Just look into it. But do it quietly."

"If you know something and you're withholding—"

"I'll make it worth your while. You'll get your big case."

I end the call and look at the phone, tense, wait to see if she calls back. I don't know if I made the right call, but I know I can't just sit on information like that.

She doesn't call back.

I get ready for bed and lie awake, mind still turning.

There's one thing that won't stop nagging me. One thing that doesn't make sense.

Alice hasn't found a new cul-de-sac.

That's the piece of information that kicked this all off to begin with. That led me to Madeline, which led me to everything else. But the Kanes are the only ones on the cul-de-sac who aren't moving.

Unless Alice lied about that, too.

As tense as I am, eventually sleep overtakes me.

Tomorrow I'll figure it out. Tomorrow I'll get the answers I need.

———

I WAKE TO AN ALARM. Not a fire alarm, nothing blasting like that. Quiet, but persistent. From the Echo, downstairs.

I blink at the clock on my bedside table. 3:23 A.M.

I have no idea why the alarm's going off. I didn't set it. I only set that alarm when I'm in the kitchen cooking, and I certainly haven't been doing much of that lately.

I climb out of bed, slide my feet into slippers, head for the stairs.

I can turn if off from the app; the kids are always telling me to do that. But I think it's easier to just use my voice.

I'm near the bottom of the stairs now. The kitchen's dark, the only light coming from the screen of the Echo Show. **Your timer is done.**

"Alexa, stop the alarm," I say, my voice heavy with sleep.

The alarm goes silent.

I turn to head back upstairs—

It starts again. That persistent chime.

"Alexa, stop the alarm," I say again, sharper this time, and I head the rest of the way down the stairs. Guess I'll have to unplug it, figure out tomorrow what's going on. I reach for the switch on the wall, and light floods the kitchen—

Immediately it goes out. The room is plunged into darkness.

A cold shiver runs up my spine.

"Alexa, turn on the lights," I say.

Light floods the room—

And then cuts out, and it's pitch black again.

Every nerve of mine is on alert. I go utterly still. Listening for any sound. I can't see a thing.

All of a sudden, music starts blasting. Full volume. Rock, or heavy metal, something that sounds frantic and intense.

"Alexa, stop," I say, practically a yell, so my voice will carry above the noise.

The room goes silent.

My heart's pounding now.

I don't hear anyone, don't sense that anyone's here. It's got to be the app. Someone's controlling things from afar.

I move toward the counter. I need to unplug the Echo, make this all stop—

Words flash across the screen, big and bold and red.

A message.

Back off.

THIRTY-ONE

I RIP THE CORD FROM THE WALL, AND THE screen goes black, the message gone. I'm breathing hard, my pulse pounding. I can still see the words in my mind.

Back off.

I yank all the smart plugs out of outlets. Turn on every light around me. This time they stay lit. I pull a flashlight from the junk drawer, just in case they go out again.

Then I walk around the townhouse, make sure all the doors are locked. Windows, too.

I find my way back to the kitchen and stand in the center of the room, just staring at the Echo, that blank screen, fear coursing through me.

I know Des's secret now. And Sean's. Secrets they've kept hidden for years. Their deepest, darkest secrets. Ones they thought they'd take to the grave.

Hoped to take to the grave. They didn't know they were talking to me.

But someone knows.

Alice?

Quds Force? Reza Karimi?

And then another thought hits me. **Madeline.** I told her to look into Des. Could **she** have done this? Or could she have tipped off Des, or Sean?

Someone did this. Threatened me, proved they can **get** to me, even inside my own home.

Alice would never do that, would she?

And Sean and Des, they're my old neighbors. My friends. **They** would never hurt me.

But they've already proven they're willing to take extreme steps for their families. What's to say they wouldn't take another?

Or that their **spouses** wouldn't?

How well do I know them?

How well do **any** of us know our neighbors, really?

I walk upstairs to my bedroom. Into the closet. I reach up to the highest shelf, pull down a black shoebox, open the lid.

Inside is my Glock.

I've always kept it in a safe. But the safe's been emptied, moved to storage. We tried to minimize what we were bringing to the rental.

I take it out, check to make sure it's loaded.

I'm not backing off. I'm putting an end to this.

THIRTY-TWO

WHEN DAWN BREAKS, I'M READY TO GO. Dressed in work clothes—pants today, and a loose top, because I've tucked the gun into my waistband. My phone's in my back pocket, ready to start recording.

Alice is up at five every morning to work out in their home gym. I know her routine. I know everything about her. Or I thought I did, anyway. Just like I thought I knew Sean, and Des.

I turn onto the cul-de-sac at five-thirty. My house is lit brightly, every exterior light illuminated. The others are softly lit, like usual, even though **nothing's** usual.

I pull into Alice's driveway. Turn the phone's audio recorder on, slide it back into my pocket.

Forget any plans. Mail, or anything like that.

This needs to happen fast. And my best chance of getting a confession is talking to her directly.

I'm incredibly tense walking up to the door. I can imagine Des at her window, watching me. Sean, at his.

And Madeline, too. Inside the house that used to be mine.

I knock lightly—I don't know if Charles is still sleeping—and Alice comes to the door in her work-out gear, face flushed and glistening with sweat, a towel slung over her shoulder. She looks surprised.

"Beth!"

"Hey. Do you have a minute to chat?"

"Of course. Always. Come on in." She stands aside, motions me in.

I walk into her foyer. This house I know so well, as well as if it were my own. How was this happening right under my nose and I missed it?

She uses the towel to blot the sweat from her face. She's still breathing hard. She walks into the kitchen, straight to the fridge, opens it, pulls out a bottle of water. "Can I get you anything?"

"No thanks."

She pulls off the cap and takes a swig. "I'm try-ing out this new modified CrossFit program. It's killer."

"I bet."

She gives me a quizzical look. "What's going on,

Beth?" She caps the bottle and slides onto one of the bar stools.

I do the same. Onto my usual one. I can feel the gun against the small of my back. I listen for any sound of Charles, but the house is quiet.

"I know about you, Alice," I say quietly.

She watches me blankly. "You know about what?"

"You. What you've done." I want to set the tone here. That we're going to be direct with each other, like we always have been. No secrets. No lies. She's going to admit the truth, and I'm going to have it all recorded.

"What have I done?"

She's good. She's still maintaining that blank look. And quite honestly, it makes me **angry**.

Maybe I should take a step back, ease into this, use our friendship to my advantage. But I can't pretend right now. Can't say I'll help her, or protect her, when she's my target—**and** a traitor.

"You're The Neighbor," I say.

"Whose neighbor?" She doesn't even miss a beat.

I stare at her. How can she look so calm, so thoroughly untroubled?

Because she's spent her life lying.

"Beth, is this about Maddy again?" Her brow is furrowed with concern. "Poor Maddy. After the other night—"

"No. It's about you."

"What **about** me?"

"You're working for Iranian intelligence. Recruiting spies. **You're** the person I've been searching for, for all these years."

She blinks. Her mouth opens just the smallest bit, almost like she's trying to summon the words to respond. "You're serious?" she finally says.

"Cut the act. I know the truth."

She stares at me, then raises a hand to her forehead, presses her fingertips into it, like she's thinking.

"Beth, I'm worried about you. First you accuse Maddy of all kinds of things, and now . . . now I don't even know **what** you're saying. That I'm a **spy**?"

I hear the sound of footsteps at the top of the stairs. I don't respond, just watch her, and listen. The footsteps are coming down the stairs, coming closer—

"Oh! Beth," Charles says, walking into the room and stopping short. He's in flannel pants and an undershirt, hair mussed with sleep. "I didn't know you were here."

His gaze shifts past me to Alice. A look passes between them, the kind I used to exchange with Mike. A wordless conversation. And it's about **me**.

"How are things?" he asks me brightly, ambling toward the coffeemaker.

"They're fine." I want him to leave so I can get back to my conversation with Alice. It's taking every ounce of my strength to act calm, like everything's normal, but I know it's the best chance of getting Alice to confess. Just two friends talking. She doesn't have to know I have a gun, that I'm recording every word she speaks.

He reaches for a mug from the cabinet, sets it down beside the coffeemaker. Looks from me to Alice. "You know, you two are obviously in the middle of a conversation. I didn't mean to interrupt."

I'm silent.

He nods. "Right. I'll just head up for a shower now, grab some coffee when I'm done. It was nice to see you, Beth."

"You, too."

He leaves the mug on the counter, heads back toward the stairs. I listen to the sound of his footsteps trailing off as he climbs them, until the sound disappears entirely.

"Beth, I think maybe it's time for you to see someone," Alice says gently. "A therapist, you know? Someone to help you sort through all these big changes in your life—"

"I know you tried to blackmail Jim. And I know you **did** blackmail other people. Our **friends**. You threatened their children. How could you do that?"

She stares at me. "I would never do that."

"You're a judge. How **dare** you make people turn on our own country?"

"This is crazy."

"Just tell me why you did it."

"I didn't **do** anything. Beth, I have **no idea** what you're talking about."

"Then I have no choice but to go to the Bureau."

She throws up her hands. She looks perplexed, incredulous. "Okay. Go to the Bureau. I don't know what else to say, Beth."

Dammit. She's a good liar.

Of course she is. She's been at it for fifteen years, at least.

This is useless. She's not going to confess, like Sean and Des. She's smarter than that.

I stand up, head to the front door. She doesn't move from her own stool, just watches me go.

"Beth, I'm worried about you," she says.

I stop at the door and turn to face her. "You **should** be worried. But not about me."

I GET BACK INTO MY car and sit in her driveway, staring ahead, my breath coming fast. I didn't get a confession. I didn't get the proof I wanted, the proof I needed. She didn't admit **anything**. There's nothing on the audio recording to implicate her in what I **know** she must have done.

I slam my fist against the steering wheel and start

the engine, then back out of her driveway, speed down the street, away from the cul-de-sac.

In my mind I picture Alice in her house, a smug smile on her face. Des in **her** house, watching me from the bay window, and Sean doing the same. **Traitors**.

A sick feeling is settling into my stomach. I didn't back off, and they know it now. **Alice** knows it.

I drive to the Kent School, park in the lot, sit there with the engine off, silence around me.

How do I get proof if she won't admit it?

And then it hits me: the money trail.

She'd have been paid, and paid well, for whatever she's doing. And she'd have used that money to pay off her debt. Those student loans would be erased. Much sooner than they otherwise would have been.

I need to find proof of **that**.

Their accounts are with America First Bank. All of them, student loans included. They're the ones who recommended the bank to us. Mike had his accounts there, too, so it was an easy choice for me to switch when we merged our finances. And I'm glad I did; their customer service is top-notch.

I google the number and place the call.

"Good morning! America First Bank, this is Mona. How may I help you?"

"Hello. I'm calling with a question about the payoff status of my student loans." I can pretend to be Alice. No problem.

"I'd be happy to help you, Ms. Bradford. May I please have your Social Security number for verification purposes?"

Dammit. This hasn't happened before. Must be some new system. They have my number, and it's linked to my account. I can't pretend to be Alice. I don't know her Social, anyway.

Maybe I should hang up. But if I hang up now, it'll look like I'm trying to do something wrong. I don't want them to flag our accounts. I shouldn't have called from my cell.

"Ma'am?"

"Sure," I say, and rattle off my own Social.

"Thank you," she says. And then, a moment later, "I don't see a record of student loans for you, Ms. Bradford. Are you calling about your husband's?"

"You know what, something came up. I'm sorry, I'll have to call you back." I end the call.

Well. That didn't work. I glance at my watch. I ought to head in. But it's like I can't summon the energy to do so.

I feel like I've reached a dead end. Like there's nothing else to do. Maybe I need to contact Agency security. Just come clean about everything. I have the audio recordings of Sean, and Des. I have proof that **they're** guilty.

But Madeline would get me cut off this case in a matter of moments. She'd be in charge, and the Bureau, and they'd blow it. If **I** can't get a confession out of Alice, they sure as hell won't be able to.

And this network is **good**. We've been chasing The Neighbor for fifteen years. Alice's tracks are covered. What if the only evidence of what she's done lies with Reza Karimi?

If I come clean, Alice gets away with this.

That's not an option. I have to do something.

And I have to do it soon, because she knows I'm onto her. And I don't know what she might do about it.

THE WORKDAY PASSES QUIETLY, UNEVENT-FULLY, and I drive home from work, numb. I still don't have a solution.

I park in front of the rental and sit. I feel as trapped as I've ever felt. Like there's no way to come out of this unscathed.

Finally I force myself out of the car. Up to the front door. I unlock it, step inside—

There's a manila envelope on the floor of the foyer. Slipped through the mail slot.

Beth Bradford written in black marker, block letters.

I close the door behind myself, lock it.

My heart is pounding.

I pick up the envelope, slide a finger under the seal.

There's a single sheet of paper inside. I pull it out with trembling hands.

More block writing. The same kind that was on Jim's note.

Want to know the truth? Meet at the river. Tonight, midnight. Look for the chalk X in the clearing. Come alone, or I leave.

THIRTY-THREE

THIS IS DANGEROUS. HEADING TO AN ISOLATED spot in the middle of the night—**obviously** it would be a mistake. I've been digging around, unearthing secrets. I'm a threat right now—to Alice, to Sean, to Des. To Reza Karimi.

I stare at the letter in my hands. I could take this to Agency security. But they'd call in the Bureau. They'd have to—it's the FBI's jurisdiction. And the Bureau would bungle it. They'd turn it into a major operation, and it would be obvious I wasn't coming to the clearing alone.

I want to know the truth. I **need** to. Alice sent this, didn't she? Maybe she didn't want to come clean in front of Charles. Maybe she wants to beg me not to turn her in.

Or maybe she's luring me to the woods to silence me.

If there's one thing I know for sure, it's this: she's not the person I thought she was.

I lay the note down on the table. Head upstairs, change into jeans and a sweatshirt, lace up hiking boots. Slide my phone and a flashlight into my back pocket, and then the Glock into my waistband.

It might not be Alice. It might be people she's working for. It might be an ambush.

One way or another, I'm going. I need to know the truth. But I'm going **now,** because I need to get there first. I need to have the upper hand.

As I head for the door, a single thought fills my mind. A memory, from last year:

Nothing good happens in the woods at night.

IT WAS THE DISTANT BARK of a dog that woke me. I blinked away sleep, and saw razor-thin streams of light filtering through the blinds on the rear window. Not daylight, either—it was still the dead of night—but the artificial kind. The Kanes' motion detection security light, the one aimed at their backyard.

I looked over beside me in bed; Mike was still fast asleep. I climbed out of bed, went to the window, peeked through the blinds.

Preston.

He was in a dark hoodie, head bowed, walking quickly away from his house, through his backyard.

I turned and looked at the clock on my bedside table, those fluorescent green numbers. 11:56 P.M.

What was Preston doing heading out at midnight? He was seventeen, for God's sake.

I sat back down on the edge of the bed and shook Mike. He grunted in his sleep.

"Wake up," I whispered.

"What?" he mumbled, his eyes still closed.

"It's Preston," I whispered. "He's leaving his house."

"Huh?" It's like the words were having trouble penetrating the fog of sleep.

"Mike, it's midnight. Preston's headed into the woods."

His eyes blinked open, then he struggled upright, propping himself on his elbows. Then he climbed out of bed, looked through the blinds. "I don't see him."

"He was just there. I should call Alice." I fumbled for my phone.

"No," Mike said. "Let me call Charles."

"Why?"

"Come on. You know he'll handle it better, whatever it is."

"What **is** it?" Every terrible prospect flooded my mind. Drugs. Running away from home. Meeting up with people he shouldn't—

"I don't know. But Alice will fly off the handle. You and I both know that."

"Well, whatever's he out there doing . . . maybe she **should** fly off the handle. Nothing good happens in the woods at night."

"Whatever it is, Charles will deal with it."

Mike picked up his phone. Placed the call, held the phone to his ear. I could hear it ringing on the other end.

No answer.

"Must be on silent," he said, ending the call. Then he got out of bed, pulled on jeans over his shorts, a sweatshirt over his T-shirt. Slid into shoes. "I'll walk over. If Charles is going to go after him, I might as well go with him, anyway."

I sat back down in bed, wide awake. Preston was a good kid, just like his sisters, just like **my** kids. Honors classes, good grades, involved in extracurriculars. Applying to highly ranked colleges, hoping to follow his parents and sisters to Yale. He wasn't the type to be doing anything unsavory. If that were Tyler out there, I'd want to know.

Then abruptly I stood up and left the bedroom, headed down the hall to Tyler's room. Stood at his doorway and looked in. He was sound asleep.

Preston should have been, too.

I went downstairs to the kitchen, made myself a cup of decaf tea, sat at the kitchen table, waiting.

Mike came back thirty minutes later. Stepped quietly through the front door, locked it behind himself. He must have seen the light from the kitchen, because he walked that way, instead of heading straight upstairs.

"Everything okay?" I asked.

"Yeah." He pulled off his sweatshirt, laid it over the back of one of the chairs.

"What was it?"

He shook his head. "Stupid teenage stuff."

"What **kind**?"

"He went down to the river with a six-pack of beer. I guess he'd made plans with a buddy to drink it."

"What?"

"I know. Like I said, stupid teenage stuff."

I was quiet. I'd watched Preston grow up. Still pictured him as a little boy sometimes, same as Tyler. It was hard to believe he was doing something like that.

"It could have been a lot worse," Mike said.

"I know," I murmured. And it was true. It could have been drugs, something like that. Beer was a pretty minor teenage transgression. But still.

"Look, don't mention it to Alice, okay? I don't think Charles is going to."

"Really? She should know."

"That's between them. Charles is going to handle it."

"You wouldn't keep a secret like that from **me**, would you?"

"Of course not." He looked indignant.

"Okay," I said reluctantly. I didn't like keeping secrets from Alice. But Mike was right. This was between them. This was **their** family, luckily. My own teenage son was safe in his bed.

"And don't mention it to Charles, either. He's pretty embarrassed. Let's just pretend it never happened."

Of course he was embarrassed. If there was anything that was important to Charles, it was how his kids looked to other people. Top of their class, best on their teams, admission to the best schools.

"Consider it forgotten," I said.

I brought my mug to the sink, then followed Mike upstairs, turning off the kitchen lights behind me. Feeling thankful for the family I had, kids who wouldn't have done something like that, a spouse who wouldn't keep a secret from me.

And realizing the Kanes weren't as perfect as they looked to the rest of the world. They had secrets. **Even from each other.**

I WATCH FOR A TAIL as I drive to Langley Park, but don't see anyone following me.

I park on the far edge of the lot, trek into the woods, down to the bank of the river.

My nerves are frayed. I know this is dangerous. I can't get it out of my head that Reza Karimi's people might be luring me down here to kill me.

Or that **Alice** is. My best friend.

I hope she just wants to explain where she was coming from, why she did what she did. And I want to hear it. More than anything.

Because when I turn her in, I need to do it with details. Right now all I have is speculation. Convincing speculation, sure. The fact that she knew those secrets about Sean and Des. That she picked dead drops in the neighborhood. That she had massive student loan debt, and that was the personal reason from her past that made her insist on funding college savings accounts for her targets.

And I think maybe because part of me wants to believe there's some other explanation. That I'm **wrong,** and it's **not** Alice.

I walk along the river in the direction of Langley Oaks. My senses are on alert. I'm incredibly aware of my surroundings, conscious of the gun at my hip, but I'm not overly afraid, because it's early. They'll expect me to wait for nightfall.

I make my way to the clearing near the curve of the river, the place where Alice and I brought the kids sometimes, when they were young. Let them climb the boulders, dip their toes in the running water.

I'm at the bend in the river now, and the clearing is in sight—

There, straight ahead, on one of the boulders, a jagged one, is a big X written in fresh white chalk.

I come to a stop, heart pounding. Instinctively I reach for my gun.

They knew I might come early.

I hold the gun taut, listening intently for any sound above the rush of the river water. Looking this way and that, turning in a slow circle, searching for anyone who might be nearby.

But I see nothing. I hear nothing.

They're not here now, but they've been here.

And they'll be back, later tonight.

Gun still tight in my hand, I find a spot behind some trees and brush, concealed, I hope, but with a direct view of the clearing, of that big white X.

Then I hunker down and wait.

NIGHT FALLS, AND DARKNESS DESCENDS. The moon is full and sits low above the clearing, casting just enough light that the X is still visible.

I have my flashlight at the ready, and the gun, too. The dirt below me is cold, and the chill in the air cuts through my sweatshirt. I listen for sounds.

There's one. I raise the gun instinctively, aim at the sound, my pulse racing. But it's just a branch falling from a tree, landing with a thud.

I lower the gun, and wait.

Another sound: a crackle of leaves. I raise my gun again—

It's a squirrel, darting by.

I check my watch. The minutes are creeping by slowly, but steadily.

Ten, then eleven.

Just past eleven-thirty, there's another sound. The crunch of dry leaves. I raise my gun.

Another crunch, and another. Slow, methodical. Coming closer, from the opposite side of the clearing, the direction from which I came. This is the sound I've been waiting for. **Footsteps.**

My heart is pounding. I look through the sights, into the darkness of the woods. Can't see anything, but I'll be able to any minute now.

I listen to the sound of the steps. Just one set.

A gust of wind whips through, sends the branches shuddering. The footsteps fall silent.

I hold my breath.

Light filters through the brush, the beam of a flashlight pointed at the clearing. The footsteps begin again.

They're almost at the edge of the clearing. My finger tightens around the trigger, because I need the upper hand here.

A person steps into view.

I'm expecting to see Alice, but it's not Alice.

It's **Charles.**

THIRTY-FOUR

"BETH?" HE SAYS. HIS VOICE ECHOES, SEEMS jarring, too loud in the quiet of the woods.

He takes another few steps into the clearing. The flashlight's in his hand, a beam of light extending out from it. But there's nothing else in his hand. No weapon.

I don't move. I'm trying to process this.

Charles sent the note.

"Beth? I know you're here."

He turns in a slow circle. There's just enough light from his flashlight, and from the moon, to see him. He's as tall and imposing as ever, and looks tense.

"Come out. I need to talk to you."

I don't move.

"**I'm** the one you're looking for, not Alice."

I could leave. I could stay hidden in the brush

until he moves on, and then I could move on. It would be the safest thing to do.

"It's not what you think, Beth."

I came here knowing it wasn't safe. I came here because I needed to know the truth. Because I need proof.

Silently I reach for my phone with my free hand, press the record button. Slide it into my pocket, then steady the gun with both hands.

I take a deep breath, try to slow my racing heart. Then I stand up, step around the brush into the clearing, gun extended in front of me, Charles in my sights.

He turns toward the sound, the beam of the flashlight swinging in my direction.

"Drop the light!" I yell. "Hands up!"

The light stays fixed on me. I can see him, but not as well as I need to, not as clearly. The light's too bright.

"Drop it now, or I shoot!"

He drops the flashlight. It rolls away from us, lands near the boulders. I blink, my eyes adjusting again to the darkness, lit by moonlight, made brighter from the beam of the flashlight reflecting off the rocks.

I can see him more clearly in my sights now. His hands are up, palms facing me. "Alice doesn't have anything to do with this," he says.

"It was **you.**" I shift my gaze so that I'm looking

at him over the sights now, but I keep the gun trained on him.

"It's not what you think. You've got it all wrong."

I don't have it all wrong. It makes sense. Just as much sense as Alice. If **she** knew Sean's and Des's secrets, he probably did, too. He was close to the dead drops. **His** life was affected by her student loans, just as surely as hers was.

"I heard what you said to Alice. About blackmailing our **friends**. Threatening kids. That never happened."

"I don't believe you." The words slip out before I can censor them. But it's true. I don't. If he didn't do this, why would he bring me here?

"I blackmailed Jim. But he was the only one. I swear to you, Beth."

A current of unease runs through me. It's always seemed strange, that particular pitch. The stakes weren't high enough; the target didn't have enough to lose. Seemed too much like the work of a novice. And The Neighbor wasn't a novice. The Neighbor knew **exactly** how to recruit. Did it dozens of times over a decade and a half, all completely under the radar, never detected, until that one. Until Jim.

Maybe it always seemed different because it **was.**

"Alice doesn't know anything about any of this," he says. "She has no part in it. And as for me . . . Look, I haven't **done** anything. Nothing that's against the law."

"Acting as an access agent for a foreign power is most certainly against the law."

"I didn't know who I was working for. I swear."

I scoff. "I don't think that's going to sway a jury. You're the head of CTC, for God's sake."

"That's just it. I'm the head of CTC. Why the **hell** would any foreign power want to use me to recruit other people?"

Another gust of wind whips through. A shiver runs through me.

"We're friends, Beth," he pleads. "You and me. You and **Alice**. Don't do this."

My gun's still pointed at him, and I have no intention of lowering it.

"Tell me what happened," I say. "How they got to you, what they asked you to do."

"It was a year ago. **They** blackmailed **me**. Sent me pictures and video of Preston. Through the mail, on a flash drive."

"Preston doing **what**?"

"Dealing." He looks ashamed when he says it. **"Drugs."**

"What did they ask of you?"

"To accept a job. One that would be detailed later."

"And you agreed?"

"I didn't have a choice."

"You **always** have a choice."

He shakes his head. "Those pictures, that video,

it would have destroyed Preston's future. Alice's, too. I mean, come on, a federal judge whose son is a drug dealer? She'd have had no choice but to resign. Same for me, probably. You think they'd let me hold on to my clearance if my son was in jail?"

This sounds more like The Neighbor.

"How did you let them know your decision?"

"A chalk X at the bottom of the driveway. I found some of the girls' old sidewalk chalk in the garage."

"Then what?" I ask. "What happened next?"

"They made a deposit. Into Preston's college savings account. Lord knows we needed it, but I sure didn't ask for it. Didn't want it."

I nod. He knows that changes the nature of the activity. Gives it the appearance of payment.

"Then nothing else, until a month or two ago. I got an email. Said I needed to recruit someone." He shakes his head. "That wasn't the sort of job I expected. But it was better than them asking for classified information. I wouldn't have done that, you know. I'd have gone to the authorities." He says it defensively.

I don't know if he would have or not. Frankly, he doesn't know it, either.

"I was supposed to let them know who it was, and they'd take over communication."

"So you picked Jim. Sent him that blackmail video." **Charles** was the neighbor Jim waved to that night. The one Jim must have been too drunk to remember.

"Yeah. Then I emailed them his name."

The way Charles was recruited, the blackmail they used, the deposit into the college savings account, it sounds like The Neighbor.

Charles **isn't** The Neighbor.

Charles was **recruited** by The Neighbor. Same as Sean and Des.

The Neighbor just wanted something different from him. Didn't ask for classified information. Asked him to recruit someone.

That was his mission.

But he's right: it doesn't make sense. He would have been far more valuable providing classified intelligence. The Neighbor must have had a reason. I just don't know what it is—and Charles doesn't, either.

In any case, it's another lead, a good one. Especially the deposit, and the emails, because they're recent. I'm sure The Neighbor's savvy enough to use every trick in the book to hide their true origins, but you never know. Maybe there will be some nugget, some crumb, that could lead us to the target.

"Look, I don't feel good about this," Charles says. "It's a complete disaster. Frankly, I hope whenever they get in touch with Jim, he tells them to go to hell. But I couldn't do that. It would have destroyed my family."

Charles doesn't know Jim has already gone to the authorities. That his attempted blackmail was a complete failure.

But it doesn't seem like he'd mind a whole lot, either.

I look around at the clearing. In my mind I can picture Preston down here with that six-pack of beer. Charles was supposed to take care of it. Would Alice have done things differently? Would she have gotten Preston straightened out before it was too late?

Was that secret between them part of the reason Charles is in this mess?

"That time you and Mike caught him down here with the six-pack. That was just the beginning, wasn't it? That should have been a sign of things to come."

He shakes his head. "What six-pack?"

A noise draws my attention. A call, indistinct, in the distance, from the direction of the neighborhood. A man's voice.

Someone's out here in the woods.

"We have to leave," I whisper. Because whoever it is, whoever's approaching, I don't want them to see me, don't want them to know I'm here.

"Are you going to turn me in?" Charles asks, in a panic.

"**Madeline?**" The voice in the distance is clearer this time.

"We need to get out of here," I say again. I head for the trees, in the direction of Langley Park.

I glance back and see that Charles has disappeared into the woods, too, in the opposite direction.

"**Madeline!**"

I go still, because I'm afraid the man heard me. I wait, and I listen.

"Madeline, are you out here? You can't keep disappearing like this."

The voice is closer now. I peer through the trees in the direction of the sound—

Josh steps into the clearing. He walks to the jagged boulder, the one with the chalk X, stares at it. Then he reaches down, picks up the lit flashlight. He swings the beam around, and I duck back behind the tree before the light reaches my section of the woods.

"I can't do this anymore," he calls out.

I peer around the tree again. He's still in the middle of the clearing.

"I can't live like this. This is our **neighborhood**. Our life. Our kids." His voice breaks. "I just can't do it."

He stands still a few moments longer. The only sound is the rushing river.

Then he hangs his head, and starts off into the woods, back toward the neighborhood.

I listen until his footsteps disappear into the distance.

My heart is pounding. He thinks Madeline's out here. **Is she?**

Why is she?

He said she keeps disappearing. Does she keep coming down here, to the river? What's she doing down here?

I start walking again, as quietly as possible, gun tight in my hand. Back toward Langley Park.

The closer I get, the more I pick up my pace. I'm nearly at the parking lot now—

"Stop right there."

Madeline steps out from behind a tree, right into my path.

And she has a gun pointed directly at my chest.

THIRTY-FIVE

I GO STILL, FEAR AND ADRENALINE RACING through me.

"It's just me," I say. We're on the same side, she and I.

She doesn't move.

We **are** on the same side, aren't we?

"Drop the weapon," she says.

I gave her information, for God's sake. That tip about Des.

My own gun is at my side. I briefly consider whether it's possible to raise it—

"**Now.**"

I let go, and it falls to the dirt with a thud. I know how she's been trained. The moment I lifted my own gun, she'd have shot hers.

She lowers her gun to her side. Watches me.

In the darkness it's hard to read the expression on her face.

"Why are you here?" she asks.

"I'm looking for a traitor."

She smirks.

"Why are **you** here?" I ask.

"Same."

In the distance there's a howl. A dog, maybe, or a coyote.

"Did you look into Des's record?" I ask. "The polygraphs she's done?"

"You think I didn't do that ages ago?"

I don't know what to say. My heart is beating fast.

"It was a dud tip, Beth. And you know it. There's nothing suspicious about Des's polygraphs."

"Then we're missing something—"

"Did you and **Charles** have a good chat?" she asks.

I say nothing.

"I saw him leave his house," she says. "The benefit of being a neighbor. Figured I'd see **who** he was meeting with."

"Charles is an old friend," I say. Let her think whatever she wants. I'm not about to give her another tip. I don't trust her. Just look at her, sneaking around in the woods, **repeatedly**.

With a gun.

And that smirk.

"Last I checked, it's not illegal to have a **conversation** with someone," I say.

"It is if you're impeding an investigation. Or if you're working for a foreign intelligence service."

"I thought I wasn't a suspect."

"Maybe I was wrong."

We stand on the worn path and eye each other, neither of us speaking.

"Sean broke into my house," she finally says. **"Armed."**

"Oh yeah?" I say evenly.

"You tipped him off, didn't you? You sent him after me?"

"I don't know what you're talking about."

A gust of wind whips through, rustling the leaves on the trees.

"We're getting close to figuring out who blackmailed Jim, you know," she says. "We're going to find who's behind it."

"Good," I say.

"It's going to be better for you if you come clean now."

If I come clean? "I have nothing to come clean about."

"Oh, really? So why the midnight rendezvous with Charles?"

I say nothing. It'll come out eventually. And right now I have a bigger target to catch.

Her phone vibrates in her pocket. She switches her gun into her left hand, pulls out her phone with her right. Reads something, then slides the phone back into her pocket.

"I need to go." Her voice sounds tense.

It's Josh, I'd be willing to bet.

"I know you're up to something," she says, taking a step toward me. "And I'm going to figure it out."

Then she reaches down and picks up my gun, slides it into her waistband. Turns, starts off through the woods, back toward the cul-de-sac.

THIRTY-SIX

AS SOON AS I'M BACK IN MY CAR IN THE LANGLEY
Park lot, I lock the doors. But I don't start the car,
don't make any attempt to leave. I just sit in the
silence, try to make sense of the thoughts running
through my head, of everything that just happened.

Charles isn't The Neighbor.

Alice isn't The Neighbor.

And Madeline—Madeline suspects that **I** have
something to do with this. That I'm interfering in
the investigation. Or that **I'm** The Neighbor.

If I don't get to the bottom of this soon,
Madeline's going to find a way to stop me. I know
she is.

I stare out at one of the darkened fields. The
T-ball field. It's small, with a low set of metal
bleachers behind home plate. It feels like a lifetime

ago Tyler was playing on that field. So much has changed since then.

So many people aren't who I thought they were.

Sean, Des, Charles. They were all part of this. They were all keeping secrets.

From their friends, their neighbors. From their own **spouses**.

I lift two fingers to my temple and try to rub away the beginnings of a headache. It's like there's too much information floating around in my head. Too many puzzle pieces, none of which seem to fit together in just the right way.

I was so sure when I came out here that Alice was The Neighbor. Then Charles.

It made sense. They knew our neighbors' secrets, were close enough to use those dead drops.

And then there were all those deposits into college savings accounts. Alice, with that student loan debt—

My gaze zeros in on those bleachers behind the T-ball field. The spot, all the way on the right, where Mike and the girls and I used to sit.

Life-changing student loan debt.

The kind we were lucky enough not to have.

Weren't we?

IT WAS TYLER'S FIRST SEASON of T-ball, and we were in our usual spot on the bleachers. Aubrey was reading, Caitlyn was drawing, and Mike and I were watching the game. We'd suppressed laughs as Tyler hit the ball off the tee and ran to third, then again as he got so dizzy twirling in circles at shortstop that he fell down. Right now he was in center field, sitting down and picking blades of grass.

"Well," I said to Mike, a smile on my face. "I think it's safe to say a baseball scholarship is out of the question."

Mike looked back at me, stone-faced. "He won't need a scholarship. None of them will."

"I'm kidding," I said, the smile still frozen on my face.

"I know." He turned away and looked straight ahead, out to the field.

I turned my gaze there, too, confused. Maybe he was just stressed about saving. We'd set up college accounts for all three kids, put in what we could. I thought we were ahead of the game. Maybe he didn't agree.

"I think we're doing okay," I said. "You know, with saving."

"We're on the right track."

"I used one of those online calculators. If we start rolling Tyler's daycare costs into savings when he starts kindergarten, we're in good shape. For state schools, anyway. And if they choose a private college, maybe some student loans—"

"No loans." He turned to me, an intense look in his eyes.

"Well, I don't think we'll need them. I just mean as a last resort—"

"Our kids aren't taking on student loans. Period. I don't want them saddled with that for the rest of their lives. It'll **change** their lives."

I raised my eyebrows. I wasn't sure where this was coming from. He was obviously in some sort of bad mood today. Probably not the best time to have a serious discussion—

A peal of laughter from behind me and a chuckle from down the row pulled my attention back to the field. I looked to see what people were laughing about—

Tyler was doing somersaults across the field.

"Oh God," I groaned, and looked over at Mike with a smile—

He was still staring straight ahead, unseeing, lost in another world.

THE STREETLIGHT ABOVE BEGINS FLICKERING, and I blink, pulled back to the present. The field's empty again, the bleachers bare.

And there's a tightness in my chest that wasn't there before.

I reach for my phone, google the number for America First Bank. Twenty-four-hour customer service; it's one of the things they're known for. I place the call. One ring—

"America First Bank, this is Elsie. How may I help you?"

"Hi. I'm calling with a question about student loan payoff status."

"Certainly, Mrs. Bradford. Can I have your Social Security number for verification purposes?"

I rattle off the number, then add, "But actually, the loans aren't in my name. They're in my husband's. I can give you his Social."

"No need, Mrs. Bradford. I can see that you hold joint accounts."

There's a pause.

"It appears the loans were paid in full. Quite some time ago."

They were. He paid off the debt just after we were married, right before we merged finances.

The debt he always described as manageable. The debt I didn't know details about.

"Can you tell me," I say, "what was the final payment?"

"Two hundred sixteen thousand, seven hundred fifty-eight dollars. And change."

Oh my God.

"Can you tell me where the money came from?" I ask, forcing out the words.

"I'm sorry?"

"The account that the payoff came from?"

"No. I'm sorry. I don't have that information."

"Okay."

"Is there anything else I can help you with, Mrs. Bradford?"

"No thanks."

I set down the phone on the passenger seat. Close my eyes, take a deep shuddering breath.

Mike knew about Sean's secret, and Des's, because I told him.

Mike knew Preston was dealing drugs. Probably saw him doing it that night, down by the river. Never went to Charles's house like he said. Came back and lied to me.

Just like he lied to me about that student loan debt. Two hundred thousand dollars of debt isn't manageable, not by a long shot.

I filled out financial disclosure forms for the Agency every year, but I didn't know about the debt, so I never reported it.

The CIA interviewed him before we were married, but he must have lied to them, just like he lied to me.

The only way you pay off debt like that, in one lump sum, is through a massive influx of cash. And there's only one way I can think of that Mike would have come into that kind of money.

But my own **husband** can't be The Neighbor. It's just not possible.

There must be some other explanation. I was

wrong about Sean, and Des, and Charles. They weren't The Neighbor. They were recruited.

Was Mike recruited, too?

Oh God, I hope he was recruited. Because the alternative is much, much worse.

THIRTY-SEVEN

I REACH FOR MY PHONE, FIND HIS NUMBER, still first on my speed dial.

"Beth?" he answers. I can hear the sleep in his voice. "Is everything okay? Are the kids okay?"

"The kids are fine. But listen, I need to talk to you."

There's a pause. I can almost picture him squinting at the numbers on the digital clock. "Now?"

"Yeah. I'll head over to your apartment."

"Why don't I come over to your place instead."

"I'm already in the car. I can be there in fifteen."

There's another pause. "I'm not at the apartment."

"Where are you?" As soon as I say the words, though, I know.

"At Britt's."

"Right."

Was the apartment just for show? Has he been

staying with **her**? If he's spending the night, it's serious, because she has a kid—

A realization hits me like a slap.

"Does Britt live on a cul-de-sac?"

I can hear noise in the background. Sheets rustling. Britt shifting in bed maybe, wondering who he's talking to in the middle of the night.

"Yeah, she does. Why?"

The Neighbor has found a new cul-de-sac.

I blink out the windshield, at the T-ball field in the distance. Suddenly it feels like my whole life was a lie.

"Why don't you meet me at Langley Park. Tyler's old T-ball field."

"Now?"

"Yeah."

There's a creak of springs in the background, like he's climbing out of bed. "Okay. Half hour?"

"See you then."

I SIT DOWN AT OUR usual spot on the bleachers. Second row, all the way on the right. The lights in the parking lot cast a faint glow over the bleachers; the field itself lies in the shadows. I sit in the silence and stare into the outfield, try to picture Tyler there, as a little boy. His antics. His goofy grin. The little uniform shirt, tucked into baseball pants.

And then I picture Aubrey and Caitlyn beside me. Drawing, reading. So small and young themselves.

And Mike.

I always prided myself on the fact that Mike and I didn't keep secrets from each other. We weren't like Des and Darryl, Alice and Charles. We were **better** than that.

But the whole time, Mike was keeping the biggest secret of all.

And what a secret it was. He recruited our **friends**. He exploited their pain, used their secrets against them. What kind of person does that?

In just under half an hour, I hear a car approach. I press the record button on my phone, slide it into my back pocket, and watch the entrance to the lot.

It's Mike's car, just as expected. Headlights wash over the field as he pulls in. He parks a space over from my car, turns off the engine, steps out. Raises a hand in an awkward wave, walks briskly toward me.

"Hey, Beth."

"Hey." I motion to the spot on the bench beside me. He sits down. Looks at me quizzically.

I say nothing, turn to face the field. I don't know where to begin.

He follows my gaze, and we sit there silently for several moments.

"We spent a lot of time here over the years," he finally says. "On fields like this."

"We sure did."

Out of the corner of my eye, I can see he turns to face me again. "Beth, are you okay?"

I don't look at him, don't say a thing.

Of course I'm not okay. I'm not okay with any of this. The fact that my marriage was built on lies, that it took me **this** long to find my target, and he was right next to me, all along.

But I'm about to take the first steps to make this okay. I'm going to get a confession, bring it to Agency security, make sure he faces consequences.

I turn toward him. "Why'd you do it, Mike?"

"Do what?"

"You know."

"Is this about Britt? Because—"

"It's not about Britt."

He watches me evenly.

"You're the person I was looking for, all along," I say.

I can see the realization in his eyes. That I **know**.

"I don't know what you're talking about," he says, but the words are empty.

"You were in debt," I say. "You had massive student loan debt when we met. And you never told me."

"It's not exactly first-date material."

"Maybe not. But you hid it from me. You lied to me."

"I didn't lie. I told you it was manageable. That

I was covering it. That we'd keep our finances separate—"

"But it **wasn't** manageable. That kind of debt is **not** manageable."

"I know." He looks down at his hands. "I mean, I didn't know when I took it on."

"Your parents didn't pay your way." I state the obvious.

"They didn't save a dime. They were underwater themselves. Refinance and refinance again. Borrow and borrow and borrow."

"I wouldn't have guessed," I say honestly. They looked like they were comfortable, financially. More than comfortable.

"Exactly. Because that's how they wanted it to look. Because it was all about keeping up with the Joneses. They were making a fair amount by the time I went off to college, but it was barely enough to keep up with their own debt. All it meant was I didn't qualify for financial aid. Loans were the only way I was going to college."

He sounds bitter.

"It didn't seem so bad at the time. I was going to be a lawyer. I was going to **Yale**. I'd be making big bucks soon enough. But turns out it **wasn't** soon enough. When I met you, I was paying over sixteen hundred a month, and that was barely touching the principal."

"You were drowning."

He nods.

"Why didn't you tell me?"

"I was embarrassed, at first. I was afraid you'd run."

"And then?"

He stares off into the distance. "And then it was too late."

"It was never too late."

"It was, though. One lie is all it takes."

My eyes flutter closed, a memory overtaking me.

"It spirals from there," I say quietly.

He matches my tone. "You can't take it back."

TYLER WAS EIGHT THE FIRST time I saw Mike truly lose his temper with one of our kids. It was a Saturday morning, and Tyler and Preston were playing in the cul-de-sac. Mike was in the office, working, and I was in the kitchen cleaning up from breakfast when Tyler burst in. "Mom, can we have juice boxes?"

"You just finished breakfast," I told him. "Not right now."

"Fine," he huffed.

I went back to washing dishes, and heard him leave the room.

A few minutes later, Mike stormed out the front door, returned with Tyler, who looked chagrined.

"What's going on?" I asked, drying my hands and walking over to the foyer, where they stood.

Mike didn't even look in my direction; he was laser-focused on Tyler. His hands were balled into fists at his side.

"How **dare** you lie to me?" he asked Tyler.

"Mike, calm down," I said. I'd never seen him like this. He was always so patient, so mild-mannered.

"No. This is between Tyler and me." His eyes were flashing.

Tyler looked scared.

"I'm going to ask you again, did you bring a juice box outside?"

"No," Tyler said weakly.

Mike took a step toward him.

"Mike, it's just a juice box," I said. Tyler must have snuck one out when I wasn't looking, and Mike saw it from the office window.

He spun toward me. "It's not **just** a juice box. It's a lie, Beth! He lied to us!"

I glanced at Tyler, who was shrinking back into the corner of the room.

"I know," I said, trying to be calm, trying to make **Mike** calm. "But, Mike, it's a very **small** lie. I think you're overreacting."

"One lie is all it takes, Beth." He was breathing hard. I could see his nostrils flaring with each breath. He didn't look like the man I knew, not at all. "It spirals from there. And you can't take it back."

His hands were still balled into fists at his side.

"You can't take it back, Beth."

THIRTY-EIGHT

"IT SPIRALED," I SAY NOW. "YOU LIED TO ME, and it spiraled out of control."

"Yes."

The word hangs there in the silence that follows.

"I was making payments, trying to get ahead of it, before we were married. I was going to tell you, I swear."

"And then?"

"And then came that paperwork. The form from the CIA. The interview."

The permission-to-marry form. "Did you tell them about the debt?"

"No."

Lie number two.

"I didn't want you to find out that way. And I was afraid they'd make you choose between me and your career."

They must have taken him at his word. Didn't dig into his past. **Or someone dropped the ball.**

"If you'd just been honest with me, I would have picked you," I say quietly. "We could have chipped away at it. We would have been okay."

"It's easy to say that now. But we wouldn't have had this." He gestures toward the field. "This community. We couldn't have lived in McLean with the debt I had."

"We would have been just as happy somewhere else."

"Would we, though?"

I look down at my hands. That was almost a confession. We're almost there.

He clears his throat. "Luckily, I got an inheritance. Was able to pay it all off."

Dammit.

"Oh?" I say. "From whom?"

"An uncle."

"Which uncle?"

"Uncle John."

"There was no Uncle John."

"Well, he wasn't **technically** an uncle. A close family friend."

He's lying, obviously. But this is the cover story. And I have a feeling it's backstopped. That Reza Karimi really could have made it look like an inheritance from someone named John.

"It was Iranian intelligence," I say.

"Beth. That's crazy." Again, the words are flat. He's not even trying hard to deny it.

"You agreed to work for them in exchange for that money."

"I don't know what you're talking about."

"You recruited **our friends**."

"I did no such thing."

Why won't he just admit it?

"You even recruited your **best friend**. Charles. How could you do that?"

A flicker of discomfort crosses his face.

"And now you've found a new cul-de-sac. Britt's cul-de-sac. You're going to insert yourself there, make friends, recruit a whole new network of spies—"

"Enough, Beth. I think it's time you get some help."

"No. It's time you tell me the truth. You owe that to me. After twenty-five years of marriage, twenty-five years of **lies,** you owe that to me."

He looks away, out to the field. Behind us, the streetlight flickers.

"Remember how Tyler used to spin out there in the outfield?" he finally says.

I follow his gaze and say nothing.

"Walk with me, Beth."

"What?"

He gets to his feet, extends a hand toward me.

"Walk with me out to the field."

"Why?"

"Can you just do it for me? Please?"

Fine. If this is what it takes for him to talk. I ignore his hand and stand up—

"Leave the phone."

I go still and meet his eye.

"There's no one here but us. Leave the phone."

The way he says it, the look on his face, it's clear: he knows I'm recording.

There's not a chance I'm going to get a recorded confession at this point. He's not going to confess anything as long as my phone's on me. Either this conversation ends right now, or I get a confession and it's not recorded.

I want the confession.

I pull the phone from my back pocket, set it down on the bleachers. Then I walk with him, across the field.

He comes to a stop in the middle of center field, turns to face me. "Don't do this, Beth."

"Don't do what?"

"Turn me in."

I don't say anything.

"Think about the kids."

"Were **you** thinking about the kids?"

"Every day."

He looks so open and honest right now. Why couldn't he have been like that years ago?

"How did they do it?" I ask. God, I wish I had the recorder. But even without it, I just want to **know**.

"An envelope came. In the mail, just after we were married. Said they knew I had lied. That when it came out, you'd lose your job, and your clearance. That you'd leave me. Or—" He takes a deep breath. "Or they could erase it for me. Pay off the student loans. Said to think of it as a favor. And that I could return that favor in the future. **Like borrowing a cup of sugar from a neighbor**."

"And you agreed." I can hear the disappointment in my voice.

"No. I mean, I was tempted. But I figured they got in touch with me because of **you**. And I wasn't going to betray you."

He looks like he's waiting for some reaction from me. I don't give him one.

"So I emailed the address they gave me. Told them that. That I wanted you out of it completely. That I'd never betray you."

"And?"

"And they said they'd never ask me to. So I agreed."

I nod slowly.

"I figured nothing they asked could be **that** bad, right? I mean, I didn't work for the CIA. I didn't have access to classified information." He clears his throat again. "Next thing I knew, the loans were completely paid off."

"And then?"

"Nothing. No communication, for **years.** I figured they'd forgotten about me. Until we moved to Langley Oaks. Then I got another letter in the mail. With the **favor** they were calling in."

"Which was?"

"I was to recruit. 'Spot and assess,' was how they described it. Not technically illegal."

"It was if you knew who you were working for."

I can tell from the look on his face he **did** know.

How could he do this?

How could he turn on his country like this?

"I told them no. That I wouldn't recruit Sean, or **any** friend. That I wanted out. Figured I'd be in deep shit. Might even go to jail. That you might lose your job. But . . ."

"But what?"

"I had to do it, Beth. I had to do what they said."

The truth crystallizes in front of me.

They used the children, didn't they?

CAITLYN WAS SIX WHEN WE nearly lost her.

She and Aubrey were playing tag with Piper and Paxton, Jada and Jasmine. Six kids running through all the backyards of the cul-de-sac, one to another, hiding in bushes, searching, squealing in delight when they spotted their friends. I was keeping an eye through the back windows whenever they were in our yard, and I knew the other parents were doing the same.

After they'd been out for a while, Aubrey walked in through the back door.

"Where's Caitlyn?" I asked.

Aubrey shrugged.

"Is she still playing?"

"Everyone went in."

Aubrey wandered over to the pantry to look for a snack. I stared after her. "Aubrey!"

"What?"

"We need to find your sister."

"She's probably just hiding."

"Go look for her, okay?"

Aubrey rolled her eyes and headed for the door.

I reached for the phone, dialed Alice. "Hey," I said when she picked up. "Is Caitlyn in your yard? Aubrey came back without her."

There was a brief pause, and I imagined Alice was walking to her window. "Don't see her. I'll have Piper and Paxton head back out and look."

"Thanks."

I dialed Des next, asked the same thing, received the same answer.

Now I was starting to panic. I joined Aubrey in the backyard, called for Caitlyn. Across the street, I could hear Des calling her name, too.

"Where did you last see her?" I asked Aubrey.

"I don't know. In our yard, I think. Here." She was starting to look a little afraid.

"Caitlyn!" I yelled again, louder this time.

Mike must have heard the commotion, because he came outside. "What's going on?"

"We don't know where Caitlyn is."

The panic on his face was instantaneous. "Caitlyn!" he yelled.

I heard the same word echoed from the Kanes' yard next door. Alice's voice.

The panic was full-fledged now.

"When did you last see her?" Mike asked me. There was a look of fear on his face I'd never seen before.

"I don't know. Ten minutes ago?"

He spun around and strode toward the woods. "Caitlyn!"

We were all looking, everyone on the cul-de-sac. Every minute that passed was more terrifying than the last. My daughter was gone.

Alice rejoined me, then stayed by my side, comforted me. "We'll find her," she kept saying. But each time she repeated the words, they sounded ever so slightly less confident, less assured.

"Should we call the police?" I finally asked. My voice sounded unnaturally high-pitched. I couldn't believe I was saying that, **thinking** that. Losing children, that happened to **other** people. Not us.

"I don't know," she said. And I hated the response, because Alice always knew what to do.

I called Mike's cellphone, but he didn't answer. Scanned the woods for him, didn't see anything.

I could hear the chorus of Caitlyn's name being called, more distant now, from all directions. How did **she** not hear it?

Where **was** she?

"I'm calling the police," I said.

"Okay," Alice agreed.

I dialed the numbers, 9-1-1, my hand trembling, my finger moving toward the send button—

"Beth, look," Alice said.

I looked up. There was Mike, walking back through the woods—

And there was Caitlyn skipping along beside him.

Oh, thank God.

I dropped the phone, ran over, wrapped my arms around her.

"Where were you?" I asked. "You know you're not supposed to go into the woods by yourself!"

"A lady lost her puppy, Mommy," she said. "I was helping her look."

I met Mike's eyes over her head. He was pale, and looked just as shocked as I felt. How had we not taught our daughter better than that?

What if it had been someone luring her into the woods? We could have lost her forever.

"Never do that again, Caitlyn," I said. I pulled

her close again, feeling her warmth against me. She was so small, so vulnerable.

I had never been more terrified in my life. Until that moment, I don't think I'd ever truly considered the possibility that one of my kids could be taken from me.

I realized something else, too: that I'd do absolutely **anything** to keep them safe.

"THAT DAY CAITLYN WENT OFF into the woods," I say quietly.

He nods. "They'd warned me, the day before. **We'd hate to see anything happen to your children.**"

"You didn't **tell** me?"

He throws up his arms helplessly. "What was I supposed to say? I was terrified. But I didn't know if they were bluffing."

"And then she disappeared."

"It was them, Beth. I'm sure of it. And I knew right then and there I'd do anything they asked of me."

I don't know what to say. I remember that feeling I had, when Caitlyn was lost. That I would have done anything to protect her.

This is like some kind of nightmare.

"The kids are safe," he says. "They have been, all these years. I did what I needed to do."

Silence falls over us. Would I have done anything

differently, in his shoes? Part of me feels sympathy for him. Gratitude, even. But more of me is **angry**. It's his fault the kids were even **in** that position.

"Was it just them? Sean and Des, and then Charles?"

"Yes."

He looks like he's telling the truth. But I've thought that for the past twenty-five years, and I've been wrong.

"What did they give you?" I ask. "What kind of secrets?"

"I'm not telling you that."

"You **owe** me." I sound deadly serious. And I **am**. He **does** owe me.

He nods slowly, like he agrees.

"Sean. It was the backup power supply?" I ask.

"Yeah. Pictures of the system. The various generators. Sketches. Specs. Everything about it."

"And Des?" I ask. "Who'd she let in?"

"Let in?"

"She passed someone on a polygraph. Who?"

"No one that I know of."

He looks honest. But that can't be the truth.

"Was it tips, then? How to lie and still pass?"

"It was nothing about polygraphs."

"What was it then?"

"IT security."

Confusion ripples through me.

"They had her go across the hall, map out desks.

Take covert cellphone pictures of the computer towers."

So it wasn't about polygraphs. It was about **proximity**. The Bureau was all over anyone who worked in IT security. And all the while, Reza Karimi was using someone across the hall.

"What were they specifically interested in?" I ask. "The lines? The—"

"USB ports."

USB ports. Very few Agency computers have them; part of keeping the network secure. Only a small number of officers across the Agency have data transfer privileges, access to ports. And everything that happens on those computers is monitored in real time.

Karimi was barking up the wrong tree with Sean. And if all he was getting from Des was the location of computers with USB ports—

Maybe he wasn't as close to penetrating the network as we thought.

"Look, Beth, it's over now."

I shake my head. "It's not—"

"It is. For me, anyway. I'm done, Beth. I'm not The Neighbor anymore."

"How are you just **done**?"

"They said I had to wait until Tyler was off to college. I couldn't leave until then."

"Couldn't leave the job? Or **me**?"

"Both."

The words feel like a knife. That's why Mike ended things right after Tyler left. He'd been biding his time. That's why he'd taken up with Britt in the meantime. The marriage was over, in his mind, long before. He just wasn't allowed to leave.

"They said before I left I was responsible for securing a replacement. A new Neighbor."

A new Neighbor. I can't believe what I'm hearing.

"That with a replacement I'd be done, and they'd protect me."

"So you recruited Charles."

"I wanted to leave the Kanes out of it, but then I saw what Preston was doing out in the woods. . . . Charles was my way out."

"He's your best friend."

"And I knew he'd do anything to protect his family's reputation. Preston behind bars would have been the ultimate disgrace."

He found Charles's weakness, and he exploited it. Just like Sean, and Des.

"I'm not The Neighbor anymore, Beth. I haven't been for the past year. Charles was my last recruit. If you're looking for The Neighbor, it's Charles."

"That doesn't erase what you've done."

"Maybe not. But there's no point in turning me in, Beth. There's no proof I've done anything illegal."

"Your handler has the proof." **Reza Karimi** has the proof, not that Mike has any idea who he's been interacting with. Who's behind it all.

"And he'll protect me."

"You believe that?"

"Absolutely. He promised me."

He promised me.

"**How?** How have you been communicating with them?" I ask.

"Does it matter?"

"Yeah. It does."

He shrugs. "Email."

Email. Like I always thought.

Mail was the method of outreach, of establishing contact. That's what Karimi meant, all those years ago. **Pass The Neighbor the exact words I say, through means that I can't use.** Mail was the means he couldn't use, because he wasn't in the U.S. He had someone transcribe his letters, drop them in the mail. And then after that, it switched to email.

Mike was communicating directly with Reza Karimi.

"So there's a record of **everything**," I say. "A written record."

"He'll protect me. He said he would. Said my replacement was in place."

"He has **blackmail** on you, Mike. He's not letting that go."

"He will." The words are confident, but there's a hint of doubt in his expression.

And there should be. There should be **more**. I know Reza Karimi, and I know Karimi's not just going to let this go. There's always a way to leverage a network into something else.

I shake my head, frustration boiling inside me. "You're not going to get away with this, Mike."

He gives me a sad smile, one that looks almost condescending. "I already have."

THIRTY-NINE

HE HASN'T. HE HASN'T GOTTEN AWAY WITH IT, and he's not going to.

I get back in my car and leave the lot. Drive through darkened streets toward home, hands tight on the wheel. Eye the turnoff for Langley Oaks. Then the one for the rental—

I keep driving.

I'm going to go straight to headquarters. I'm going to march right into CIC, and I'm going to tell them everything. Turn over the recordings so they have proof.

I stop at a red light. The roads are empty, no one around.

The light turns green and I head through the intersection—

A shrill blast. An incoming call, the ring amplified through the speakers of the car, the phone connected to Bluetooth. The number appears on the screen on the dashboard.

Unknown.

A blocked call in the middle of the night. No doubt it's **them**.

I press the green button on the screen, because I want to hear what they have to say.

"Hello?"

Nothing. No words, no sound, just silence.

I tap the red button, end the call.

They don't scare me.

I press down harder on the gas, hear the engine churn in response. Still no one around, no cars on the road—

Another shrill blast. I glance at the screen— **unknown**—and answer the call. "What do you want?"

Silence, again.

I jam my finger at the screen, end the call.

"Piss off," I say aloud, and I accelerate even more.

They're trying to scare me. Just like they were in the rental, with the alarm and lights and the blasting music. They want me to know they can get to me.

I know it. And I'm not afraid.

I keep driving. Closer to headquarters now—

A chime this time, through the sound system. Incoming text.

The words appear on the dashboard screen.

Turn around. We'd hate to see anything happen to your children.

A SHIVER RUNS UP MY spine, and my foot eases off the gas, almost instinctively. I coast, the needle on the speedometer dropping, and look around. No other cars on the road, but they know where I am, where I'm headed. What I'm about to do.

There's an intersection up ahead. The light is yellow, then turns to red.

I press the brakes, come to a complete stop.

The car is utterly silent. The words have disappeared from the screen, but they're clear as ever in my mind.

I can keep going, tell CIC everything. Best-case scenario, they arrange for security for my kids. How long will it take? These people are here **now**. They see me, they know where I'm going. They could be at Aubrey's house before I even step into the security office. And Caitlyn, she's overseas. Would they be able to guarantee her safety?

The light turns green, and I don't lift my foot from the brake.

The threat to **me**, it didn't work. But the threat to my kids, that's another story.

They know **exactly** what they're doing.

Finally, reluctantly, I move my foot from brake pedal to gas. Then I press down—

And pull a U-turn.

At the next red light, I reach for my phone, open a group text with the three kids.

Be careful today.

Caitlyn responds an instant later. Why?

It's morning in London; Aubrey and Tyler are no doubt still sound asleep.

The light turns green, and I consider the question. **Why?** Because I was warned to stop digging around, and I didn't. Because someone threatened to hurt you as a result.

And because I'm still not going to back off.

I take the turn toward Aubrey and Austin's townhouse and press down hard on the gas.

There's nothing more important than my kids. But staying quiet isn't the way to protect them.

Mike **thinks** he protected them. But all he did was dig himself in deeper and deeper, and now the kids are in jeopardy again.

I'm not going to do the same thing.

I'll let them **think** I'm going to. Let them see me turn around. Let them think they won.

But they didn't win.

I swore an oath. I have a responsibility.

I'm going to put an end to all of this.

FORTY

I KNOCK ON AUBREY AND AUSTIN'S FRONT door, the sound echoing in the night silence. There's no one around; the row of townhomes are dark on the inside, softy illuminated outside by porch lights, the streetlights in the parking lot.

There's no answer.

I knock again, louder this time. They're fast asleep, I'm sure.

I wish this were all some sort of nightmare I could wake up from.

My kids have been threatened.

Mike was The Neighbor.

Mike, my own husband.

I missed it. And I wasn't the only one, either. The Agency should have caught it.

But he lied to them, just like he lied to me.

He recruited our friends. Destroyed their lives.

A light turns on inside. Footsteps, shuffling toward the door. They pause, like someone's looking out the peephole. Then the door opens.

Austin's there, in flannel pants and a white T-shirt, bare feet. "Beth?" He squints at me.

Aubrey comes up behind him, cinching a robe around her waist. "Mom? What in the world is going on?"

"Can I come in?"

"Yes, please," Austin says, flustered, opening the door wider.

Aubrey reaches for my upper arm as I step through the door, leads me toward the kitchen. "Are you okay?"

"I'm fine. Did you get my text?"

"Text? No." Her brow is creased with worry.

"Listen, you need to be careful. You and Austin, and Caitlyn and Tyler, too."

She stops short, drops her hand from my arm, gives me a scared look. "Why?"

"You just do."

She casts a glance at Austin, then focuses on me again. "What on earth is going on?"

"Just . . ." What am I supposed to say? "I just want you all to be careful. Watch your back, you know?"

She sinks down into a chair at the kitchen table, her eyes never leaving mine.

I pull out a chair across from her and sit down,

avoiding her gaze. Pull my phone from my bag, check it. There are the kids' faces, when they were young, and the time. Still no response from Tyler. I lay it on the table in front of me.

"Why don't you and I talk, Mom?" Aubrey says gently. "Why don't you tell me what's going on?"

God, where do I even begin?

"You and Dad split up, didn't you?" she asks.

I blink at her. If only that were **all** that's going on. "Yeah."

She reaches across the table, reaches for my hand. I let her take it.

"Can I get anyone some tea?" Austin asks from the other side of the room, clearly uncomfortable, clearly not wanting to be part of this conversation.

I shake my head, and Aubrey doesn't take her eyes off me. Austin drifts away, out of the kitchen.

Aubrey gives me a sympathetic look. "Is there any way around it?"

I shake my head. "He lied to me. For a long time. It's not something we can come back from."

She nods slowly.

"I'm sorry, honey. I'm sorry that this is happening." I'm sorry for who her father truly is, what he's done. I'm sorry that **she's** now in danger because of it.

"Don't apologize, Mom," she says. Her eyes look watery.

I nod quickly. I can't tell her what I'm really apologizing for, not yet.

"Mom, I just want you to be happy. I want that for Dad, too. Happy, and safe, and healthy. That's all I want—"

A sound outside, a pop. I stand so abruptly the chair falls backward and hits the floor—

It was a car backfiring in the distance. "Sorry," I murmur, reach for the chair, standing it straight again.

Austin is back. He and Aubrey exchange another glance—

"Austin, why don't you and my mom go sit in the living room. I'll make us a pot of tea—"

"No tea, Aubrey. I'm just here to make sure the two of you are being careful."

She gives Austin a pointed look.

"Come on, Beth. Let's go sit," he says.

Aubrey turns her back to me, reaches for the kettle.

Fine. I follow Austin into the living room, sink down into the couch. He sits on the love seat, leans forward, hands clasped in front of him. "Anything I can do, Beth?"

"Watch out for Aubrey," I say quietly. "This is serious, Austin."

"Are you in trouble?" He matches my volume. I can hear Aubrey moving around the kitchen.

"It's my job. It's—" I realize I don't know what

Aubrey's told Austin about my job. "There are some people who want to get back at me. . . ."

"Are you serious?"

"Yeah."

"Well, have you gone to the police?"

"It's not that easy. It's—"

Before I can finish the thought, the lights around us cut out, and everything goes dark.

IT'S PITCH BLACK; I CAN'T see a thing. It's like that night in the rental all over again, except worse now, because it's not **me** they're threatening, it's my kids.

"Aubrey!" I call. "Come in here."

"I'm looking for a flashlight," she calls from the kitchen. I can hear her rummaging around in a drawer.

I stand from the couch, begin feeling my way toward the kitchen, pulse racing—

A beam of light appears. Aubrey's holding a flashlight, walking toward me.

"Make sure all your doors are locked," I say.

"Mom?" For the first time, I see fear on her face.

"Do it!"

"It's the whole neighborhood," comes Austin's voice. I spin toward him, and Aubrey's flashlight swings in the same direction. He's at the living room window, looking out.

He's right. It's all black outside. No lights from

neighboring townhomes, no streetlights, the parking lot is dark—

"Phone's out, too," Aubrey says. She's holding her cellphone, looking at the screen. "No reception."

It's more than just the neighborhood. I'm sure of it. This is bigger than just me, just us.

I brush past her, back to the kitchen table. Feel around for my phone, then my bag, drop the phone inside, zip it back up.

"Mom?" Aubrey asks, her voice rising in concern. "Where are you going?"

"Work." I sling the strap over my shoulder, and head toward the door.

"In the dark?" Her voice is bordering on panic now.

"You two stay here, keep the doors locked, and **be careful**." I pause at the door and turn around, give Aubrey a quick, fierce hug. "I love you."

"Love you, too, Mom. But can't you wait until the lights come back on?"

"I don't know when that'll be," I say, and I let myself out the door, head for my car, parked in the pitch-black lot.

Because this wasn't random, accidental, something that'll be a quick fix.

This was a **cyberattack**. This was Quds Force activating their malware, shutting down our electrical grid, and our cell towers, too.

This is all part of Reza Karimi's plan.

FORTY-ONE

THE CITY IS DARK. STREETLIGHTS ARE OUT; traffic lights, too. The only light comes from my headlights, and those of the occasional car I pass on the way to headquarters. They're few and far between; it's still the middle of the night, and most people, thankfully, seem to have enough sense to stay off the roads.

My brain is churning, working desperately to figure out what's happening, how this plays in. How this gets Reza Karimi closer to hacking into the intranet. Because I **know** this is connected somehow.

We're entirely reliant on the CIA backup system now, aren't we? The system that Sean O'Malley runs, the one he told Reza Karimi about.

The system will be strained. It'll be providing all the power to the entire Langley campus, keeping everything running. Maybe the strain will create some sort of loophole. Cause the generators to go into overdrive, something like that. I have no idea; I don't know the system.

But Sean does.

I don't know how the electrical grid's been shut down, either. If they've hacked in and commandeered the system, or, worse, if they've somehow **destroyed** the system, a scenario that could take weeks or, God forbid, **months** to repair. And I don't know how far it extends. Is it just DC? The whole East Coast? **More?**

Aubrey said cell towers are down. Radio stations apparently are, too; the car stereo system is streaming nothing but silence.

When I approach headquarters, there's light, almost like a beacon in the darkness. But it's not reassuring, because they're going to use that to their advantage. I can feel it. And I need to go in there and come clean about everything, figure this all out before it's too late.

There's extra security at the gates, more uniformed guards than usual, long guns in hand. They look tense.

I show my badge and they wave me through. There are more cars in the lot than I'd expect at this time of night, more than just the overnight teams. I park in the nearest empty space, hustle toward the entrance—

And I see Cy, heading toward the doors himself, albeit at a slower pace. He turns slightly as I catch up to him. "Beth," he says, tipping an imaginary hat in my direction. "They've finally done it. All hands on deck, eh? Even us Kent School folks."

"That's right."

He must have been called. Must think I was, too. We must have proof it was Iran. Not that there's any doubt in my mind.

"One last hurrah before I retire," he says.

At that I slow slightly, match my pace to his. "Yeah?" This is news to me.

"Not that there's much of a place for me here anymore." He shrugs. "But one last time being close to the action." He gives me a sad smile.

Suddenly I see Cy in a new light. He didn't want to be at the Kent School. He wanted to be part of something important, but he was cut out. Sent away. I have more in common with him than I thought.

But it's not too late for either of us.

"Don't head to CIC," I tell him. "You're right; they won't have anything for you to do. Get down to Facilities."

"Beth, what—"

"Karimi's trying to use the backup power supply. Talk to people down there, see what you can figure out."

He stares at me, stunned.

"Just trust me," I say, and continue past him, breaking into a jog toward the entrance.

"I do," he finally calls after me, and the words send a fresh rush of adrenaline through me.

It's tense inside the lobby, more security here, too, everyone moving faster than usual.

I badge through the turnstiles, then briskly walk the familiar route to CIC.

I hold my badge to the reader at the door to the vault, even though I know it won't work. It doesn't.

I pound my fist against the door.

A moment later, it's pulled from the inside. There's a guy standing there, a thin guy with a goatee, someone I recognize, but whose name I don't remember.

"Beth," he says.

"Hi," I say. I wait for him to move out of my way, but he doesn't.

"Excuse me," I finally say, taking a step toward the door, ready to squeeze past him—

He steps to the side, blocking my path. "I'm sorry, Beth. I don't think you have access here."

"I have information," I say. "I need to talk to Dale."

He doesn't move. "I'm sorry. I'm not allowed to let you in."

"Look, I just need—"

"Beth." It's Annemarie, coming up behind the guy with the goatee.

"Annemarie, I need to talk to Dale."

"Beth, you know you can't be here."

I can see other people inside the vault watching now, from the hallway, or peering over cubicle walls.

Goatee is still blocking my path.

This is ridiculous. We're in the middle of a cyber-attack. **Reza Karimi's** attack. I push past Goatee into the vault.

"Beth," Annemarie protests. "You're not allowed to be here."

"Don't you have bigger concerns right now?" I keep walking past her, toward Dale's office—

Dale steps into the hall, into my path.

"I need to talk to you," I say.

"Call security," he says quietly to Goatee, who's right behind me.

"That's fine," I say. "I **want** security. I need to talk to them, and to you."

There's silence around us. I glance around, and there are more sets of eyes on me now—

The whiteboard. There it is, on the far wall. With writing, in blue.

The Neighbor will protect him.

I stare at the words, try to make sense of them. The Neighbor will protect **who?**

Mike?

Charles will protect **Mike?**

Who cares right now. Reza Karimi has set his

plans in motion. This is what it's all led up to. I need to do something—

"They're using the backup power system," I say. "The generators. That's how they're going to get into JWICS. It's somehow connected—"

"Beth, why don't you have a seat in my office," Dale says. He glances at the whiteboard, and I wonder if he just wants to get me away from it, but it's too late, I've seen it, whatever it is, whatever it means.

"Why aren't you listening to me?" No sooner have I said it than there's a click from the vault door, the lock unlatching, and two burly uniformed guards push through, into the vault. They look around, and they seem to know instantly that it's **me** they were called for. They're on either side of me within seconds.

"Thanks, gentlemen," Dale says. "Beth was just about to come into my office."

"I'm not going anywhere."

You could hear a pin drop in the vault right now.

"It's the backup power supply, Dale. The generators. That's how they're getting in—"

Movement catches my eye. **Madeline,** stepping out of Dale's office, eyes on me the whole time, face impassive.

"Dale, this is the information The Neighbor's been collecting—"

"Beth—"

"You have to trust me."

He hesitates. "**Why?**"

"Because I know who it is. The Neighbor."

He watches me, expressionless. I can feel the guards on either side of me, close to me.

"It's **Mike.**"

He crosses his arms. "Mike?"

"My husband. **Ex**-husband." That description isn't quite right, either. "**Soon-to-be** ex-husband."

Dale's eyes shift to one of the guards behind me. Madeline is staring at me.

"Look, I know that sounds far-fetched. But it's true. He **admitted** it. He's been The Neighbor all along."

"Your soon-to-be ex-husband."

"Yes. But he's not The Neighbor anymore. There's a new Neighbor."

"Oh? And who's the new Neighbor?" He says it slowly, evenly.

"Charles Kane."

He takes a deep breath in through his nose, then exhales. "Charles Kane. The director of CTC?"

"Yes. He's my next-door neighbor."

Dale nods slowly. "I know. Charles talked to us the other day."

"He did?"

"Yes. Told us he has concerns about your mental

well-being. That you came to his house and accused his **wife** of being The Neighbor."

The words make me go still. He's trying to make me look unstable. And it **worked**. I can see it in Dale's eyes. I can feel it, from the guards. From everyone in the vault, listening.

"I thought it was her at first," I say. "But I was wrong."

He nods again.

"And Madeline Sterling? You thought it was her at first, too, didn't you?"

I glance over at Madeline. She's still quiet, and there's a hint of a smirk on her face. "Yes."

The vault is silent. I look around, and the people watching look away. Even **Annemarie** looks away.

"Beth, you do realize how all of this sounds, don't you?"

"Yes," I say. I know it sounds crazy. But it's not. It's true. "Listen, I can prove it."

I reach for my bag, pull it open, and the guard to my right moves toward me, but Dale stops him with an extended hand.

It's not a weapon, for God's sake. It's my phone. I pull it out and hold it up.

"You're not allowed to have that here." Dale states the obvious.

Madeline moves forward abruptly, takes it out of my hands.

"Give that back."

I reach for it, but she moves it away from me, walks with it back toward Dale's office.

I turn to Dale, panicked. "I recorded Charles's confession."

I can see the surprise on his face. He looks at the guards, each one in turn, eyebrows raised.

"I don't think we should do this," Madeline says. "It's a breach of protocol. We don't know what she's bringing in here."

"I'm bringing in **confessions**," I snap.

She holds my gaze and says nothing.

"Let's see it," Dale says.

I walk over to Madeline, take my phone right back out of her hands, unlock it in one swift move—

The background's different. The picture of my kids isn't there. Just the default background, like when the phone was brand new.

And the icons look different, too. It looks like a new phone, straight out of the box.

"This isn't my phone," I say. I look up at Madeline. "Give me my phone."

Her brows arch up. Her eyes never leave mine.

"What did you do with my phone?" I say, my voice rising in pitch.

"Beth, that's the phone I just took from you."

"It's not. This isn't my phone."

"You unlocked it," Dale says.

I look again at the screen. Search for the app

with the audio recordings, swipe left, but it's not there either.

It's gone.

I look up at Madeline. "What did you do?"

She stares at me. Out of the corner of my eye, I see one of the guards moving closer.

"You wiped it, didn't you?"

"Beth, calm down," Madeline says.

"Don't tell me to calm down!"

The guard is beside me now. There's a hand on my elbow.

I look up at Dale, and his expression has completely changed. The anticipation is gone. And it's not even suspicion that's taken its place. It's **sympathy**. "Beth, it's okay."

"No, it's not. It was just **here**."

I should have made a copy. Should have backed this up. But it doesn't even matter right now. The only thing that matters is stopping whatever's about to happen. Stopping Reza Karimi.

"Look, I don't know exactly how they're going to do it. But they're using the power system. That's how they're getting into JWICS. You have to trust me on this one—"

"We're going to get you the help that you need."

"I don't need help." A realization hits me, and I spin toward Annemarie. "The backup system. What'd you find out?"

She shrinks back like a deer caught in headlights. "There's no way in, Beth."

"Then we're missing something. Reza Karimi found it. I'm telling you, this is it."

Annemarie looks at Dale helplessly.

I turn back toward him. "We're missing something, Dale. And if we don't figure it out soon . . . Look, I'll give you every detail they told me. You'll be able to prove it."

Dale's eyebrows are arched, like he doesn't believe a word I'm saying, like I'm crazy.

"Mike. Look at Mike. He—"

"Mike contacted us, too, Beth. He said . . . he said you've been having hallucinations."

Hallucinations? I haven't been having hallucinations. I mean, sure, sometimes I feel like I can picture the kids when they were younger, but that's not **hallucinations**. And how **dare** he share something like that with my boss?

He wants it to look like I've lost it. He wants that, and Charles wants that, and Madeline—

My eyes dart around the vault. Madeline, Annemarie. The whiteboard.

The Neighbor will protect him.

They're winning. Reza Karimi is winning. He's attacking us, and he's about to get into our system, and we're not going to be able to stop him.

I feel desperate. Terrified. No one will listen to me, and nothing is clear—

Suddenly everything goes dark.

The entire vault is plunged into blackness. Silence descends; there's no hum from the air-conditioning, from computer towers.

In my mind I see Sean. That day so long ago, out on the cul-de-sac, when I was first getting to know the neighbors. His shy smile. **I'm just the guy who keeps the lights on.**

The guy who keeps the lights on knows how to shut them **off**, too.

I was so sure Reza Karimi wanted to use the power system to insert malware, somehow worm his way into JWICS.

But that wasn't what he wanted. **This** was the plan all along. Making the Agency go dark.

"It's him," I say, my voice echoing in the silence. "It's Reza Karimi. And he's coming for the network."

FORTY-TWO

EVERYONE STARTS MOVING. I CAN'T SEE IT, BUT can hear it. The shuffle of feet, desk drawers opening, closing again. Somewhere someone finds a flashlight, then another, and thin beams of light break through the darkness in the vault.

The security guards rush from the vault.

"Is Quds Force going to storm the place?" comes a male voice. He gives a nervous laugh.

No one answers. No one else laughs.

Madeline switches on a flashlight, aims it at me. I blink into it until I can see her face. She's expressionless, watching me.

"Is there airflow in here right now? We're in a windowless vault, for God's sake," says a female, deep in the vault.

"Prop open the door?" comes a reply.

What is Karimi's plan? It feels like all the pieces are there, and I just need to fit them together, make sense of them.

Karimi used Sean's information to knock out the power system—

Karimi used Des, too. But not to get anyone through a polygraph. To take **pictures** across the hall in IT security—

"We gotta get these lights back on," comes another voice.

"No," I say. The word slips out, abrupt and unexpected. "We need to keep them off."

I CAN FEEL EYES ACROSS the vault settle onto me. Can see it, from what little illumination there is, from the way flashlight beams land on me.

"What are you talking about?" comes a voice. Goatee, I think.

I search out Dale. "Make sure we **do not** restart those generators. Cut power to the building. That grid's coming back to life."

"I don't know if we can do that." He sounds flustered.

"Someone needs to try."

It all makes sense now. It's all clear. And it's terrifying.

"This is how they're getting in," I say.

Those words from that intercept ages ago float through my mind. They didn't make sense then, but they do now.

" 'When they see the light, it will all be over.' Remember that, Dale?"

"When the power comes back on, they're in our network," I say.

"How?" Goatee asks.

"We need to get down to IT security."

Everyone's staring at me. Dale, Madeline—

No one's moving.

"Give me a light!"

Someone tosses a flashlight my way.

I catch it and head for the door.

I RUN DOWN DARK HALLS, winding my way toward the security division, the beam from the flashlight bouncing in front of me, lighting the way. I know this part of the building; I've met Des here to walk together to the cafeteria for lunch. This is where she works—and that means cyber security is right across the hall.

"Beth, wait." It's Annemarie's voice.

"Wait for us." Dale, too.

I can hear their footsteps behind me. Can see light from another flashlight. But I'm not waiting. I need to get there as fast as I can.

The vault doors along the hall are all propped open; we weren't the only ones concerned about airflow. There are no labels beside the doors, nothing to indicate what lies behind each one.

I find the door I recognize, the one where I've met Des, and I head straight through to the one across the hall.

It's dark inside, but my light finds figures, a group of three people standing in the center of the vault. Three young guys in jeans, night owls by the looks of them. The late shift. They stare at me, wide-eyed.

"You can't come in here," one says.

I ignore him.

The vault's big. Annemarie and Dale enter right behind me, breathing hard—

And **Madeline.** She followed, too. She's the one with the flashlight.

"Check every computer with a USB port," I say. "There's going to be a flash drive in one of them."

I head left, and Annemarie follows. Dale and Madeline head in the opposite direction.

"You can't be here," one of the young guys says again.

"Who else has been here?" I ask, my voice urgent. I don't stop to look at him, to wait for a response. I'm searching each computer, shining my flashlight at each tower.

"No one," the guy says, bewildered.

"None of them have ports," Annemarie says, from the next aisle over. I can hear the fear in her voice.

"Some of them do. Keep looking."

I search all the way through one aisle, turn down the next. Annemarie's in the next one over. Panic is rising inside me.

Nothing in this aisle, either, or the next. I head to the one after that, near the middle of the vault—

Madeline's at the other end of it, working her way toward me.

"Nothing?" I say, my voice desperate. If we're already meeting in the middle, if they haven't found anything, either—

"Nothing."

Annemarie's right, there are no ports on any of them—

I move my flashlight to the next computer—

Finally. One with a port, but it's empty—

Another, right next to it, also empty. I move my flashlight to the next—

There it is.

A flash drive connected to a port.

I found it.

Another beam of light lands on it. Madeline's flashlight. I glance up and we make eye contact—

And then I lunge for the flash drive, pull it from the port, then yank every cord from the back of the tower—

The lights flicker back on.

A hum fills the room, air-conditioning and computers restarting. The whole room is filled with light.

I sit back on my heels, the flash drive tight in my fist, tension draining from my body, leaving me shaky.

Dale comes up behind me, and Annemarie, too. The three tech guys come over, too, but keep their distance, looking uncertain, and wary. Madeline's still beside me.

The computers around me flicker to life, screens morphing from black to blue.

I watch the one in front of me.

The screen stays dark, and the tower is silent.

FORTY-THREE

CYBER RUNS DIAGNOSTICS ON THE FLASH drive, on a standalone computer, of course, one that'll be discarded. No prints except mine on the outside, but Reza Karimi's are all over the inside. Technically, anyway. It's the work of Quds Force, without a doubt.

It's him.

And it would have worked, according to our smartest techies. The code would have evaded our safeguards because the power was out, would have wormed its way into our system as soon as power was restored.

When they see the light, it will all be over.

We were within seconds of Reza Karimi winning, gaining access to our classified system, just like he's always wanted.

After I pulled out that flash drive, handed it over

to authorities, I sat through a thorough debrief. Told Agency investigators everything. Every last detail.

This time, no one acted like I was crazy.

Dale attended the debrief. Sat in the back of the conference room, listening. When I'd said all there was to say, answered every question the investigators threw at me, an uncomfortable silence descended. One of the investigators finally cleared his throat. "We'll have to address the fact that you ran an unauthorized investigation," he said. "We'll have to find an appropriate course of action."

"You're right," Dale said. Everyone turned to look in his direction. My heart sank. How was he taking their side? "And I propose that the appropriate course of action is for us to say **thank you**."

The investigators exchanged glances. "I'm sorry?" one of them said.

"We owe Beth a debt of gratitude. She prevented catastrophic damage to the intelligence community. Stopped a massive disclosure of classified information."

"Yes, but—"

"And we owe her an apology, as well. Because the 'unauthorized investigation' wouldn't have been necessary if we'd listened to her. Trusted her."

Dale made eye contact with me, offered me a nod. I nodded back. **Apology accepted.**

The door to the conference room opened, and

Cy slipped in, stood near the door, expressionless. He must have heard by now that I didn't have access to the Frozen Piranha intercepts. Must have guessed that I convinced him to give me information I couldn't access myself. I felt a surge of guilt.

"The bigger question," Dale went on, facing the investigators again, "is **who** inserted that flash drive. What are you doing to get to the bottom of **that**?"

One of the investigators shifted uncomfortably. "Well, we're going to commence a full investigation—"

"Actually," Cy interrupted from the back, "that's why I'm here." I see the hint of a smile pull at his lips. "We **did** get to the bottom of it. It was a young techie in Facilities. He had slipped out, came back to his vault right before the power came back on. Acting real nervous. I started chatting him up, and"—Cy puffs out his chest—"the kid admitted everything. It was blackmail. A note in the mail. Kid thought anything on that flash drive would be caught by our systems before damage was done."

Silence falls over the room. I'm struck again by just how close we came to disaster.

"Well," one of the investigators finally says, seemingly searching for words. "That's wonderful news. Admirable work, sir."

Cy tips an imaginary cap, smiles broadly. "It was

my pleasure. Glad to have helped. But it was really a matter of being in the right place at the right time, and for that we can thank Ms. Bradford."

Cy winks at me, and I smile back.

I don't know who tasked the young analyst, but I have a sneaking suspicion we'll find out it was Sean, given that it was someone in Facilities.

I also don't know if Karimi will ever trace this disruption back to me. I hope he doesn't. And I hope to God that if he does, he never takes it out on my kids. I insisted the Agency get a security detail on each of them, just in case. It'll only last a short time, I know, but it's better than nothing.

After the debrief, I'm stopped by a colleague in the hallway, and then another, and a steady stream after that. The same people who watched me in the vault like I was crazy, now approaching to congratulate me, and apologize. No hard feelings, I tell them all. And it's true. We're all doing our best here. I'm just relieved we stopped Karimi in time.

I'm still in the hallway when Madeline approaches. My CIC colleagues have all drifted away; it's just the two of us.

"Bureau's working on warrants," she says. "They'll probably be moving soon."

"Good."

It **is** good. Part of me is sad for them, these people I thought I knew, and thought I loved. **Especially** because part of me understands why they did what they did. Because if there's one thing I had in common with my neighbors, it's that we all would have done anything for our families. But they deserve to face the consequences of their actions.

"Sean, Des, Charles," Madeline says. "You were right about them."

"And Mike."

"Mike isn't The Neighbor, Beth."

I stare at her, incredulous. "He admitted it to me. I **told** you that."

"Nothing you've said about him seems to be checking out so far."

"Look at the loans. That should be the most obvious—"

"He **did** get an inheritance, Beth."

I don't even know what to say. "It's backstopped, then. Dig deeper."

She says nothing. I can tell she doesn't believe me.

"Why would I **lie**?"

She shrugs. "I think you have a grudge against Mike. Just like you have one against me."

"It's not that, I swear—"

"Or you're covering for someone."

"Why would I turn in my friends and cover for someone else? It doesn't make sense."

She watches me without saying a word.

I shake my head, and I start to walk away—

She places a hand out in front of me, stops me. Gives me an icy look.

"You know, Beth, the thing is, anything you accused Mike of doing, **you** could have been doing it yourself."

This is preposterous. This is **bullshit**.

"What the hell are you talking about, Madeline?"

She gives me a long look. Then she removes a folded sheet of paper from her back pocket, opens it, hands it to me.

It's an intercept, from just minutes ago, from Frozen Piranha. I skim the summary description; the encryption protocols changed again, a sure sign they feared they'd been compromised, but our tech gurus used the signatures to break the new encryption. It's a conversation between Reza Karimi and the Iranian official in DC. I focus in on the exact words.

Operation failed, the official said.

Worry not, Karimi replied. We're leveraging the network into something new.

I glance up at Madeline. She's watching me carefully.

And The Neighbor? the official asked.

She's completed her first task, Karimi said. It's almost time for her to begin recruiting.

"What do you make of that, Beth?" Madeline asks.

I reread the words, a knot twisting in my stomach—

She plucks the paper from my hands, refolds it along the creases, slides it into her pocket, her holstered gun visible at her hip.

Then she gives me one last smirk and heads away.

FORTY-FOUR

I STAND ALONE IN THE HALLWAY AND STARE at the door Madeline just walked through, the one that leads into my vault.

Her.

That's the first time they've ever used a pronoun.

The Neighbor's a **she.**

Or rather, the **new** Neighbor's a she.

Those recent intercepts, when Karimi has been talking about The Neighbor, he hasn't been talking about Mike **or** Charles. He's been talking about someone else entirely.

Someone who's still active. Who's just completed a task, who's about to start recruiting.

I think back to that conversation with Annemarie, in my Kent School office. When she pointed out that Madeline would have been too young when The Neighbor was first recruited.

She's not too young **now**.

She's not too young to be The New Neighbor.

She found a new cul-de-sac, just like they said.

She was **here,** happened to be here the very night the power went out, happened to be right next to that flash drive, right before I discovered it. She was in on it, wasn't she? Maybe **she** was even the one who planted it, after that techie brought it down to the vault, or she was trying to cover for him, at the very least.

She's been my biggest roadblock since the beginning. She's the reason I was removed from the case. She's one of the people who reported me to security, who's trying to make me look crazy. She's protecting Mike.

The Neighbor will protect him.

And now the latest intercept. **She's completed her first task. It's almost time for her to begin recruiting.**

Her first task. Was it **this**? Planting the flash drive? Protecting Mike?

Accusing **me** of being The Neighbor?

And now she's almost ready to begin her own recruiting.

Mike's gone, and she's taking over.

I was right all along, wasn't I?

Madeline's The Neighbor.

I run that last intercept through my head again. Reza Karimi's own words.

We're leveraging the network into something new.

He has more in mind for Madeline. He's not done with her yet. And neither am I.

I'm going to get back on this case, and back to hunting my target, proving who she is, and what she's done.

That's my next chapter.

FORTY-FIVE

A CARAVAN OF VEHICLES, MARKED AND unmarked, make their way onto the cul-de-sac, piercing the early morning stillness, their engines the only sound on the silent street.

Inside the O'Malleys' house, Sean and Erin sit across from each other at the kitchen table. Erin uses both hands to wipe away the tears that are dampening her cheeks. "You should have told me," she whispers.

"I know," he says quietly. The twins are upstairs, and neither of them want the kids to hear.

"How bad was it?" she asks. "What you gave them?"

"I didn't think it was that bad. I swear, Erin. But . . ." He trails off.

More tears fall, and this time she doesn't bother to wipe them away. Just nods, her chin quivering.

"How long?" she asks. She can barely force out the words.

"Prison, you mean?"

"Yes."

"I don't know. I don't know if I'll be back," he says, his voice breaking.

Her eyes fill with pain. It's a haunted look, and one that's eerily familiar. Sean remembers it well, from that fog she lived in for so many years, before they had the twins. He reaches a hand across the table. "I'm so sorry, Erin."

She looks at his hand, open to her, and then shakes her head, looks away. Leaves the table without another word.

ACROSS THE STREET, DES AND Darryl stand on opposite sides of the master bedroom. Darryl's shoulders are tense, the anger simmering inside. He doesn't look at her.

"What will you tell the girls?" she asks.

"The truth."

"How do you think they'll take it?"

"How do you **think**, Des?" He finally meets her eye. There's so much anger in his look it sends a chill through her. "They'll be disgusted. They'll want nothing to do with you. Neither do I."

He shakes his head and walks out of the room.

She stares after him, then walks to the window,

looks out, down at the cul-de-sac below, blurry through the tears in her eyes. Cars line the once quiet street.

Light from the Kanes' house draws her attention. She blinks quickly, wipes away the tears that fall, and sees Alice standing near her bay window, looking up. Their eyes meet.

Des holds her gaze for several moments, wondering if **she** could be the one behind this. The fact that she doesn't know is all the answer she needs. She's done with Alice, with **all** the neighbors, forever.

Not that she has much of a choice now.

Someone pounds at the front door.

Des pulls the blinds closed and walks away.

WHEN THE BLINDS SNAP SHUT, Alice turns to Charles. "What do you think they **did**?"

He's standing behind her at the bay window, doesn't take his eyes off the street. "I don't know," he murmurs.

She looks back out the window. There's a team heading toward the front door of the O'Malleys' house now, too. SWAT, with body armor and long guns.

"What's **happening**?" she murmurs.

Charles doesn't look at her, doesn't take his eyes off the cul-de-sac.

"I gotta call Beth." She reaches for her phone.

"Maybe just wait," Charles says, placing a hand over hers, lowering the phone.

"She won't believe this. I don't believe this." Alice looks out the window again, watches the teams of agents at her neighbors' doors.

"Alice—" Charles begins, haltingly, his voice strained.

Alice doesn't seem to hear him. "What happened to our cul-de-sac? These families, our neighbors . . . they all seemed so **perfect**."

Charles looks over her head, out the bay window. Watches as a swarm of officers begin to make their way up his own driveway.

"Sure looked that way," he says, his voice flat. And then, more quietly, "I guess that was the whole point."

FORTY-SIX

One Month Later

MADELINE STANDS ALONE AT THE BAY WINDOW, looking out at the cul-de-sac. The Kanes' and the O'Malleys' and the Johnsons'. Perfect houses. FOR SALE signs in each perfect lawn.

The houses are dark, and the street is quiet. No one's around, as usual.

No one but her.

Even the house she's in, the Bradfords' house, is quiet. The sort of quiet that doesn't exist, **shouldn't** exist, with three small children. But the children are gone. Josh took them.

And when he did, she threw herself into work, because at least if she could catch The Neighbor, it would all be worth it. But she hasn't. Sure, they've arrested three people. Three neighbors. Sean and Des and Charles. All charged with espionage, their families disgraced, faced with sky-high legal costs. But they're all **recruits.**

The identity of The Neighbor is still a mystery.

Madeline knows who it is, though. It's **Beth.** Madeline feels it with every fiber of her being.

Beth wanted them to believe it was Mike, the soon-to-be ex-husband. But there's not a shred of proof he's done any of the things she accused him of.

And everything she claimed he did, she could have done herself. She knew the secrets of her neighbors' pasts. She knew how to use their children to terrify them into submission.

But right now, Beth's the hero. She cracked the case, found the recruits, stopped the attack. As soon as her teaching stint is over, CIC's going to welcome her back with open arms. They're even willing to overlook her baseless accusations about Mike, sweep them under the rug, and she's not pushing the issue. It's obvious she's desperate to get back into CIC.

Madeline has tried to tell them the truth. That Reza Karimi is leveraging the network into something else, something bigger, that Beth is **part** of it, not the hero at all. But no one's listening. They think it's all in her imagination. The stress of so much change all at once: losing her husband, her kids, her mission. Becoming obsessed with the woman who came before her.

She's been placed on a new leave of absence, one she doesn't want.

Beth's at the center of it all, Madeline's certain.

And Beth had **this**. This life that Madeline wanted. She got to raise her kids here in this home. She had a career, and a husband, and friends who sat on lawn chairs in the street and drank wine and watched their kids play in the cul-de-sac. She had it all.

And all the while, she was The Neighbor, wasn't she?

Now look at the cul-de-sac. It's nothing but an empty street.

It's all Beth's fault. Madeline hates her for it.

And Madeline's going to prove she's The Neighbor, if it's the last thing she does.

EPILOGUE

"WONDERFUL THAT YOU CAN SEE THE cul-de-sac from here," the Realtor says, standing at the bay window, looking out at the quiet street. She turns and smiles at Aubrey. "This is such a lovely one, too. So social. If you and Austin have kids, I'm sure they'll be down there playing all the time."

Aubrey instinctively touches her abdomen, hidden beneath a flowy top. "That sounds nice."

"I think you made a wonderful choice with this home," the Realtor says, gesturing toward the empty house behind them. Austin's somewhere in here, upstairs maybe, making sure everything's perfect before they sign the papers at closing. But Aubrey was drawn to that window.

The Realtor holds out a key. "And I know you've been waiting quite some time for this day to arrive. You found this house, what, two months ago?"

"Yeah." Aubrey hesitates, then almost reluctantly takes the key from her.

She turns back to the window, looks down at the street again. There's a young girl on a pink bike pedaling around the cul-de-sac now, handlebar streamers trailing behind her. "I grew up playing on a cul-de-sac, you know."

"Did you?"

"Yeah. My mom and dad used to sit out there in lawn chairs, watch us."

The mention of her dad makes her mind drift. Back to the day she got that envelope in the mail, the one addressed to her in black marker, block letters. With the note inside:

Your father has been an access agent working for Iranian intelligence for the past fifteen years. His involvement will become public—and he will be imprisoned as a traitor—unless you agree to help us.

And then behind it, the email exchanges, the student loan payoff receipt. And copies of the notes that came later. **We'd hate for anything to happen to your children.**

Her father had wanted to protect **her**. To give **her** a better life. How could she not do the same for him?

What do you want from me? she wrote back.

Nothing right now. Your word is enough.

She didn't tell a soul, not even Austin, because she didn't want him involved. She didn't know if he'd understand. And because she knew she had no choice. It was her father. Family came first.

I'll do it, she wrote.

Eventually, they came back, and they asked for more. Asked her to take over her father's role, become The New Neighbor.

No, she told them.

And then it came. The envelope, with proof of what she knew, what she had agreed to cover up. And even more chilling, a picture of her ultrasound photo, the one that was hanging on her fridge at home, and a message:

They're so fragile when they're young. We'd hate for anything to happen.

She'd been terrified. She and Austin hadn't told a soul about the baby, hadn't sent out that picture. They must have been in her home, or her medical records, and either way it was chilling, because it showed just how easily they could reach her family. She cried her eyes out. But now she **really** couldn't tell Austin. And she certainly couldn't say no.

She agreed to become The New Neighbor.

Her first task was silencing her mother. She's the one who reset Beth's cellphone, wiped it clean, while Beth was in the living room with Austin.

And she's the one who sent those warnings.

Back off.

We'd hate for anything to happen to your children. It had worked on her, and her father; how could it **not** work on the woman who raised her?

The next task is to make her first recruitment. There are plenty of targets to choose from; the new house is in the shadow of Fort Meade, and most of the neighbors have some tie to the NSA.

Use the children, her handler had said. **It's the best way to get to know the neighbors.**

"Maybe you'll do that someday, too," the Realtor says.

Aubrey spins toward her. "I'm sorry?"

"Maybe someday **you'll** sit out in that cul-de-sac, watching your own children."

"Oh. Yeah. Maybe I will."

She turns back to the window and watches the girl on the bike, pedaling faster now, so innocent, so carefree.

"Sounds like you're following in your parents' footsteps," the Realtor says with a smile.

"One of my parents," Aubrey says quietly, no smile on her face, none whatsoever. "Just one."

ACKNOWLEDGMENTS

A heartfelt thank-you to everyone at Ballantine, especially Kara Cesare, Karen Fink, Taylor Noel, Kim Hovey, Kara Welsh, Kelly Chian, and Jesse Shuman. Huge thanks, too, to The Gernert Company, particularly David Gernert, Ellen Coughtrey, Anna Worrall, and Rebecca Gardner. And a big shout-out to the CIA PCRB and to my friend Karen Boyer for giving this book an early read.

To my husband, Barry, and our three wonderful kids, James, William, and Emma: I love you! Much love, too, to the rest of my incredible family, especially Mom; Dad and Janine; Kristin, Jason, and Noah; Dave and Johanna; Donna; and the Sullivans, Walls, Clevelands, and McCullars.

As always, this is a work of fiction. I have wonderful neighbors, and there's not a spy among them.

ABOUT THE AUTHOR

KAREN CLEVELAND is a former CIA counterterrorism analyst and the New York Times bestselling author of **Need to Know, Keep You Close**, and **You Can Run**. She has master's degrees from Trinity College Dublin and Harvard University. Cleveland lives in North Carolina with her husband and three children.

karen-cleveland.com
Facebook.com/KarenClevelandAuthor
Twitter: @karecleve

 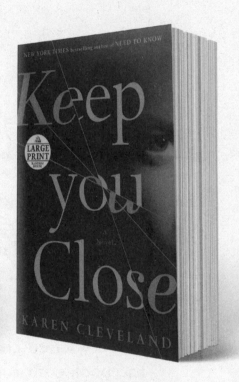